Caledonian Privateer

by

Gail MacMillan

Caledonian Privateer

COPYRIGHT © 2011 by Gail MacMillan

Cover Art by *Tina Lynn Stout*

The Wild Rose Press
PO Box 706
Adams Basin, NY 14410-0706
Visit us at www.thewildrosepress.com

Publishing History: previously published by Awe-Struck Publishing, 2008
First English Tea Edition, 2011
Print ISBN 1-60154-941-5

Published in the United States of America

"Let me go, you great brute!" Emma kicked and clawed. "I won't go back, I won't! You'll have to kill me first!"

"Madam, at the moment I have no intention of taking you anywhere, back to whatever you're referring to included. And I definitely have no desire to murder you."

She looked up at him. She saw only the black silhouette of a tall, broad-shouldered man wearing a long, dark riding cloak. Water spouted off the wide brim of his hat. His face was hidden by the darkness.

Emma's thoughts began to clear. If he wasn't one of the squire's men, then who was he? A highwayman. That was it. He had to be a highwayman. Surely no one else would be abroad at midnight in a raging storm. But if he was a highwayman and she told him who she was and why she was trying to escape, he would sense a reward for returning her. She must keep her true identity a secret. It was her only hope.

"I was at a fete," she said, pushing tangled, wet curls from her forehead. "I chose not to wait for a carriage when I decided to leave before the others."

"An interesting tale. And, where, pray tell, are you going alone on foot in a storm?"

"I'm going to London."

"To visit the Queen?" His tone was jesting.

"Hardly. I'm taking passage on a ship that will be leaving the docks for the Caribbean."

"With no luggage? Not a single portmanteau? You intrigue me, madam. Allow me to offer you a ride to the nearest inn. It's a most inhospitable night, and from what I can discern, you're not dressed for it. Perhaps when we're comfortably settled before a roaring fire you'll see fit to tell me the true story of your adventures."

Praise for Gail MacMillan

Dedication

Remembering Molly

Chapter One

Rain and sleet lashed Emma's cheeks and mingled with the tears of terror and despair coursing down over her cold skin. Stumbling through the midnight darkness of the storm-lashed night of May 17, 1812, casting furtive glances over her shoulder, she fled down the hill from the mansion behind her, its windows ablaze with light from the hundreds of candles lit for the Squire's party.

The road led to London, and at the London docks there were ships. Among them she would find one to take her to the Caribbean and safety at her brother's mission.

A bolt of lightning illuminated the black sky as thunder rolled, shaking the ground beneath her scarlet slippers. Uttering a strangled cry, she plunged ahead, glancing back over her shoulder once again into the darkness in a vain attempt to discern pursuers.

The next instant she hit a rock-hard, hair-coated wall. Reeling backward, she floundered to her knees and struggled to right herself. The horse she had run into screamed and reared, churning up the wet road with slashing hooves as it cavorted in front of her, blocking the road. Worse still, it had a rider. One of Squire Falkner's men, she had no doubt!

Panic forced her to her feet and to a lunging attempt to pass the snorting, prancing animal. Her attempt failed, and its rider leaped to the ground and seized her by an arm.

"Let me go, you great brute!" Emma kicked and clawed. "I won't go back, I won't! You'll have to kill

1

me first!"

"Madam, at the moment I have no intention of taking you anywhere, back to whatever you're referring to included. And I definitely have no desire to murder you."

She looked up at him. She saw only the black silhouette of a tall, broad-shouldered man wearing a long, dark riding cloak. Water spouted off the wide brim of his hat. His face was hidden by the darkness.

Emma's thoughts began to clear. If he wasn't one of the squire's men, then who was he? A highwayman. That was it. He had to be a highwayman. Surely no one else would be abroad at midnight in a raging storm. But if he was a highwayman and she told him who she was and why she was trying to escape, he would sense a reward for returning her. She must keep her true identity a secret. It was her only hope.

"I was at a fete," she said, pushing tangled, wet curls from her forehead. "I chose not to wait for a carriage when I decided to leave before the others."

"An interesting tale. And, where, pray tell, are you going alone on foot in a storm?"

"I'm going to London."

"To visit the Queen?" His tone was jesting.

"Hardly. I'm taking passage on a ship that will be leaving the docks for the Caribbean."

"With no luggage? Not a single portmanteau? You intrigue me, madam. Allow me to offer you a ride to the nearest inn. It's a most inhospitable night, and from what I can discern, you're not dressed for it. Perhaps when we're comfortably settled before a roaring fire you'll see fit to tell me the true story of your adventures."

Emma hesitated. Then, above the howl of the wind and the slash of rain, she heard them. Baying like the hounds of hell, the squire's dogs were on her trail.

"So someone has set his dogs upon you. Madam, you interest me more and more." He drew his horse to him and mounted. Holding down a hand, he kicked his foot from the stirrup. "Climb up behind me. We must ride like the wind."

Emma paused. "Why?" she asked suspiciously.

The barking drew closer, more intense.

"Listen! Do you need any other reason to take a chance on me?"

She grasped his gloved hand. As he drew her upward, she managed to get her foot in the stirrup and scramble into position astride behind him on the great horse.

"Hold tight!" he ordered. With a jolt that all but unseated her, he sent their mount bounding off into the night.

It was a mad, violent dash through blinding rain, bruising sleet, and nightmarish thunder and lightning. Clinging to the stranger's well-muscled body, Emma lost the sound of the hounds' baying. She wondered if they'd left them far behind or if perhaps their cries had simply been drowned out by the wild night and the pounding of the horse's hooves.

Only the feeling of strength in the stranger's body and the powerful motion of the great horse beneath her gave her any sense of reality. Emma Prescott could never have imagined herself a participant in this mad dash for freedom.

She knew the danger was far from over. The horse had only to stumble or his rider lose control. She repressed a shudder. Death would be preferable to being found defenseless and on foot by those vicious dogs.

Shortly Emma felt the rider slowing the horse; then its motion told her they were descending a bank. She slid sideways, all but falling off the animal's slick wet rump.

"Hold fast!" the man snapped, and she gripped his muscular body with renewed vehemence. Their mount's hooves splashed into a stream, and she flinched as ice-cold water sprayed up under her gown.

"Hold tight!" he ordered again. His legs and thighs moved against her, urging the horse back into a gallop, only this time it was a careful canter as they kept to the water.

She understood. The dogs would have difficulty following them along a stream, especially one swollen by the torrential rain.

For some time their course followed the brook before the rider turned his mount up an incline. Again Emma struggled to keep from sliding to the ground as the big animal heaved itself up the bank and onto a road. She had never held another human being as tightly as she held this stranger.

She had little time to reflect on the decorum or lack of it in their present position. His heels whipped back, sending the animal leaping forward once again into a full gallop. Another brilliant bolt of lightning rent the sky, and the horse threw back its head, snorting and rattling its bridle.

"Easy, Laddie, easy," he soothed. "Just a bit farther and you'll have food and shelter."

Before long he drew rein. Glancing around his broad shoulder, Emma saw the dark silhouette of several stone buildings. An inn or farm, she decided.

"Get down," he ordered holding the blowing horse steady.

She stuck one foot in the stirrup he had freed for her, slid her other leg over the horse's wet hindquarters, and, with the stranger's hand keeping her from falling into the mud, dropped with a bump to the ground. The man dismounted and paused to pat the horse's heaving sides.

"Thank you, my lad," he said. "You've done me

proud this night."

He turned to Emma in the driving rain. She still could see nothing of his features under the brim of the hat that spouted rivulets of water. A shiver ran through her as horrible visions of her rescuer's possible physiognomy rushed over her exhausted mind. Scarred from disease or battle, grotesque from birth, perhaps he was a creature even more horrifying than the one she'd fled only hours earlier.

"I'll make arrangements for us in this inn for the remainder of the night. Follow where I lead, and do not contradict if you wish to remain safe from whatever villains are on your trail."

Leading the horse, he headed for the door. Emma hesitated, then followed. She had little choice. But what had he meant when he'd said not to contradict him?

He had to bang on the door several times before a short, disgruntled-looking man with heavy side-whiskers, drink-reddened cheeks, and a bulbous nose opened it a crack.

"What do ye want?" he growled. "It's nigh on midnight, time all respectable folks were in their beds."

"Open this door, you miserable cur, before I break it in!" her companion shocked Emma by snarling. "My lady wife and I have ridden far this night, and we'll have food and shelter for us and our mount or you'll pay dearly."

His threats hit their mark. The landlord opened the door to admit them. Holding a candle, he wore a nightshirt that swept the stone floor.

"Come in, then, if you must." He scowled. "But, mind, I don't give cover to highwaymen and their doxies. Be you one of them?"

"Well, perhaps this night you will." Emma's companion pushed the little man aside. He strode boldly into the dimly lit common room, where a fire languishing on the hearth held the night shadows at bay.

As Emma followed her companion inside, he swept off his hat and turned to look at her. She saw him start as he saw her clearly for the first time. The deepest blue eyes she'd ever seen stared at her from a sun-browned face with strong, regular features like those of the Adonis she'd seen in her father's books.

"Well, well," he said, a corner of his mouth quirking as he looked down at her.

She swallowed hard, realizing what he saw. The crimson dress and cloak trimmed with ermine, although drenched and mud-splattered, could give only one impression.

"Your wife, eh?" The landlord leered at her. "Didn't think gentlemen married her kind. But then, you're likely no gentleman. Ah, well, it's nothing to me. She's your choice, Mister..."

"Captain Morgan Reynolds," he startled Emma by declaring. "Captain Morgan Reynolds of the *Ula*. My ship lies at anchor in the Clyde. I'm eager to return to her. Thus, we'll be leaving early in the morning, at daybreak. Now, rouse your lady, if you have one. We need food and drink and a room for the night. I assume your stable hand is long since abed, so I'll attend to our horse."

He went back out into the night as a plump woman with a thatch of gray curls sticking out from under a nightcap came into the room, pulling a faded robe over a nightgown.

"Bless my soul, child!" she exclaimed as she saw Emma. "Come and sit by the fire. Ben, build up the flames. Can't you see she's half frozen?"

She drew Emma across the room to stand by the big stone hearth that dominated the far wall, while her husband, grumbling, rekindled the embers languishing there. Apparently business flagged,

Emma thought as she allowed herself to be led along. The only other customer apparent sat in a far corner, in the shadows, hunched over a glass and a bottle. He appeared too far gone in his cups to notice the new arrivals.

"Let us get you out of that wet wrap." The landlady drew the drenched cloak from Emma's shoulders. "Oh my!" She gasped as she surveyed what lay beneath. Embarrassed, Emma put a hand to her breast in an effort to cover cleavage the plunging neckline did not.

"The gentleman said you're his...wife?" Disbelief hung in her words.

"Yes...yes, that's correct." She'd been ordered not to contradict. "Mrs. Emma Reynolds," she steadied her tone and stuck out her chin defiantly. "We've been married nearly a year."

"Well, well." Her gaze raked Emma up and down. "There's just no tellin'..." She turned on her husband suddenly. "Ben, go check on our guest and his horse." When he had gone out, pulling a coat over his nightshirt and muttering, she continued, "I'll hang your cloak near the fire to dry. Sit down and warm your bones. I'll not have you catching your death in my establishment, no matter..."

Emma obeyed as the woman went to a sideboard and began to rattle among the dishes. *She thinks I'm the captain's doxy. It little matters. As long as I'm with him, no matter what my status, I'm under his protection.*

The landlady returned and placed bread and cheese on the table beside Emma. With a final demeaning glance at Emma she went into a pantry and returned with a bottle of wine.

"This is the best I can do at this hour," she said. "In the morning, I'll see to it you have a proper breakfast before you and your...husband take to the road once more. He isn't a highwayman, is he, dearie?" Her tone became plaintive, almost whining. "Ben and me, we're terrible afraid of harboring any of that lot. The squire what lives several miles from here in the big house can be dreadful to anyone caught hiding robbers."

"No, he isn't." Emma, ravenous and exhausted, was willing to say anything that would assure her food and a place to lay her weary head for the night. "He's a sea captain."

Ah, well, then, good." The woman seemed relieved by Emma's answer. "The squire is a dangerous man, make no mistake."

Yes," Emma breathed.

"What's that?" The woman was instantly alert again. "Do you know him?"

"How could I? My husband and I are only passing through this county. We're acquainted with no one."

The door opened, and the man who'd called himself Captain Reynolds returned with the innkeeper.

"Food and a fire," he breathed doffing his hat and cloak. "Just what we need, Mrs. Reynolds. Innkeeper, you and your lady may retire. We're capable of eating and drinking on our own."

"Aye." The landlord headed for the stairs, leaving a trail of muddy tracks across the board floor. "Your room will be the one at the top of stairs to the left. Come along, woman. We've lost enough sleep."

"We'll see you in the mornin', sir and madam." The woman bobbed a curtsy and followed her husband.

"Well, madam, shall we sample this elegant repast?" Captain Reynolds picked up the bottle and filled the two glasses on the table. Then he sank into the chair opposite Emma and proceeded to pull off his boots. They were high and made of rich leather.

The footwear of a well-to-do man. Are sea captains rich? I've never met one.

The cost of his boots didn't seem to matter to him as he threw them carelessly beside the hearth and picked up his wine goblet. With a weary sigh, he stretched his stockinged feet out toward the warmth. He took a long swallow before turning to Emma.

"Well, drink up, Mrs. Reynolds, and if you've a mind, serve us each with bread and cheese. I'm weary, but I don't intend to go to bed hungry."

"As you wish, sir." Emma moved slightly forward on her chair and began to cut the food into servings. She felt his gaze raking over her as surely as if they'd been his hands.

"You're staring, Captain," she said. "Do I interest you so greatly you cannot focus on anything else in this room?"

"At the moment, madam, you most definitely do interest me, not only above anything in this room but in my life. You have the deportment of a lady, yet that gown and the dressing of your hair label you a woman of the evening. A courtesan, most likely, for no common doxy would be arrayed as you are. Were you mistress to some wealthy milord? Did you fall from favor and were therefore forced to flee? Did you perhaps take one of his young lackeys as your lover and he discovered the fact? And, by the way, what is your name? You haven't yet introduced yourself."

"Hush!" she indicated the man slumped over the table in the corner. "We're not alone."

"As good as." He glanced dismissively at the room's other occupant. "He's beyond caring or eavesdropping. Now, come, introduce yourself, lady, and tell me truly why the Lad and I found you stumbling down a back country road in a storm at midnight, pursued if not by the hounds of hell at least by the dogs of someone sufficiently disgruntled to set them upon you."

9

"You ask an inordinate number of questions." Emma sliced the bread with greater vehemence than necessary. "My name is Emma...Smith. If you have such a low opinion of me, why did you bother to rescue me?"

"Because no matter what you did, no one including yourself deserves to be left to the mercy of English dogs." The words were uttered with such sudden, dark anger they gave Emma pause in cutting the loaf, the knife poised above it as she glanced over at him.

"Ah." She feigned an understanding she did not possess as she handed him a plate of bread and cheese.

"So you won't tell me who you were fleeing or why, Emma...Smith?" His eyes twinkled wickedly as he drew out her name. Breaking off a bit of cheese, he tossed it into his mouth.

"And I don't imagine you want to tell me why you were abroad at such an ungodly hour wearing a black cloak and hat?" She fluttered her eyelashes.

"Touché!" He chuckled and his handsome countenance, previously grim and foreboding, was suddenly transformed. "Let us remain exactly what we are...mysterious creatures of the night. Now eat, drink. I've ridden far and hard, and I long for a couch."

They finished their meal in silence, but Emma became alarmed at the amount of wine he consumed. What if he became demanding? What if, once they retired to that room they would share, he sought payment for rescuing her?

Then the thought struck her. She had more than one way of paying him. Surely the ruby-and-diamond necklace secreted in her bodice would be sufficient ransom to keep him at bay.

Her green eyes narrowed as she chewed on her cheese. Perhaps he'd be content with a single stone.

She could not afford to surrender the entire piece. She had to pay her passage to the Caribbean. She'd have to find time alone to extract only the gem she felt would satisfy him. There was one particular ruby...

"Come along, Mrs. Reynolds," he interrupted her scheming. "Let us seek whatever form of bed this elaborate establishment has to offer us."

He picked up his boots and headed for the stairs. She hesitated.

"Well, come along, come along!" he said impatiently. "I'm too weary to show any interest in you this night. Even if I weren't, there's a lady whose affections I value much too highly to risk losing for a single roll in the hay with an Englishman's whore."

Emma nearly choked as she swallowed back her reactive response. She dared not anger him, not while he represented her safe passage out of the county.

Holding a candle, Captain Reynolds led the way up the narrow, dusty stairway and shoved open the plank door to the left at its zenith.

"Behold, the royal chamber," he muttered as a raw-beamed room with a board floor, a bed built against one wall, and a single chair and table was revealed.

"It appears clean." Emma advanced past him and ran a hand critically over the bedcover. "But where will you sleep?"

"Ah-ha! So even though I saved you from marauding hounds and a fate probably worse than death, you still have the audacity to assume I'll allow you the bed to yourself. Madam, I admire your spirit."

"Sir, a gentleman would most certainly grant a lady a bed." She turned to him in the flickering candlelight. How satanically handsome he was. If she were in the market for a lover...

"But, madam, you're no lady."

Emma drew herself up angrily. She turned her back on him to draw open the covers. She pulled the topmost one from the bed, grabbed a pillow, and threw both into his arms.

"There!" she said. "We're sharing the bed."

He paused a moment, the blanket and pillow clutched to his chest. Then he burst out laughing.

"Whatever your name is, you've got courage, I'll give you that. Any man who chose to keep you would have his hands full."

"Make yourself comfortable on whatever part of the floor you choose," she ordered sitting down on the edge of the bed and pulling off her delicate but muddied slippers. "It little matters to me."

Turning her back to him, she raised her skirts to remove her wet stockings. Then she scuttled under the covers. With the quilts pulled to her chin, she wriggled out of her dress, then disappeared beneath the covers. Bedding roiled and rolled. Finally her hands emerged at the foot to throw stockings and dress over the end board, and, after another convulsing of bedding, her head appeared at the top.

"Quite a display of modesty for an English doxy." His mouth kinked into an amused grin. "Perhaps you've been deceiving me, and you're not a trollop after all." He drew a deep breath and threw his blanket and pillow against the closed door. "At any rate, you'll have to forgive me if I don't demonstrate the same modesty. I'm weary and have little energy or patience for it."

He unbuttoned his shirt and threw it over the chair. Emma caught a glimpse of a broad, lightly furred chest before she pulled the covers over her head and rolled to face the wall. She heard him moving about, feet shuffling. Was he removing his trousers? *The man has no sense of decorum whatsoever! Perhaps he is a highwayman. Perhaps the name Captain Morgan Reynolds was nothing but a lie to throw the innkeepers off his scent.*

She heard him settling near the door. To prevent intrusion? Was his precaution simply that of a traveler in a strange inn, or did he perhaps have enemies? She shuddered. They didn't need any more. Squire Falkner provided more than enough danger.

Once convinced he slept, she withdrew the necklace from her bodice. The storm had blown away, and the jewels glittered and gleamed in the shaft of pale moonlight peering into the room. These gems had the power to either save her life or end it. She heaved a great sigh, pulled a pin from her hair, and began to pry at the large central ruby.

It proved a difficult task. Each time she made the slightest sound, she glanced at the man lying in the quilt near the door. His heavy breathing, punctuated by the occasional snore, assured her he slept. She heaved a silent sigh of relief when the stone finally fell free.

After she'd hidden the stone beneath her pillow, she returned the remainder of the necklace to its hiding place. She could only hope the single gem would be sufficient to convince Captain Reynolds to guide her to London.

Sleep eluded her. What lay before her in the morning haunted her until she knew she had no other choice.

"Captain Reynolds," she called. "Captain Reynolds." She could not sleep until she'd fixed a bargain with him.

"Madam, I'm bone weary." He turned toward her with a muted groan. "Can't whatever is troubling you wait until morning?"

"I want you to take me to London." She felt her heart hammering at her ribs. "I can pay you."

"Oh, you can, can you?" He pulled himself up on

an elbow and looked over at her. "Just what form of barter are you offering?"

His words reeked of sexual suggestion. She struggled to prevent retorting with an equally rude repudiation. She could not risk antagonizing the one person who at present appeared capable of helping her.

"This." She pulled the gem from beneath her pillow. It winked in the moonlight.

Lithe as a cat, he came to his feet and crossed the room. Naked to the waist, wearing only skin-tight undertrousers, he was an earthy, virile creature. Emma felt her breath catch in her throat.

He held out his hand, and she let the stone drop into his palm. He moved to the window, where he rolled it about in his hand, staring down at it.

"I assume this was a gift from a well-satisfied lover? You must be quite a woman to warrant such a reward."

Anger surged through Emma, but she managed to contain it. "Its source is of no importance. If it will induce you to take me safely to London, I'll be satisfied that it's been well spent."

"I believe it will, madam. I definitely believe it will." A smile creased his face as he hefted the ruby in his closed fist and headed back to his improvised bed. "Go to sleep. You may consider your safe passage to London assured."

She turned on her side to sleep and an involuntary yelp of pain escaped her.

"Our wild ride is taking its toll." He chuckled. "You'll have to accustom yourself to the saddle. We've two days' ride ahead, and no time to pause for aches and pains."

"Never fear, sir, I'll keep pace," she replied haughtily.

"Somehow I feel certain you will." She heard him rolling himself back into his improvised bed.

The amusement in his tone rankled even as his assurance of taking her safely to London lulled her to sleep.

****

When Emma awoke the next morning, the first rays of a new day were slanting in through the window. For a moment she stared about, trying to recall where she was and how she came to be in this strange, sparse room. As memory returned, she rolled toward the door where she'd heard her rescuer settling for the night. He was gone, the quilt neatly folded atop the pillow on the table.

She sat up, her heartbeats quickening. Had he deserted her?

Then she heard noises from outside the inn. Clutching a quilt about her, she went to the window. Below, in the muddy and straw-strewn dooryard, she saw the man who called himself Captain Morgan Reynolds arguing with the landlord. Tied to a hitching rail beside them were two horses, one the big black on which they'd ridden the previous night, the other a small sorrel mare.

"It's an exorbitant price for such a little horse," Captain Reynolds snapped. "She's too small to be of any real value, definitely not the kind of animal most travelers would choose. You'll be hard pressed to sell her...especially if, as I suspect, you didn't come by her through honest means. The sooner she's gone from your premises the better, I'll wager."

"Perhaps we both have a bit to hide." The landlord squinted up at the captain in the brightness of the sunbeams rising over the stables. "You and your doxy have the appearance of avoiding the law, as well, but without another mount to bear her away from here, you could be in deep trouble."

"My good man." Emma felt her breath catch in her throat as Captain Reynolds grabbed the smaller man by his shirtfront, all but lifting him off his feet.

His words were a snarl. "Don't threaten me. I assure you that, highwayman or no, I can be a very dangerous man. Now take what I offer for the mare, dress her up with that sidesaddle I saw hanging in your stable—no doubt another less than legal acquisition—and be grateful I have seen fit to pay you at all."

"No need to get nasty." As the little man capitulated, Captain Reynolds let him sink fully back onto his feet. "I'll see to it while you and your good lady partake of the breakfast the woman has prepared for you." He straightened his shabby shirt and squared his shoulders.

As Captain Reynolds turned away, the innkeeper made a demeaning gesture behind his back. Emma was glad her rescuer hadn't seen it. She didn't fancy murder first thing in the morning. Or any time, for that matter.

Emma scuttled away from the window and looked for the dress she'd left hanging over the end of the bed. It was gone. In its place lay a dark green velvet riding habit, accompanied by a matching plumed hat. The crimson gown was nowhere to be seen.

Hearing the captain entering the inn below, she realized now was not the time to waste speculating on where that awful dress had gone and how its replacement had appeared. She struggled into the green velvet dress. As she buttoned it, she was delighted to discover that it fit decently well. Aside from being a tad too long, it might have been tailor-made, and she looked well in it, she decided, swirling about before a small, crazed glass on the wall. But her hair—it was a riot of undressed curls tumbling about her shoulders and down her back. She gathered it up in her hands and was endeavoring to bring it into some sort of order when booted footsteps on the uncarpeted stairs announced his approach.

"Mrs. Reynolds?" He'd paused outside the room. "Are you ready for breakfast? We must eat and be on our way."

"Yes." She crossed the room and opened the door with one hand, the other holding her hair up in place.

"Well." He looked her up and down, his gaze as sensual, as tactile, as if it were his hands and not his gaze examining over her. "The dress becomes you, madam. I only regret that the landlady, among her stores of no doubt ill-gotten booty, didn't have any suitable riding boots."

"My slippers will do." Emma returned to the bed, sat down on its edge, and donned them over stockings that had dried during the night. "There." She stood. "As soon as I pin up my hair, I'll be ready."

"Leave it." The words were deep and sensuous. He advanced across the room toward her. Something in his eyes and demeanor shocked her, sent her pulses racing. "You look lovely just as you are." He reached out to take between his fingers a tangled ringlet that fell over her shoulder. Their gazes met, and she drew a sharp intake of breath.

"You are one very beautiful woman, Emma Smith or whoever you are. Allow me."

He drew a length of green ribbon from his pocket and gently turned her about. She felt his hands carefully gather her hair into a mass at the nape of her neck, felt his fingers scrape her bare skin as he tied it back. His hands fell to her shoulders, and for a moment she thought he'd draw her into his arms, back against that hard, virile body she'd become all too aware of during the previous night's ride. The next instant they fell away and, when she whirled, she saw him striding toward the door.

"Come along. We must not give your pursuers

time to regroup, refreshed from a night's rest."

His change of mood was as sudden as a mug of ice water dashed into her face. Thrown off balance, she could only follow.

"I saw you purchasing a mount for me." She managed to find words as they descended the stairs. "I assume you also paid for this traveling costume."

"You paid for both." He paused and leaned close to speak softly into her ear. "Remember our bargain. It's all part of seeing you safely to London." He quirked her a conspiratorial wink and continued down into the common room.

She followed him, her too-long skirts sweeping through the dust. The landlady waited beside a table laid with ham, bread, and tea.

"There's food," the woman said sourly before returning to her duties near the hearth.

"Come, sit." Captain Reynolds pulled out a chair for Emma. "Will you serve this elegant repast, madam?"

"Of course, my dear." Emma took up their charade, cocked her head coquettishly and proceeded to pour out tea into the cups provided.

For a few minutes they ate in silence. Then, as Emma's gaze swept around the common room, she saw her ermine-trimmed cape and dress hanging near the door. *I should take those along. Even though I detest the outfit, it* is *all I have, aside from the clothes on my back.*

She turned to the landlady. "Do you have a sack? I should like to pack my dress and cloak for the journey."

"There'll be no need, my love." Captain Reynolds took a final swallow of tea and arose. He strode across the room, bundled Emma's clothing into a ball, and flung the lot into the flames languishing on the hearth.

"Oh, no, sir!" The landlady gasped. "Such finery,

sir! Such wanton destruction!"

"And you were thinking they'd fetch a fine price if we left them for you." Captain Reynolds took a poker and shoved the blazing garments deeper into the flames. "No such good fortune, landlady. I've always detested that particular ball gown. When we reach civilization, I plan to buy her an entirely new wardrobe, one suited to her station in life."

He turned to the angry, distressed woman, the poker half raised in his hand. "Do you have any more protests to offer, mistress?"

Mumbling and scowling, she turned away.

Emma felt her heart hammering at her ribs. This was the second time in a half hour she'd witnessed her companion making threats. She'd have to tread carefully in his presence.

"Come, wife." He turned and headed for the door. "We have a long, hard ride ahead of us today, if we're to get to Scotland before the Sabbath."

"Scotland?" Emma was taken aback. Surely last night he'd said he would take her to London.

"Aye, to where my ship lies waiting in the Clyde. Surely you remember, my dear."

He cast a conspiratorial glance at Emma, and she understood. They had to disguise their trail.

"Certainly, my darling. Scotland by the Sabbath it is."

Chapter Two

In the inn yard the landlord waited with the two horses. His scowl told Emma he would be glad to see the backs of her and her companion.

"Many thanks, landlord." Captain Reynolds' words reeked of sarcasm as he tossed the little man several gold coins. "You've been anything but a genial host."

As the innkeeper scrambled to retrieve them from the muddy yard, the captain turned to Emma and made a stirrup with strong brown hands. "I'll hoist you aboard."

She looked up at the saddle, at the pretty little horse standing ready, and hesitated.

"Well, come on, come on!" he barked. "We've a lot of ground to cover today."

"No need to be impatient, my darling." Emma slanted him a coquettish glance as she put her slipper into his cupped hands. He'd chosen their guise. She'd show him she was capable of keeping up her part of the deception. "You were not so hasty last night."

"Argh!" He scowled at her. "Get aboard."

She smiled sweetly in return, gripped the saddle, and felt herself being propelled upward, seemingly with as little effort as if she'd been a feather. She landed indecorously on the sidesaddle and had to scramble to right herself in the unfamiliar appliance.

"Comfortable, Mrs. Reynolds?" The captain watched, a sardonic smile quirking his lips, as she struggled to find a comfortable seat.

"Yes." Emma drew herself up with dignity and gathered the reins. Praying she wouldn't plummet to the ground the moment the mare began to move, she fluttered her eyelashes as she looked down at him. "Ready whenever you are, Captain."

"Farewell, landlord." He mounted in a single, fluid motion and turned the stallion toward the innkeeper. The little man jumped back, shielding his face from the prancing animal. "Rest assured I won't recommend your accommodation to any fellow travelers we may encounter."

With a disgruntled mutter, the man turned toward the stables.

Captain Reynolds clucked to his mount and headed out of the stable yard at a trot.

Emma remained where she was.

"Come along, Mrs. Reynolds." He swung about to face her. "We have a lot of miles to cover before nightfall."

When Emma remained immobile, he urged his mount back to her side.

"Well?" he asked, exasperation surfacing in his tone.

"I can't ride," Emma hissed. She couldn't risk the landlord overhearing. He'd be even more suspicious if he learned her so-called husband didn't know she couldn't ride.

"Damnation! Just cluck to the animal and hang on. You'll soon get the knack of it." He whirled his impatient stallion about and gave Emma's mare a slap on the rump. The animal jolted into a brisk trot, all but unseating her.

Clinging to mane and reins, Emma felt certain she'd be tossed at any moment as she bounced out of the inn yard and into the rutted road beyond.

"You'll soon get the knack of it, Mrs. Reynolds," he flung at her as he cantered past. "Or else end up on your backside on the road."

Nasty, vulgar man! Bouncing so hard she feared she'd permanently injure private parts of her anatomy, Emma had to allow her mare to follow the man masquerading as her husband out along the road leading northward, toward Scotland. She'd show him. She'd master riding or die in the effort. Certainly she wouldn't give him the satisfaction of seeing her land on the road on what he had so rudely declared her "backside."

****

Emma finally fell in with the rhythm of the mare's gait. As she began to feel increasingly competent, she realized they were still riding north.

"We're still going north, sir," she said. "Shouldn't we be turning toward London by now?"

"I'm well aware of our direction, madam," he flung over his shoulder. "I believe it's wisest to leave a good beginning of a northern trail for the hounds that will surely be reapplied to your retreat this morning. There's a stream up ahead. Once we reach it, we'll turn south in its flow. After a couple of miles in the water it will be safe to take the highroad to London."

He nudged his horse with his heels and sent the great animal forward at a canter. Emma urged her mount and followed him, clinging to the reins.

At noon they rode out of the stream and dismounted in a meadow to rest. Aching in every bone and muscle of her body, Emma dropped to the grass. As he came to stand over her, legs set firmly apart, arms akimbo, she squinted up at him, a dark outline against the midday sun, and asked, "Why?"

"Why what, madam?"

"Why are you continuing to help me get to London? You know now that you can easily outride me and leave me to my own devices."

"As I've already told you, I'm not in favor of

anyone being pursued and attacked by hounds, especially English hounds." He pulled off his hat and sank down beside her. "And, you are paying for my services."

"Even more reason for you to desert me. You already had the ruby. You could have saved yourself the bother of my company and been the richer for it." Emma looked over at him, green eyes cool and appraising.

"Yes, I could have." He placed his hands behind him on the grass and leaned back, supported by them. "But I've always welcomed an adventure. You intrigue me. A woman running alone through the night, pursued by dogs—what could you possibly have done to inspire such a vindictive response? I've known men to turn out their mistresses when they became old or fat, but you're neither. Did you take another lover, a younger man, perhaps? Did you have him living on your master's favors? That would enrage a man."

"No!" Emma swung away from him, her mind racing. She had to come up with some reason for her strange circumstances, something he'd believe as surely as he believed her a lady of the evening.

"Then you tell me. I've exhausted my repertoire of possibilities."

"There are some things..." Emma hoped she wasn't flushing as she conjured the lie. "There are some things...certain acts...even a mistress cannot countenance."

"Ah." He pulled himself upright. "You must be new to the profession, indeed. In my experience, women like you will do anything for money."

Emma whirled on him. Her hand shot out and she would have slapped him soundly across the face had he not been quicker.

"Easily offended, are you?" He caught her upraised arm and bent it backward until she cried

23

out in pain. "Behave yourself, madam," he said, releasing her. "Or, I warn you, I'll take your mare and ride off, leaving you to make your way to London the best way you know how."

"You're no sea captain!" Emma raged, nursing her shoulder. "Sea captains are men of honor! They'd never treat a lady so despicably!"

"A lady, yes. But you, my girl, are by your own admission no lady." He arose and took a sack from a bag behind his saddle. He tossed it in her direction. "We'll eat and be on our way."

****

As he watched Emma Smith laying out their noon repast, Morgan Reynolds studied her carefully. She moved and spoke like a lady, but her physical response to his questioning branded her quite ready and willing to fight like the doxy she declared herself to be. Her former protector had to be a man of wealth. That crimson gown and cape had been of the best quality. Perhaps he'd been sufficiently rich and powerful to have been able to take whomever he chose as his mistress. Perhaps Emma Smith had been no doxy to begin with; perhaps she was merely a young lady who had fallen on hard times, who'd seen no other way of providing for herself and possibly her family. If such was the case, Emma Smith was more to be pitied than scorned.

Stop troubling yourself about it, he told himself. *Once you reach London, you need never see her again.*

London. He turned his back on Emma and went to loosen the horses' girths to allow them to rest more comfortably. London meant Vanessa and all of her charms he'd been missing so acutely. He thought of his rooms there, elegant rooms that taxed his purse but were such a haven of love and physical pleasure even he, frugal Scot that he was, could not regret a single penny. She would join him there shortly. The thought made his pulses quicken, his body harden. He remembered the fine home he'd built for her in New Brunswick. Built but not furnished. He touched the gem in his pocket. This fortuitous trinket would buy a fine collection of elegant pieces to finish their home in a style befitting Vanessa Cameron, soon to be Vanessa Reynolds.

He ran his hand over his stallion's arched neck and drew a deep breath in an effort to still his rising lust. In two days she'd be his bride.

To distract himself, he turned his thoughts to the mission that had brought him to the north of England. It wouldn't be easy facing his sister with the news that he'd failed to find her long-lost son. Or that he'd failed to take revenge on the man who'd stolen him from her so many years ago.

He turned back to Emma, suddenly impatient with her. If it weren't for this unplanned traveling companion, he could ride like the wind and be completing his wedding arrangements with all speed.

"You appear vexed, Captain."

"Eat up," he snapped. "I plan to be in London no later than tomorrow noon."

"As do I." Seemingly unperturbed by his shortness, she indicated the food she'd set out. "But you won't be in top form to pursue that goal unless you're properly nourished. Come, sit, eat. The sooner you do, the sooner we can once more be on our way."

Her coolness rankled him. With a sound of disgust, he sank down beside her, snatched up a slice of the proffered bread, and bit into it angrily.

"Much better." Her tone was placating, with a ring of self-satisfaction that reminded him of a governess Vanessa had once had.

"If I did not know better, I'd think you were a vicar's daughter turned governess," he muttered.

25

"You have much of the same annoying manner."

"You flatter me, sir. I can assure you my education has been largely self-acquired, and I've not been trained to tutor children." She began to gather up the remains of their meal.

"Ah, well, no matter. Perhaps you can affect that persona once you get to the Caribbean, and it will enable you to get decent employment."

She arose and snapped the cloth sharply, almost under his nose, to clear it of crumbs. "Perhaps I will, sir, perhaps I will."

****

Shortly they were once more on the road to London. As he watched her struggling to manage her mare, he felt a reluctant admiration seeping through his annoyance. Alone in the world, riding into an unknown future with a man who saw fit only to snap at her and belittle her, she demonstrated an unrelenting courage he could not help but respect. If he weren't an affianced man about to be married to the most beautiful, most bewitching woman in the world, he might be tempted.

****

The inn at which they stopped that evening was a respectable establishment with a tidy yard and freshly swept common room. A delicious meal of venison stew, excellent red wine, and fruit tart with thick cream satisfied their hunger and thirst. Afterward they were shown to a large upstairs room scented with the soap of a recent cleaning. A wide, white-sheeted bed with its head between a pair of sparkling windows dominated the space, while a dresser and armoire dominated opposite walls. In one corner was a bathing tub.

"Will you be requiring water?" the landlord inquired, indicating the latter.

"My wife would appreciate the opportunity," the captain responded, before Emma had an opportunity to speak. "Please see that it is provided at once. Meanwhile I'll return to your common room and sample a few tankards of your excellent ale."

"Certainly, sir. Immediately, sir." The landlord left quickly as Emma rounded on the captain.

"How dare you presume to speak for me?" she snapped.

"Last evening our accommodations offered scant facilities for ablutions." He stretched his shoulders, his words weary and hinting of exasperation. "Furthermore, I assume you're stiff and sore after a long day in the saddle. A hot bath will make you feel much better."

"And if I do avail myself of this elixir, how can I be certain you will remain in the common room a decent length of time for it to work its magic?"

"Madam, I'm bone weary myself." He turned and headed for the door. "I need a few tankards to revive me, the consumption of which will keep me away until well after your bath water has gone cold. Of course..." He swung back as he stepped into the hallway. "I expect you will have bolted the door. There are other men staying at this inn who may not be as immune to your charms as myself."

The door closed behind him. As she heard his booted footsteps descending the stairs, she opened the buttons on her spencer and stretched stiff limbs. He'd been correct. She needed a long, soothing soak in a tub of warm water. The thought of its medicinal effects took away the last of her apprehensions. When the steaming buckets of water arrived, she could barely wait for the landlady and her serving girl to leave before she bolted the door and began to pull off her dusty clothing.

She slipped into the tub with a sigh of pure pleasure. Nothing could have been more appropriate, she thought, stretching out. Traveling with Captain Morgan Reynolds had its good points. As she relaxed, her thoughts turned to the morrow and what she would do once they arrived in London. She'd have to remove another jewel from the necklace and seek out an establishment willing to convert it into coin. Next, she'd need to find a ship to take her to the Caribbean. If that ship were not sailing immediately, she would have to find lodgings until it did. It was all a huge muddle, something she didn't want to deal with at the moment. Satiated by a fine meal, good wine, and now this lovely bath, Emma closed her eyes.

****

"Mrs. Reynolds, can you hear me? Let me in. I'm tired and need my rest."

His voice brought her back to the moment with a start. Clutching a washcloth to her breast, she scrambled upright in the tub of lukewarm water. She'd dozed.

Shivering, she arose and wrapped herself in one of the large bath sheets the landlady had left on the nearby chair.

"Mrs. Reynolds, will you open this door, or must I kick it in?"

Emma felt a shudder run through her body. He sounded inebriated.

"I'm coming." Tripping over her dragging wrap, she scurried to the door and slid back the bolt.

"Thank you." The two words held no hint of gratitude. He strode in, pulling off his coat and flinging it over the chair. His cravat hanging loosely about his neck gave him the appearance of a man who'd been too long in his cups. "Now, madam, I suggest you climb into our bed and turn your face to the wall if you feel propriety won't countenance watching your husband bathe. I'm tired and dusty, too. The landlord and his manservant will shortly arrive with fresh water."

"Surely you jest!" Emma clutched the towel to

her chin and stared at him aghast.

"Surely I do not." He sat down on the chair, pulled off his boots, and flung them across the room. Coming unsteadily to his feet, he began to unbutton his vest and shirt.

"Oh!" Emma fled across the room, climbed into the bed, and, with the towel still clutched about her, turned her face to the wall. "You have no sense of decorum whatsoever, sir. I cannot imagine..."

"Oh, I'm quite sure that, given the nature of the trade you would have me believe you indulged in, you have no need to imagine."

Stifling a retort, Emma burrowed into the bedcovers and fumed silently while she listened to the sounds of the arrival of fresh bath water.

He was singing, singing some sort of ribald sea chantey. Emma struggled deeper into the bedding, trying not to hear, but found she couldn't breathe. As she surfaced, the smoke from the cigar he'd lighted tickled her nose. She sneezed.

"Bless you, Mrs. Reynolds." He broke off his song and slurred out the words.

Peering out from beneath her quilts, Emma saw he held the cigar in one hand while the tankard of ale the landlord had brought along with the bath water occupied his other. By the time he sought his couch, he'd be roaring drunk. His inebriation could also cause them to be late setting out in the morning.

"Can't you please bathe more quietly?" she snapped. "And don't you think you've had quite enough ale? You've said we must ride hard and fast tomorrow if we hope to reach London. We both need our rest."

"Ah, madam, don't worry about me. I'll be as fresh as a daisy. As for my singing, I can switch to a lullaby if that would be of any help in your finding Morpheus."

"No, no, no!" Incensed, Emma rolled over and sat up, holding the covers to her throat. "Just please finish your ablutions and go to bed!"

"Ah, go to bed, not come to bed." Stretched out in the tub, water to his waist, bare feet sticking out over the end, cigar in one hand, drink in the other, he grinned crookedly.

"A not-so-subtle indication as to where I may seek my rest. Very well, I'll go to bed."

He placed the tankard on a stool beside the tub and started to rise out of the soapy water. Emma, with a cry of annoyance, turned to face the wall. He gave a throaty chuckle, sensuous in its depth. An involuntary tremor swept over her.

He was an incredibly handsome man, with a kind of dark charm she suddenly realized she'd have to struggle to deny. If she allowed herself to submit to it, she'd be no better than the doxy she was impersonating.

She heard him drying himself, pulling on his undertrousers, and then she felt a quilt yanked from the bed. A second later the pillow beside the one on which she rested her head was snatched away.

"Forgive me, madam," he replied to her grunt of displeasure. "But since you've made it abundantly clear you won't allow me to share the bed, I must be allowed some level of comfort on the floor."

She heard him adjust quilt and pillow near the door, then grunt as he lowered himself onto the makeshift couch. Within seconds he was snoring.

Emma arose on one elbow, glared over at him in exasperation, pounded her pillow into another shape, and sank back into the bed to fall exhaustedly into a dreamless sleep, confident the necklace was well hidden in the folds of her gown.

****

When Emma awoke the following morning, he was gone from his place by the door, his quilt and pillow neatly piled on the chair. Eager to be once more on their way, she arose and dressed. As she pinned on her hat, she heard booted footsteps on the stairs, followed by a knock at the door.

"Mrs. Reynolds, it's well past dawn. Make an effort to get down to breakfast as quickly as possible." The last sentence rattled with annoyance, but before Emma could retort, she heard his footsteps retreating down the stairs.

He is totally insufferable! She stabbed the last pin into place. Yet she dared not rankle him. He was her only means of getting to London and, even though she'd paid him for the service, he would have no difficulty deserting her somewhere along the way. Like just now, for instance, when she'd overslept.

But he hadn't. Surely that said the man had some integrity. He'd also left her unmolested these past two nights, even though they'd shared a room and assumed the role of husband and wife.

She patted her hair as she stared at the young woman in the glass above the bureau. Without being immodest, Emma judged herself not unattractive.

What was she thinking? She whirled away from her reflection, annoyed. Did she want this handsome, devilish stranger to make advances toward her, to try seducing her into his bed? Certainly not. His failing to do as much was no reflection on Mistress Emma Prescott's charms. He'd told her there already was a lady in his life, a lady to whom he was devoted. So there!

With a whirl of green velvet, Emma pulled open the door and, head held high, strode regally down the stairs.

A half hour later they were on the road. At midmorning they paused beside a stream to rest the horses, and Captain Reynolds wandered off to stretch his legs. Emma took the opportunity to rub her mare's velvety nose and plant a kiss on her cheek. "Good Bonnie," she murmured.

"You've named her?" His voice close behind made her whirl.

"I've always fancied the name," she said, trying not to appear startled.

"A fine Scottish name it is," he surprised her by replying, a sudden burr entering his speech. "Aye, she is a bonnie little lassie, I'll grant you that."

"You're a Scotsman!" Emma looked up at him, astonished.

"And is that a crime in dear old England?" His tone became instantly bitter and sarcastic. "If it is, it will only be another offense in a long line of offenses your people have seen fit to heap upon us."

"My people?"

"You are an English wench, are you not?"

"An English lady, sir." Emma drew herself up proudly.

"Really?" He squinted down at her. "Not by my definition. Mount your Bonnie, and let's be on our way. I plan to reach London by evening, no matter what. If you can't keep up, that'll be your hard luck."

He turned away from her and swung up onto the Lad with a smoothness and grace she could not help but grudgingly admire.

****

Emma's first glimpse of London was through a haze of fog, smoke, twilight, and exhaustion as she clung to her mount, barely able to stay upright after the hard pace Captain Reynolds had set for them in the preceding hours. She should have been agog at the massive buildings and crowded populace, but she could only be deeply thankful her companion had slowed their momentum to a walk on entering the city.

His lady would be waiting for him here. He must be very much in love with her. That fact had served her well. Although he'd been free with ribald

32

remarks during their journey, he'd never once threatened her with physical intimacy.

"Hurry up, madam," he said, glancing back. "We've only a few more streets to traverse before we're at my lodgings."

"Your lodgings?" She'd expected him to deposit her somewhere, anywhere but there. What would his lady say when he arrived with her?

"Of course. Where did you think I would be bound? Tomorrow I'll find you a suitable room in the same vicinity, which is a respectable one. The value of that gem with which you paid me to guide you here will stretch to pay for your accommodations for a week or two...until you can find passage to America or the Caribbean or wherever...or you decide to return to your lover."

"I will not be returning!"

"Very well. Once I deposit you in safe lodgings, it matters little to me what you decide. Now come along. I'm weary and anxious to enjoy the comfort of my own rooms."

"But your lady..."

"My lady is not due to arrive in London until tomorrow. At present, she's visiting friends at a manor house in Surrey. You will be long gone before she darkens my doorway, never fear."

He touched his heels to his horse's side and set off at a trot through the crowded streets. Emma had no choice but to follow.

****

Captain Reynolds' rooms on the second floor of a large brick house were spacious and comfortable. In fact, they bordered on elegant. Were sea captains wealthy men? She'd heard that some were, especially those who practiced less than honorable behaviors at sea.

"Make yourself at home, Mistress Smith," he said, waving his arm to indicate the comfortably

33

furnished drawing room into which they'd stepped. "Remove your slippers and jacket. Take a seat. My landlady, Mrs. Bradley, will be along presently with refreshment. There's a bedchamber yonder, if you'd like to refresh yourself in privacy. I'll have her bring hot water. I'm sure she's already laid out clean towels. She's most solicitous to our needs."

He'd said "our." He and his lady must share these rooms as lovers. Or perhaps this lady was his wife. Although he hadn't referred to her as such, Emma could only assume this was case, given his unabashed description of their living arrangements.

"The lady you refer to...she is your wife?" Emma could not resist confirming her suspicion.

"Presently, no. But in the very near future." He went to the ledge above the fireplace, took a cigar from the humidor there, and bit off an end, then took a faggot from the fire on the hearth, lighting the cigar before he continued. "I've waited long enough. Before we sail for America next week, I plan to see her wed...to me."

"I congratulate you, sir, and wish you every happiness." Emma lowered her gaze to her hands, clutched demurely in her lap. She wondered why she suddenly felt such a strong pang of something that felt ridiculously like regret.

"Well, thank you, Mistress Emma." He turned to look at her, at first with a hint of surprise and then with a slight grin twitching a corner of his mouth. "Very prettily put. I wonder what your past was, before you became a rich man's whore. If we had more time, I'd take it upon myself to explore that avenue." He strode over to a window and smoked thoughtfully for a moment. "After tomorrow we'll no doubt never see each other again."

"No doubt," Emma replied softly. Again came that strange sensation that made her innards quiver unpleasantly.

He turned to face her. In the last light of day, filtering in through the lace curtains, his expression was enigmatic as he paused to gaze at her. Emma felt poised on the brink of something she didn't understand and couldn't define. Carriages rattled past in the street below, children yelled in their play, but inside the rooms of Captain Morgan Reynolds a static hiatus held a man and woman in its grip.

"Well." He shattered the moment by tossing his cigar into the fire and snatching up his hat and cloak. "I have errands to do this evening, paramount of which is finding you lodgings."

"Yes, errands." Emma came out of her trance sufficiently to reply in an absent monotone.

"I know a respectable house on the next street." He headed for the door. "I'll arrange for you to stay there. Then I must see to securing our wedding license and the purchase of a ring. You'll be safe here. Prepare for bed, if you wish. You can have the room yonder. I'll sleep out here. First thing in the morning, I'll remove you to your new quarters. I think it best you're gone before Vanessa arrives."

"Vanessa. Is that her name?" Emma stopped him as he put his hand on the door.

"Yes. Vanessa Cameron, soon to be Reynolds." He paused to look back at her.

"Very pretty." Emma began to unpin her hat before a glass. "It means butterfly, did you know? I hope your lady is as beautiful but more constant than her namesake."

The instant the words were spoken, Emma regretted them. She had no reason to be snide with the man. He'd been nothing but a faithful guide and caretaker. What was wrong with her?

"I assure you, madam, my intended is as constant as the sun, moon, and stars. Perhaps someday you'll find someone who inspires you to feel likewise." His words were heavy with anger. He left, slamming the door.

****

As he strode through the crowded street outside his rooming house, he struggled to swallow the outrage that chit of a girl had aroused in him. He'd saved her from a pack of hounds and guided her safely to London, and this was how she repaid him. Well, what could one expect from her kind?

He made arrangements for her to take up residence at a nearby house the following day, then proceeded to a well-known jeweler. He would purchase the finest wedding ring he could afford. He imagined the exhilaration he'd experience when he slid it onto Vanessa's slim white finger the following day. He'd loved her for so long, since he'd first laid eyes on her when he was a gangly lad of sixteen. Now, finally, the time had come.

He'd take her back to New Brunswick with him and see her ensconced in a home finer than that of her lumber baron father, much finer than the one he'd built for his sister and brother-in-law years earlier. He had to take a deep breath to contain his exuberance: by this time tomorrow she'd be his wife, and they'd be sharing the big, luxurious bed in his rooms as husband and wife.

"A fine choice," the jeweler said a half hour later when he'd made his decision. "Your lady will be delighted, I'm sure."

"I'm hopeful." Morgan drew the ruby from his pocket and held it out to the little man. "I'm also hoping you can appraise this for me."

The jeweler stuck a loupe to his eye and examined it carefully.

"A near-perfect stone," he said, finally removing the loupe and looking up at Morgan. "French-cut, I'd say, like something from the collection of their late queen."

"You can't mean Marie Antoinette?" His breath

36

caught in his throat.

"The one and only. Many of her jewels disappeared during the revolution. Some are just now surfacing here in England. I ask you again, sir, how did you come by it?"

"Since I don't look wealthy enough to have purchased it legitimately?" Morgan quirked a corner of his mouth sardonically. "If you must have the truth, sir, it was given to me by a lady for services rendered."

The little man batted his eyelids and began to fumble beneath his counter. "I'll just put your purchase in a box, sir. I wouldn't want you losing it."

Morgan felt a chuckle rising in his throat. He'd been called many things in his life, but this would be the first time he knew he'd been labeled a gigolo.

"How much will you give me for it?" he asked.

****

"I've brought your tea."

Emma arose from where she'd been dozing before the fire and went to open the door. A pleasant-faced woman with neat white hair and soft pink cheeks, bustled in carrying a tray laden with a pot of tea, scones, jam, and clotted cream.

"I trust this will suffice until breakfast tomorrow," she said, setting it on a low table before Emma. "I wasn't expecting the captain until then."

"It all looks wonderful." Emma pulled herself upright and smiled at the woman.

"Shall I pour?" The woman straightened up and looked inquiringly at Emma. She had more pressing questions in her mind, Emma reckoned, but the woman's curiosity wasn't about to be satisfied.

"No, thank you. That will be all, Mrs. Bradley." Emma picked up the china pot and smiled a dismissal.

"You'll find a robe and nightgown on the bed." Mrs. Bradley rubbed her hands on her snowy apron, reluctant to be so easily dismissed. "I was expecting Miss Vanessa, and so I laid things out for her...as usual."

"Thank you." Emma turned her attention to pouring the tea.

The landlady turned abruptly away and left, shutting the door a bit more soundly than necessary.

A sly little smile tipped Emma's lips as she stirred milk into her tea. *I do believe I'm beginning to appear quite as scandalous as I've portrayed myself to be.*

Chapter Three

Captain Morgan Reynolds whistled as he started up the steps to his rooming house. In his waistcoat pocket, the small packet that contained his bride's wedding ring pressed against his heart.

"Captain Reynolds!" A young lad ran down the street toward him in the twilight, waving an envelope. "Be you Captain Morgan Reynolds?"

"Aye, lad." Morgan, in an exuberant frame of mind, let his Scottish accent break through as the boy caught up to him. "Is that for me?"

"Aye, sir. A lady told me to watch for you and deliver it."

"Give it here, my good lad." Morgan took a coin from his pocket, flipped it to the boy, and snatched the envelope. He drew it to his nose. The familiar scent of lavender wafted over his senses. Vanessa. She'd had to write. She couldn't wait until the morrow to pour out her love.

"Thank ye, sir." The boy looked down at the coin in his hand and broke into a grin. "Bless ye, sir, ye and yer good lady."

"Be off with you." Morgan chuckled. He turned and stepped into the building's lighted foyer before he gently slid a finger beneath the flap. A smile still across his face, he unfolded the single sheet.

His expression reflected the impact of the words as he read. His happy expression froze, then slowly dissolved into the furrowed forehead and fallen mouth of shock. When he looked up, his eyes reflected the stark blankness of disbelief.

For a few moments he stood fixed in place, the

ticking of the grandfather clock beside the cloak rack the only sound breaking the silence of the entrance hall.

"No!" he bellowed finally. "No, no, no!"

He crumpled the mauve sheet into a hard ball and flung it with all his strength against a far wall. "God damn you, you deceiving, mercenary little bitch!"

He slammed a fist into the palm of his other hand, then threw back his head to gulp in great gasps of air. He felt lightheaded, caught in some sort of mad nightmare. She couldn't have done it. He'd loved her since he was a boy. He'd worked and slaved and planned to be able to ask her to be his wife. She couldn't have left him for another man, she couldn't!

He whirled and headed back out into the fast-falling darkness. He hadn't gotten drunk, rip-roaring drunk, in years, but tonight definitely was the time.

****

Alone in his rooms, humming a little ditty, Emma prepared for bed. She knew her challenges were far from over, but she'd gotten this far by her wits and a single one of the gems she possessed. The fact gave her confidence she'd be able to manage the remainder of her journey to safety and freedom. Reassured, she fell into his wide featherbed. Exhausted from their journey, she soon fell asleep.

****

"Get up, madam, damn you, get up!"

Emma awoke as his words broke over her like a roaring wave. Sleepy and disoriented, she struggled up on one elbow and stared at the outraged man looming over her. His face reddened from drink, his person stinking of spirits and cigar smoke, his shirt minus cravat and waistcoat and hanging open, Captain Morgan Reynolds for a moment appeared a stranger.

"What is wrong with you?" she asked, trying to equate his changed appearance with the man she had come to trust. He frightened her.

"Get dressed, madam." He staggered back a step. "I intend to marry you."

"What did you say?" Emma sat up, clutching the covers to her throat. "Are you mad?"

"No, no, not mad, just unwilling to be a cuckold. I need a wife, and you need passage to the Caribbean. I have a ship. I'll take you there. I will make it my sole mission in life to take you there. It won't cost you a single gem or a single night in my bed. I need a display wife, one I can show off on my arm in place of the blatant bitch who has seen fit to marry another man on the eve of our wedding."

"Vanessa married someone else?" Emma stared at him, aghast. "But you were affianced. Are you certain? Who did she marry?"

"Of course I'm certain." He sank into a chair, his bluster suddenly leaving him. "She sent me a note. 'Forgive me, Morgan, but you must understand. Lord Peter has given me a title and an estate here in England such as you never could.' Lord Peter, Good God! A stinking English aristocrat!" He dropped his head into his hands. His broad shoulders shook.

Emma jumped out of bed. Pulling a wrapper she'd found in the armoire about her, she went, barefooted, to his side. There she hesitated a moment, her fingers working indecisively above his shoulder before she dropped her hand comfortingly onto it.

"I'm so sorry," she said softly.

"Don't be sorry!" Her touch brought him leaping to his feet, raging again, but she saw more pain than anger distorting his features and wasn't deterred. "I don't want your pity. I want you to..."

"To save you from embarrassment." Emma faced him squarely. "Very well."

"What?" He stared at her incredulously.

"I will marry you...in name only...in return for your taking me safely to the Caribbean."

"Why?"

"Because you recently saved my life even before you knew I was capable of paying you to do so. And because I've seen what this woman, this butterfly, means to you. You don't deserve to be humiliated by such as her. And you won't be. In public I will be the most besotted, the most loving of wives. You may tell all and sundry that you jilted Vanessa to be with me."

"Hmph." He sat down heavily on the edge of the bed. "You would do that for me, Emma Smith?"

"Yes." She stuck out her chin. "I repay all debts as best I can."

"A woman of honor." In the light of the single candle he'd placed on the bureau when he came into the room, he looked up at her, a hint of humor entering his expression. "Ironic, is it not, that I find such virtue in a woman of the night and none in a so-called lady?"

"Go to bed." Emma found herself weakening, feeling an urge to hold him, to soothe away some of his misery. "I left a blanket and pillow on the sofa in the drawing room. You look weary. You must rest. Tomorrow," she paused and drew a deep breath, "will be our wedding day."

With a heavy sigh, he pulled himself to his feet and started toward the door. "If you change your mind in the light of day..."

"I won't." Emma faced him in the flickering candlelight and considered the madness of marrying this satanically handsome man she'd known a scant two days. *Dear God, help me,* she prayed silently. "Now go."

****

"Well?"

Emma awoke to find him standing in the bedroom doorway dressed in a white shirt, neatly tied cravat, and freshly brushed and pressed coat and breeches. She caught a scent of a pleasant soap. Nothing about him reminded her of the inebriated man who had charged into her bedroom the previous night except the bloodshot in his intensely blue eyes.

"Well, what?" She struggled up to a sitting position and tried to rub sleep from her eyes.

"Is this not our wedding day?" He crossed his arms on his broad chest.

"I said I would marry you, and I will." She came fully awake, remembering her bargain, and faced him. "Just let me wash, dress, and fix my hair, and we'll be off to whatever site you've chosen for our nuptials."

As she made to get out of bed, wrapping the robe she'd used the previous evening around her, he stepped forward and laid a hand on her shoulder.

"What?" She looked up at him, wide-eyed.

"I thank you most sincerely, Mistress Emma, but I cannot possibly allow you to marry me simply to save my pride." His voice, soft and gentle, startled her. "Last night I was hurt and angry, self-centered in my chagrin when I accepted your offer. This morning in the harsh light of day I realize how wrong that would be. Instead," he turned away and went to gaze out the window into a street Emma could hear bustling with activity, "I would like to propose a compromise. Pose as my wife until I can see you safely to your chosen destination in the Caribbean. Your pretense will be more than sufficient to pay your passage."

"But how...?" Astonished, Emma stared up at him.

"This morning we'll go out and purchase you a wardrobe befitting my lady wife. We'll then return to inform Mrs. Bradley that we were quietly wed. Each morning until we sail I'll make certain my couch in the other room is restored to order before she arrives to clean, allowing her to believe we share this bed.

"Once we're underway, it will be even easier. I will take another cabin while you use my captain's quarters. I will inform the crew that my young bride has fallen victim to a seasickness that has robbed her of all amorous interest.

"We must first sail to New Brunswick, a British colony in North America. I have business concerns in Pine, one of its settlements, as well as family I must visit. I have my own house in the area, where we'll live until we embark for the Caribbean. Well, what do you say, Mistress Emma Smith? Are you willing to enact the part of Captain Morgan Reynolds' spouse?"

"Yes." Emma got up, pulling on the robe she'd worn the previous night. "Yes, of course, my dear." She dropped him a mock curtsey and headed into the connecting dressing room.

****

Morgan watched as she quietly closed the door behind her. Then he drew a deep breath, rubbed his hands together, turned and went back out into the drawing room. He had a wife to flaunt before anyone who might feel inclined to question his failure to have the beautiful Vanessa as his bride. No one need ever know his sudden new choice of a spouse had been an Englishman's fancy woman.

He poured himself a cup of coffee from the pot Mrs. Bradley had provided and sat down with a sigh, all the feeling of smugness suddenly draining out of him. This wasn't going to be the day he'd been planning for weeks, months, even years.

His mouth quirked at the irony of the situation. Perhaps he was getting no better than he deserved. After all, he was only a crude Highlander who'd allowed himself to get so deeply in debt to finance his romance with an elegant woman that he'd have to work like a demon to right himself again.

Fool! He branded himself as he looked around at the expensive apartment. Worse than a fool. A Scotsman who couldn't exhibit the frugality for which his race was famous.

He reached into his waistcoat pocket and drew out the wedding ring he'd purchased the previous day. The ruby he'd sold to the jeweler for a generous settlement and used the proceeds to cover a portion of his debts. That would be a start. But only a start. The money from the sale of the ruby would keep his creditors at bay for only a short time. He wondered what Emma would say if she knew the state of his finances.

Today he'd have to incur more debts when he purchased a wardrobe befitting the bride of Captain Morgan Reynolds. He drew a deep breath. Such was the price of pride. He could almost hear his half-sister Iona extolling the thought. Nearly twenty years his senior, she exhibited all the economies attributed to their race.

"I'm ready, Captain."

Emma Smith, or whatever her true name was, brought him out of his reflections as she stepped into the drawing room, her riding habit brushed, her hair neatly pinned beneath her small plumed hat. For the first time he looked at her—really looked at her. Previously enamored with Vanessa, he'd barely taken note of her as a woman.

Now, as he sat staring at her, he realized she was a remarkably pretty little creature, with a lovely complexion, large green eyes framed by long dark lashes, and golden brown hair that curled quite charmingly about her face. Dressed by the skilled seamstresses he'd come to know during his experiences with Vanessa, Emma Smith could pass as a refined, desirable lady.

"You're staring." She began to don her gloves. "Am I in some way unacceptable?"

"No." He arose and brought himself back to the moment abruptly. "You look...quite acceptable. I was only about to remark that there is no need to hurry. We have all day. Sit. Please. Enjoy some of this excellent coffee. Mrs. Bradley will bring breakfast when I ring."

"Thank you." She sat down in a lady's chair across from him. "I am hungry."

"Well, then." He stepped to a bell cord beside the fireplace and pulled it twice. He returned to the table hosting the coffeepot and poured her a cup. "Cream? Sugar?"

"Cream." She offered him a soft, demure smile.

Oh, yes, Mistress Emma Smith, you'll do very nicely. "There is one small matter to be attended to before we walk out in public." He reached into his waistcoat pocket, removed the small box, and opened it. A gold band rimmed with sparkling green stones gleamed in the sunlight flooding into the room.

"It's beautiful." Emma's eyes widened.

"Yes, it is." He plucked it from its velvet nest. "Your hand, Mrs. Reynolds, if you please. If you're to pose as my wife you must have all the proper accoutrements, which of course shall include a wedding ring."

"But surely a simple gold band would have been sufficient." Emma watched as he took her hand and slid the sparkling jewelry onto her third finger. It fitted as if custom made.

"Perhaps it would have been." He held her hand and leaned back to admire its sparkle. "But since I'd already purchased this one, it seemed wasteful to buy another. At any rate," he paused and looked up at her, "emeralds match your eyes."

For a moment blue eyes gazed into green. Then Mrs. Bradley broke the moment by entering to ask if

46

they required more coffee.

****

Emma had never seen anything like the London to which Captain Reynolds introduced her that morning. In the bright May sunshine it appeared a melee of humanity as they walked through the business district. He must have caught the amazement in her wide eyes when he glanced down at her on his arm.

"You've never been to the city before today?" he asked.

"No." She gazed about, a trifle breathless from the excitement.

"Then you must see the market." At the next corner he turned right, and suddenly they were among crowded stalls, the occupants of which were crying out the merits of the items they offered for sale. The noise and energy of the place caught Emma off guard and her grip tightened on his arm.

"Enjoy it, Mistress Emma Smith." He looked down at her and smiled. "You're quite safe."

Reassured, she relaxed into the enjoyment of the moment. Fish were thrown on scales, fruit and vegetables critically examined by prospective buyers, game birds, rabbits, and domestic fowl hung dead on hooks ready for sale. Other stalls offered farm equipment, furniture, freshly baked pies and breads, and even ropes and nets.

Captain Reynolds paused before a booth that offered colorful nosegays of various varieties of flowers.

"Violets for my lady," he said throwing a coin onto the board that served as a counter.

"Aye, sir," the ragged old woman in attendance agreed with alacrity as she looked at the size of the coin. "Thank ya, sir. God bless ya, sir."

As they walked away, Captain Reynolds touched the blossoms in Emma's hands, and she noticed that his fingers were scarred.

"In New Brunswick, in spring, the fields and forest edges are blue with these minuscule marvels," he said. His tone grew bitter. "It's a beautiful country, but much like a lovely woman...it can be as dangerous and cruel as it is alluring and fascinating."

She could think of no appropriate comment as he turned her around a corner and up the steps of an establishment that bore the legend "Mistress Mildred Mason, Seamstress" above the door. It would be a long time before the hurt and bitterness the woman Vanessa had engendered left his heart.

****

Inside the building Emma was confronted by such an array of fabrics, of hustle and bustle, for a moment she felt disoriented. A number of women scurried about, spreading out material and cutting patterns, while others huddled over the tasks of sewing fabrics together. A tall, stately looking woman came forward to greet them, her dark eyes taking in Emma with a single sweeping and not altogether approving appraisal.

"Captain." She offered him her hand in such a business-like manner Emma was startled. No curtsy, no humble vendor seeking custom appeared to lurk in this middle-aged woman's soul.

"Mistress Mason." Captain Reynolds took her hand and bowed over it.

"How may I be of service, sir?" Her tone was cold. "Have you come to order more gowns for Mistress Vanessa? I have her measurements on file. We can make up anything you might fancy in a day or two."

Again she cast her cold gaze over Emma. She understood. This woman had been dressmaker to Captain Reynolds' intended. She didn't appreciate him arriving at her shop with another woman on his arm.

"No, thank you, mistress." He straightened up and looked directly at her. "I would like you to prepare several gowns for my wife, Mrs. Emma Reynolds. Five, I think, suitable for a voyage and travel in the colonies. She will also require a ball gown of gold silk, with an overlay of your finest white lace, as well as a matching cape and reticule. Everything must be ready by Monday. We'll be sailing with the tide that morning."

"Your...wife?" The woman's eyes widened to the point they looked in danger of popping out of her head. "Your wife? But surely..."

"We were wed yesterday and plan to sail to New Brunswick within the week. Can you fill my order or will I be forced to take my custom elsewhere?" His brusqueness left no doubt of the sincerity of his words.

"A tall order, sir." The woman struggled to resume her composure. "I do feel I must add, however, that you'll wish to update your account before taking on more credit in this establishment...especially when a new lady is involved." The word "new" reeked with sarcasm.

"Of course." Captain Reynolds stepped away from Emma and drew out his purse. "If you'll give me an accounting of my present debt and the proposed cost of my wife's outfitting, I'll settle with you at once."

A startled look shot over the woman's face as she viewed the money. Then she smiled primly.

"Well, of course, Captain. If you'll just give me a moment..." She turned to two of the women laying out fabric on a nearby table. "Lily, Charlotte! Look smart and measure this lady for dresses and undergarments. Captain Reynolds has commissioned a deal of work that must be done posthaste."

49

She turned back to Captain Reynolds. "Now, Captain, if you'll leave your lady in our capable hands for the next hour or two, we'll see to her complete outfit."

"Very well." He drew a deep breath. "But first, Mistress Mason, you and I will adjourn to your office and I will make good my promise to pay."

****

As Emma was measured and shown various fabrics, she wondered about the cool reception they'd received from the seamstress. There could be only one explanation. Captain Reynolds had allowed himself to be drawn into debt to satisfy the fancies of the lady Vanessa. Her ruby had enabled him to pay his bills and buy her much-needed clothing.

She wondered how much that ruby had fetched. If it would cover large amounts, it must be very valuable. What of the rest of the necklace she'd left hidden under the mattress in his rooms? Could she be carrying a small fortune? *A small stolen fortune,* a little voice in her head reminded her, and she flinched.

"Did I stick you with a pin, mistress?" Lily asked, concerned, as she stepped back from measuring Emma's waist. "I'm so sorry, mistress."

"No, no, definitely not." Emma smiled down at the nervous little shop girl. "I just had a sudden twinge."

Of guilt, she continued silently. She wondered what the penalty of the law would be if she were apprehended. Suddenly she could barely wait to be on Captain Reynolds' ship and safely on her way to America.

Then she overheard the whisper of one of the women working behind a nearby screen: "The captain finally come to his senses and got rid of the stuck-up piece of baggage what was running him head over heels into debt. Married this one for

50

money, looks like. Able to settle his account all of a sudden. He's a lucky beggar. She's quite a pretty little thing."

****

"You're very quiet." Captain Reynolds remarked as he guided her back through the streets toward his rooms. "Did you not find any fabrics or designs to your liking? Mistress Mason is one of this city's best seamstresses."

"And most expensive?" Emma glanced sideways up at him.

"And most expensive. Don't concern yourself on that score. As you observed, your outfitting has all been paid for."

"That's not what I was thinking." Emma decided to venture onto dangerous ground.

"Then what?" He stopped and turned her to face him. Intense blue eyes stared down into frank green ones.

"I was thinking that you had perhaps purchased gowns in her establishment for Vanessa. Expensive gowns that you could not afford."

"I could afford, woman, I could afford." His face darkening, he caught her by the arm and began to walk forward so quickly she had to trot to keep apace with him.

"I just thought..."

"Well, then, don't. It no longer concerns either of us."

They'd reached the house where he lived. He strode up the steps so swiftly, with her in tow, that she stumbled. *That will teach me to question him.*

****

He poured himself a dram of whiskey, then turned to stare at the closed bedroom door behind which she'd vanished in a swirl of green velvet the moment they'd reached his rooms. He'd annoyed her with his harsh treatment because she'd dared to

51

question his finances. He didn't want her to suspect, much less know, the tangle of debt in which he'd gotten himself enmeshed in his attempts to impress a woman who'd jilted him without a second thought.

None of it was Mistress Emma Smith's fault. He should knock on that securely shut panel and apologize. Because of her ruby he'd been able to settle a good many debts he hadn't anticipated squaring away for months.

But he couldn't. A pride at once fierce and stubborn held him in its grip. He was, after all, a man, and a proud Highlander, at that. He wouldn't go crawling to any woman. Not even one who'd shown all the courage and charm of Emma Smith.

Emma Smith. He turned away and strode across the room to sink into his favorite wing chair. Surely that wasn't her true name. But who was she, really, and where had she come from that dark night he'd found her on the road? How had she come by that exquisite French ruby? Had it been a gift from a well-pleased lover or—he paused over the possibility—had she perhaps stolen it? Was Emma Smith a thief? He shook his head in an effort to clear it of the jumble of questions that surrounded the woman in the next room.

Furthermore he'd convinced her to pose as his wife and promised to take her to New Brunswick, then on to the Caribbean. Yesterday, and even this morning, suffering from his excesses, it had seemed a good idea. Now he wondered.

She was a pretty woman, a beguiling woman in many ways. She had an innocently seductive manner of casting mischievous sideways glances up at him, glances that alerted his male instincts, that made him all too aware of how attractive the minx could be. Even now, thoughts were stealing across his mind, thoughts best saved for an actual wife or at least a consenting lover. But Emma was neither.

Yet...

He caught himself up on that last word. *Damn!
Don't start thinking along those lines, laddie.* He
finished off his whiskey in a single swig and arose to
get more.

Twilight was sliding across the room, and he
paused to light a lamp before he returned to his
chair. He had to admit it. He missed Vanessa to the
quick of his soul. Had she been here now, she'd be
coming out of the bedroom in one of those elegant,
exorbitantly expensive negligees, her golden hair a
soft, loose cloud about her shoulders and down her
back. She'd cross the room slowly, seductively, a sly
smile tipping her full lips, and slide softly onto his
lap. She'd slide her soft white arms about his neck
and...

He leaped to his feet. With a roar, he flung his
glass into the fireplace. Then he buried his head in
his hands and slid them back until his fingers tore at
his thick, black curls.

"Captain, are you all right?"

Emma was standing in the bedroom doorway,
swathed in one of Vanessa's more conservative
dressing gowns. Her hair hung loose about her
shoulders. *Beautiful, beautiful.* Startled, he felt his
body react.

"Yes, yes." He regained his composure and
squared his shoulders. He saw her gaze go to the
fireplace, where shattered glass glinted in the
lamplight.

"It's normal for you to feel anger." She stood
where she was, and he understood why some rich
laird would want her as his mistress. In dishabille,
Mistress Emma Smith was an enchanting woman.

"Go to bed, mistress." He turned to the
sideboard to find a fresh glass and more whiskey.
"I'm dealing with the situation."

"Hardly in a wise manner." He felt her staring

at him as he splashed the amber liquid into another glass. "One that never helps."

"And you'd know all about such matters?" He swung on her, annoyed.

"More than I care to, sir, more than I care to." She turned and went back into the room, closing the door firmly behind her.

Emma Smith became more of a puzzle each time they spoke. He looked down at the liquid in the crystal glass. With a grunt, he set it aside.

She was right. He removed his coat and unbuttoned his vest. Drinking himself into oblivion night after night would never quell the pain and longing—he avoided the word "lusting" even though he knew it was more accurate—that Vanessa Cameron had left him to suffer.

****

"Mrs. Reynolds, our supper has arrived." He knocked lightly on the bedroom door. The pheasant and champagne looked more than tempting, but he found himself wishing his housekeeper would show a little economy. But then, why would she? When he'd been sharing the apartment with Vanessa, he'd instructed her to bring the best available.

Emma stepped out into the room wearing her riding habit without the spencer and hat. Ringlets framed her heart-shaped face. Her complexion was what he'd heard described as peaches and cream, her figure excellent in the high-waisted style of the day.

"It looks absolutely delicious." Emma gave him a disarming smile.

He moved quickly to pull out a chair for her and seat her carefully at the table before he took a place opposite her.

"I apologize for my earlier behavior." He looked squarely into beautiful green eyes that met his gaze unflinchingly. "I will try to be a more civil companion in future. Or," his blue eyes suddenly lit up with a small twinkle, "you will be seeking a false dissolution of our false marriage."

"I gave my word, sir." She cocked her head. "I shan't desert you. But I will admit I prefer to live without bad humor tarnishing our relationship."

"Well said. That makes two of us. Now let's get to this delectable-looking bird. I trust you're hungry, Mrs. Reynolds?"

A half hour later, as they were enjoying coffee before the fire, a knock sounded on the door. Emma looked questioningly at Morgan, but he shook his head. "I wasn't expecting anyone."

He arose and opened the door to admit a big, burly man. The captain's equal in height, he appeared to be a good twenty years his senior. He sported bushy side-whiskers and a ruddy complexion. As he pulled off his cap, a thatch of gray curls came into view.

"Morgan, my lad, where have ye been? We've been loading the *Ula* daily. Will ye no be coming to the dock to oversee us at all? I know you're in love, but..."

His words broke off as his gaze suddenly fell on Emma.

"Beg pardon, Captain." The man's attitude of friendly camaraderie vanished as confusion furrowed his weathered brow. "I wasn't aware ye were entertaining...a lady."

"Come in, Angus." Morgan Reynolds stepped aside to admit their visitor. "I would like you to meet Emma, my wife. We were wed two days ago."

"Wife?" The man looked as if he'd been hit by a plank. Dazed, he entered the room only when Captain Reynolds took him by the arm and drew him inside. "But Vanessa...?"

"Vanessa took a sudden fancy to become the wife of a wealthy laird, while I took an equally sudden fancy to Mistress Emma, and that's the entire story." Captain Reynolds went to the sideboard, where he splashed whiskey into a tumbler. "Will ye no drink ta our health?" A thick Scottish accent colored his final sentence.

He thrust the glass into the hand of the visitor, who continued to stand transfixed, staring at Emma.

"Come, come, man. Dinna stand there looking as if a death has just been announced." Morgan picked up his coffee cup and clicked against the newcomer's glass. "Drink ta Emma and me, and wish us much happiness."

When the man still made no reply, Morgan turned to Emma, the Scottish brogue disappearing from his speech as quickly as it had come.

"My darling, this astounded man is my first mate and my brother-in-law, Angus MacLeod. He is married to my sister Iona and lives in New Brunswick with her when he's not serving with me on the *Ula*. Generally he's a good man, not nearly the slack-jawed creature you see before you at the moment."

"A pleasure, Mr. MacLeod." Emma arose and offered the man her hand. Morgan had said he had family in New Brunswick but not that he had a brother-in-law presently in England. What else hadn't he told her?

"Mistress." The mariner took her hand in his big, work-hardened one. "Forgive my behavior. It is no reflection upon your good self. I am simply amazed by Morgan's...the captain's unexpected decision." He turned to Morgan, confusion and pain mirrored in his weathered countenance.

"I'm sorry, laddie, truly sorry...about Vanessa. I wish..."

"Enough, Angus." Morgan led Emma back to her seat by the fire. "Be happy I've found a fine lady to fill the void."

"Aye, indeed, laddie, indeed." After Morgan and Emma had been seated, Angus MacLeod sat down abruptly in a chair near the door. "I never believed you and Vanessa were suited. I never..."

"We'll not be discussing it." Again the Scottish tone and the quick, hard anger she'd seen on previous occasions.

"You live in New Brunswick, Mr. MacLeod?" Emma changed the course of the conversation deftly, smiling over at their visitor in her most beguiling manner. "Do you enjoy the country? Does the climate agree with you and your wife?"

"Aye, mistress, Iona and I are very happy." He took a sip of his whiskey and appeared to relax. "It can be harsh at times, but the changing of the seasons can be beautiful. Most important, we're free to do as we choose."

"Were you not free on this side of the ocean?" His remark piqued Emma's curiosity.

"We're Highlanders, ma'am, driven from our lands to make way for English sheep." Sudden vehement bitterness filled his tone. "We nearly froze to death after our cottages were burned." He took another sip of whiskey, appeared to regain control of his anger, and continued, "In the colonies there's none of that. A man can make a life for himself confident it will be there for his children and his children's children. Speaking of which..." He turned to look hopefully at Morgan.

"No." He shook his head.

"Ah." Angus looked down into his glass, his expression falling into one of deep regret. "She'll be disappointed, and no doubt about it."

"I did my best."

"I'm sure you did, laddie. Still..."

"Enough of this unhappy talk." Morgan went to his humidor. He removed two cigars and handed one to Angus. "Tell me about the *Ula*. Is she loaded? Will we be ready to cast off bright and early Monday morning?"

"You must see for yourself." Angus accepted the end of the faggot Morgan pulled from the fire and allowed him to ignite the cigar. He drew a deep inhale and blew smoke before continuing. "You've been neglecting your duty to her and her crew, Captain. You'd best get down to the dock in the morning."

"I will, I will. We're both eager to sail. Emma is anxious to see America, aren't you, my darling?"

"Most anxious." Emma looked up at Morgan in an adoring fashion. "But, then anywhere you are I shall be happy, my love."

Chapter Four

After Angus MacLeod left, Emma turned to Morgan, who stood smoking by the window. "So you have a sister named Iona and a brother-in-law named Angus. Do you have more family of which I should be aware if I'm to successfully masquerade as your wife?"

"They're my only living relatives. And you? Who is it you're so eager to reach in the Caribbean? Is it a family member? Or yet another lover?"

"His name is Colin. He's my brother and a clergyman." Emma saw no reason to lie about the fact. He'd discover the truth when he delivered her to Eden Island.

"Ah! So you are the fallen angel of your clan."

"How dare you mock me, sir!" Emma jumped to her feet and faced him, her face pale with rage, hands clenched into white-knuckled fists at her sides. "You know nothing of what I've been forced to do, of what troubles filled my life before I met you!"

"No, you're quite right." He confronted her calmly. "I apologize. But you've led me to believe you don't warrant the consideration that is a lady's due. Have I been played for a fool? Pray tell me, Emma Smith-Reynolds, exactly who are you, and what were you doing on the highroad in a raging storm? How did someone who holds no claim to riches come by a ruby quite possibly from the collection of the late French queen?"

"French queen?" His question blew away her fury in a gust of astonishment. "Marie Antoinette?"

"Indeed. I had a highly competent jeweler

appraise it. The cut apparently is a distinctive one."

Emma turned away, a hand going to her throat, where she'd once worn an entire collection of the gems. What had she stolen? Crown jewels? The penalty for such a crime must be severe indeed. She felt ill.

She rushed into the bedroom and slammed the door shut. Her back to the panel, her breast heaving, she leaned against the closed panel. Prison! The thought sent a cold sweat washing over her entire body. She couldn't bear even the thought.

Drawing deep, slow breaths in an effort to regain her calm, she decided she had only one chance of escaping such a fate. She must provide an excellent impersonation of the captain's wife...no matter what it entailed.

****

The next morning she dressed and styled her hair with care. When she went to join Captain Reynolds for breakfast, she sat down daintily across from him and cast him what she hoped was a beguiling smile.

"You look well, madam," he said, reseating himself after having risen at her entrance. "Last evening I feared your sudden departure from my presence might indicate you were unwell. Or perhaps learning you had carried a gem that once belonged to a queen unsettled you."

"Simply a case of too much rich food and coffee too late in the evening," she replied, helping herself to bread and butter. "This morning I'm right as rain and eager to accompany you when you visit your *Ula*."

"Madam, taking you to the docks wouldn't be prudent." He paused with his coffee cup halfway to his mouth. "It's a rough part of the city, not at all suited for a lady."

"Ah." She looked over at him and lowered her

eyes so that her long lashes spread out over her alabaster cheeks. "So you'd prefer your lady wife remain cloistered in these rooms?"

"I do." He drained his cup and stood up. "I have a great deal of business to conduct. I prefer not to be hampered by a lady, even if that lady is my wife, on my arm."

"Very well." Emma leaned back in her chair and threw out her hands in a graceful gesture of submission. "I shall bide my time. Perhaps Mrs. Bradley has a bit of fancywork with which I might help her."

"You can do needlework?" He paused in reaching for his hat and looked back at her, dark eyebrows elevating.

"Certainly." She cast him a coquettish glance. "Between moments of intimacy and passion, a courtesan must amuse herself."

"Emma Reynolds, I believe you make such outrageous statements simply to confuse and vex me. Try to behave until I return. That shouldn't prove an impossible request coming from a husband you should respect...and love."

****

During the remainder of the week, Emma saw little of Captain Reynolds. He left early each morning to supervise the loading of his ship and to obtain the necessary papers for her sailing. Mrs. Bradley furnished Emma with needlework to pass the time. The housekeeper's raised eyebrows bore witness to her amazement at the young woman's competency. Emma stifled a smile. She was proving to be an enigma to the landlady as well as to her supposed spouse.

On Saturday Emma's new wardrobe arrived. She was amazed to discover several dresses she hadn't ordered among the collection of gowns, undergarments, nightdresses, capes, boots, shoes, and gloves. When she questioned the delivery man, he shrugged and said they had all been ordered for the wife of Captain Morgan Reynolds.

She carried the boxes into the bedroom. As she opened one after another she saw that the seamstress and her staff had done a remarkable job. Later, as she swirled about before the cheval mirror in one beautifully made creation after another, she decided that she, Emma Prescott, well attired, with clean hair and body, was not an unattractive creature.

In the midst of her reverie, another thought assailed her. She paused before the mirror, hands on her hips. Surely a single stone hadn't been sufficient to clear his debts and purchase all this finery. Could he possibly have discovered the necklace and was making fast and loose with its proceeds?

Startled at the possibility, Emma knelt beside the bed and felt beneath the mattress. Ah, there it was, still safe and sound. Carefully she drew it out and held it up to the light. It glittered and gleamed in the afternoon sun, as brilliant as the queen who may once have worn it. She wondered again about its worth and, more importantly, the punishment for stealing such a royal treasure.

"Mrs. Reynolds." Captain Reynolds' voice startled her.

"I'm in here." She stuffed the necklace back beneath the mattress, arose, and gave her skirts a quick brush.

"Ah!" He stood in the doorway and looked her up and down. "I see your wardrobe has arrived. That gown is most becoming. It must be a pleasant change after days of wearing that same green velvet."

"It certainly is." Emma swirled about so that he might get the full impression of her new gown. "Thank you." She paused and looked over at him, green eyes coquettishly demure.

"Your gem purchased it." He turned and walked back in the drawing room.

"Did it?" She followed him. "It must have fetched a mighty sum to allow you not only to pay your debts but also to buy me a most complete wardrobe."

"It did." He splashed whiskey into a glass from a decanter on the sideboard before he turned back to face her. "And it brings me to wonder how you came by a stone my jeweler believes came from the collection of the French queen."

"Does it matter?" Emma felt her heartbeat quicken as she struggled for a cool, calm demeanor. "It has served us both well. And the queen is long dead, so why concern ourselves about questions as to how and why?"

"I suppose I must accept that answer, since you've agreed to pose as my wife. But someday," he crossed the room and came to loom over her, "Mrs. Reynolds, I will have the truth, all of it, never fear."

****

Captain Reynolds left their lodgings at dawn on Monday morning. An hour later, two sailors came to collect the trunks he'd provided to contain his and Emma's belongings.

"A carriage will be here in an hour to collect yourself, missus," one of them informed her as he and his companion hefted the containers out of the apartment. "The captain bid us tell you to be ready prompt."

"Did he now?" Emma flashed the man a glittering smile, batting her eyelashes, and he tripped and almost fell as he passed out the doorway.

"Hi, Mike, don't ye go lookin' at the captain's missus like that!" she heard the other sailor warn as they made their way out of the house. "Ye know he's not a man to take triflin' with his ladies lightly. He'd skin ye alive, he suspected ye'd taken to lookin' at her in a special way."

Emma chuckled. She might not be the bewitching Vanessa, but in her new wardrobe and with a bit of acting she might just pass as a charming woman, the kind that just might remove the other woman from Captain Morgan Reynolds' mind. She didn't have time to speculate on why that mattered. She still had a bit of last-minute packing to do, which included the necklace from beneath the mattress.

****

When she arrived at the docks, she saw him striding about the wharf, obviously deeply involved in final preparations. Sitting in the carriage that had brought her, Emma adjusted her feather-trimmed bonnet and smoothed the skirts of her deep blue traveling costume. Captain Reynolds certainly cut a dashing figure, a man to catch the eye of even the most discerning woman.

Her driver interrupted her thoughts by opening the door and extending his hand.

"This way, mistress," he began, but suddenly a young man was by his side, a tall, handsome young man with curling golden hair and a smile that lit up his face.

"Allow me, my lady." He brushed the driver aside and put one booted foot on the step to extend his gloved hand in to her.

"I don't believe we've met, Mr...." Emma hesitated.

"Farand Thatcher, at your service. And you would be...?"

"My wife." Captain Reynolds appeared beside him. "And I'm quite capable of helping her from her carriage, Mr. Thatcher." His tone brooked no argument.

"I'm sure you are." Farand Thatcher touched his

hat and backed off. "I meant no offense, sir. Madam."
He turned back to Emma and swept her a bow.
"Until we meet again." Brown eyes twinkled
wickedly up at her.

"You're late, madam." The captain extended his
hand to her. When she accepted it, his fingers close
around hers more tightly than necessary. "I was
about to send someone to look for you. Now I find
you dallying about the docks with a dandy."

"Hardly dallying, sir." She accepted his hand
and smiled demurely down at him. "If I am tardy,
you must blame it on London traffic. You must know
by now I am not about to miss the opportunity of a
voyage to America."

Several of the sailors involved in the loading had
paused to look admiringly at their master's wife as
she alighted from the carriage. When Emma cast
them a smile, Captain Reynolds' reaction was swift.

"Get back to work!" he bellowed. "My wife is a
lady not to be stared at by the likes of you!"

As they scuttled to obey, he returned his
attention to Emma.

"I'll have no flirting with my crew," he muttered,
his tone sending a shiver wafting over Emma. "As
my wife, you must command respect. Casting
beguiling looks at all and sundry may once have
been your stock in trade, but I'll have none of it, do
you understand? That goes doubly for dockside
gigolos."

"Aye, Captain." Although her heart was
pounding a dangerous tattoo against her ribs, Emma
tilted her head coquettishly in his direction.
"Whatever you say, my lord and master."

"Argh!" He caught her by an arm and propelled
her toward the ship.

"The horses are coming with us?" she asked as
she saw two sailors loading Bonnie and the Lad.

"You seem to have grown fond of the mare, and

I'll need a good riding horse. Such are few and far between presently in New Brunswick. Now come along. I won't have my men drooling over my wife."

He drew her past the sailors and onto the deck so swiftly her shoes barely touched the boarding plank.

"The captain be powerful jealous of his new missus," one of the sailors chuckled. "I don't envy any man what takes a serious fancy to her."

****

Once aboard, Captain Reynolds guided Emma to a hatch near the rear of the ship.

"Follow me," he said and swung down the ladder beneath. She watched as he descended. When he turned to look up at her, she paused.

"Well, come along, Mrs. Reynolds." He extended a hand up to her. "We haven't got all day. I want you safely ensconced in my...our cabin before we catch the tide."

"I'd prefer if you moved off a few paces, my love," Emma said softly. "I'll not have you looking up my skirts as I descend."

"Do you think me so desperate for a glimpse of your nether regions that I'm prepared to make an utter fool of myself by tarrying at the foot of this ladder? Good God, woman, give me small credit! I have far bigger concerns, with sailing imminent!"

"Please." Emma cast him a simpering smile.

"Argh!" He strode a few feet down the corridor. "Is this a sufficient distance to satisfy your tender sensibilities?"

"Thank you." With another smile, this time reeking with smugness, Emma descended the steps.

****

As Morgan led her along the corridor toward the rear of the ship, he slowly regained his sense of humor. The minx delighted in teasing him, did she? Well, he'd play along...but only so far as it amused him.

Emma drew a sharp inhale when Captain Reynolds pushed open his cabin door to reveal a gleaming oak-lined room, complete with wide, quilt-covered bed, mahogany desk and chair, and even a large copper tub for bathing. Along one wall a narrow set of shelves was filled with books. Next to them sat their trunks. Had this perhaps been another love nest of the captain and Vanessa? Again she wondered about the cost, and her hand went to her bodice, where she kept the necklace secreted.

If her counterfeit husband had gotten himself deeply into debt because of the expensive tastes of a woman who obviously cared little for him, that was his problem. She, Emma Prescott, had the means to support herself independently. And in considerable comfort, if the amount he appeared to have gotten from the sale of a single stone was any indication of the gems' worth.

"You appear lost in thought, Mrs. Reynolds." He broke into her considerations as he turned to leave. "I'll leave you to settle in and will come for you when we set sail. I'm sure you'd like to cast a fond farewell to England's bonnie shores." The last had a ring of sarcasm. When she glanced up at him his expression had become cold and bitter.

"You seem to have no love for this country," she said.

"I've told you. I'm a Highlander by birth. Do you not know how these English have treated us over the years, how they are still destroying our lives and homes back in those hills?"

"I know a little," Emma replied. "I believe some Highlanders were asked to leave their lands to make way for sheep whose wool and mutton was needed for the military fighting in the French war."

"Asked? Have you been living under a stone, woman? We were driven out, our cottages burned.

Some of us starved, some froze in the snow. Only the most fortunate, like my sister Iona and I, were able to make our way to the coast and secure passage to America."

"I'm sorry. I've lived an isolated life. I had no idea..."

"Well, you do now. Therefore, when we get to America, I would be grateful if you'd not make an issue of announcing your own heritage. My family and friends would not take kindly to my marrying an English wench." He strode out of the cabin, banging the door behind him.

Emma slowly drew off her gloves and removed her hat. Captain Morgan was a complex man, steeped in a vibrant hatred of the English and extremely jealous of the women in his life. Had he always been the latter, or had it resulted from Vanessa's betrayal? Whatever the reason, Emma decided not to challenge it any further. At least not until he'd taken her safely to America.

****

"Are you decent, madam?" An hour later, a sharp knock on the door and four harsh words announced his return.

"Of course." Emma threw it open. "Are we ready to cast off, m'lord?"

"Immediately." He took her arm and hurried her along the corridor to the ladder. "Since I have no time to waste on your modesty, I'll ascend first and you can follow."

"You're a gentleman, sir." Emma dropped him a small curtsy.

He made a disgruntled sound as he swung his tall, muscular length up the steps.

A melee of activity engaged the deck onto which Emma emerged, as sailors rushed about their duties, coiling ropes and checking rigging. Captain Reynolds guided her through it all to the raised deck at the rear, where a helmsman stood ready at the wheel. Angus MacLeod, also on the bridge, touched his cap to her.

"Welcome aboard, Mrs. Reynolds. I'm hopin' you enjoy the voyage."

"I'm sure I shall, sir." Emma smiled at him. "With you and my husband in charge, I'm certain all will go well."

"Thank ye, ma'am. "

"Is everything in readiness, Mr. MacLeod?" The captain turned to his brother-in-law.

"Aye, sir. Shipshape."

"Then let's be on our way."

Moments later, the great ship slid out into the river, with the captain giving orders to the helmsman and Angus, the latter bellowing them to the sailors.

Amazed and thrilled at the smooth glide of the great ship, Emma looked up at the clear skies above the tall masts and drew a deep breath. At last she was on her way to a new life and safety in the colonies.

****

Emma ate a solitary luncheon brought to the cabin by a sailor who informed her the captain regretted he was too busy to join her. When she'd finished, she took the clothing she believed she'd need for the voyage from her trunks and hung them in a small clothespress near the door. She wondered if she should unpack the captain's belongings, then decided against it. She would not want him rummaging through her personal belongings. She would respect his privacy.

She paused in shaking out a warm rust-and-green traveling suit and looked over at the wide bed built into the wall. He'd said he would sleep in another cabin, claiming seasickness on her part as her need for privacy, but he'd no doubt miss the

69

comfort of his own couch.

Well, it couldn't be helped. She definitely wasn't going to offer to share with him. Determining not to be discomfited by his sacrifice, she went back to her unpacking.

****

In defiance of the excuse of seasickness he planned to use as reason for their separate sleeping arrangements, she spent most of the afternoon at the rail, first watching land fade from sight behind them, then enjoying the way the huge sails caught the breeze to propel the great ship's smooth roll forward. It was an experience not to be missed, no matter what problems she might be creating for herself that evening.

She watched the captain, on the quarterdeck, his attention focused on his ship's progress while he gave Angus orders to relay to the crew. He was an impressive man, handsome, virile, strong, and more than slightly enigmatic. She knew she had a great deal to learn about Captain Morgan Reynolds.

Late in the afternoon she returned to their cabin and lay down for a short rest on the big, soft bed. She must have dozed, for suddenly, it seemed, he was at the door.

"Mrs. Reynolds, may I come in? The steward will be here shortly with our dinner."

"Of course." Emma scrambled to her feet, patted her hair, smoothed her skirt and hastened to open the door.

His dark curls a windblown tangle, a stubble beginning to appear on his chin and jaws, he was an earthy, sensuous-looking creature. Emma felt her breath come into her body a bit too sharply.

"You've been enjoying the voyage?" He stripped off his seaman's jacket and, rolling up the sleeves of his white shirt, went to a basin on the dresser to wash his hands and arms.

"Very much so, Captain." Emma took a seat at the small eating table near the bed and fireplace and adjusted her skirts. "I had no idea it would be so pleasant."

"And what is to become of our excuse of seasickness?" He turned to her, drying his muscular arms on a snow-white towel. "Or have you decided to discard it in favor of sharing that bed yonder with me?"

"Of course not! You may simply hint that you and your new bride have had words and you've decided to sleep apart from the harpy."

"You don't think that will make me look a fool, to have married such an unpleasant creature?"

"Men make mistakes. It may be a well known fact by now that I was your hasty second choice."

"Aye, well, it might suffice." Again the Scottish brogue. "However, ye hardly look like an unfortunate choice."

"Thank you, kind sir." She dropped him a teasing curtsy. "But a pleasant façade can often hide an ugly interior, a condition of which I'm sure your men are aware. Now may we talk of more pleasant topics, for example, the beauty of this ocean voyage."

"Don't be fooled, Emma." His words went back to proper English and he spoke sincerely, as if to a friend. "This is just the beginning. The North Atlantic is full of vicious tricks, and I've no doubt we'll soon be sampling them."

There was a tap at the door, and he turned to answer it, letting in a sailor bearing a tray heavy with roast beef, vegetables, bread, and even a bottle of wine and a pot of tea.

"That will be all, Edwards," Captain Reynolds said after he'd placed it on the table in front of Emma.

"Yes, sir, thank you, sir." The man turned and headed for the door.

"Oh, and Edwards, please tell Mr. MacLeod that my wife and I don't wish to be disturbed unless it's a dire emergency."

"Aye, sir." The young seaman ducked his head, a knowing grin on his face as he turned and went out.

"What happened to your plan to plead an argument as a reason for not staying with me?" As soon as the sailor's footsteps had died away, Emma rounded on him. "'I don't wish to be disturbed unless it's a dire emergency' are hardly the words of a man who has become disenchanted with his new bride."

"Ah, well, since you chose to destroy the seasick excuse, I don't see why I have to develop another fabrication. So here I stay." He sank into the chair opposite her. "Will you allow me to offer you a glass of wine?" He picked up the bottle and held it over her glass.

"I suppose there can be no point to opposing your decision." With a small, resigned sigh, she inclined her head and he proceeded to fill their glasses.

He took an appreciative sip, then spread out his hand to indicate the laden table. "Come, eat. Cold food does no good in the belly."

"Of course." She leaned forward and ladled beef and vegetables onto a plate which she proceeded to pass over to him. "You must be hungry. Did you have no luncheon?"

"I was otherwise occupied." He accepted the food and took up his knife and fork. "Running a ship the size of the *Ula* takes considerable time and energy."

"The *Ula*. What does the name mean?" Emma paused in filling her own plate and glanced over at him.

"It means 'sea jewel,'" he said, cutting into the tender beef. "And she is just that. A true gem of a ship."

"Ah." Emma placed her food before her and tried

not to think of the necklace in her bodice.

"Is the food not to your liking?" He looked over at her when she made no move to begin eating.

"It's perfectly lovely." She came back to the moment, picked up her utensils, and lied. "I was just thinking...about America and the Caribbean, and wondering how long it will be until I see Colin again."

"A lot will depend on the weather and politics." He finished off a potato and took up his glass.

"Politics?" Emma didn't understand.

"Are you not aware of the world situation?" He looked over at her, his eyebrows rising. "Alexander of Russia has withdrawn from his alliance with Napoleon. Now Russia and France are facing each other as enemies. To the south, the war provoked by the French general's decision to replace the Bourbon king with his own brother Joseph is raging in Spain. To the north, in Scotland, there are rumblings of sedition from displaced Highlanders. Then, of course, there are the American rebels to the south of British America. Most people believe that the warmongers among them will shortly declare war. Then the seas will become a battleground. Travel to the Caribbean will become even more of a risky business than it is at present."

"Are you saying I could be trapped in British North America indefinitely?" Her forehead furrowed as she looked across the table at him.

"Aye, that you could. But never fear. As my wife you'll have a safe home for as long as necessary in New Brunswick. In fact," he leaned back in his chair and let a bitter smile kink up one corner of his mouth, "We will have a large if sparsely furnished home all to ourselves."

"The house you built for Vanessa?" Emma spoke softly and avoided looking at him. She didn't want to look upon his hurt.

"Yes." He finished off his wine and reached for the bottle. "The house I built for Vanessa." Then his tone lightened. "Come along, Mrs. Reynolds. Eat, drink, enjoy. We must leave the past behind us...on the shores of England."

****

A half hour later Captain Reynolds placed the remains of their meal on the tray and placed it in the companionway.

"Edwards will pick it up later," he said, stepping back inside the cabin. He slid the bolt into place, then turned to Emma.

"Tonight, my dear, we will share that bed yonder. I believe it's large enough for us each to have sufficient space even with a blanket rolled and placed between us for decorum. I also believe you now know me well enough to trust me to keep to myself."

She hesitated, then nodded. "Yes."

"Good. Then I suggest you prepare for bed and climb into the back. You'll be better off there, as I could be summoned in the night." He began to unbutton his shirt. Emma turned quickly away.

"Please feel safe to disrobe and don a nightshift," he said, flinging aside the garment and going to sit at his desk, naked to the waist. "I promise to keep my eyes firmly fixed on these charts and maps for the next five minutes."

Emma hesitated, then went to her trunk and took out a long-sleeved, high-necked nightgown. Going behind his back, she removed her dress and petticoats and slipped into it. Then she scampered to the bed and climbed into it.

"You disrobe with amazing speed." He looked up to see her carefully arranging a rolled-up blanket down the center. "Is that a skill of your former trade?"

"You have a vile tongue and cruder thoughts,

Captain," she snapped. "I simply saw no reason to dally."

"Oh, aye." He arose. "Other ladies with whom I've spent nights have been more inclined to fuss over their evening ablutions."

She felt her breath catch in her throat. She couldn't help staring. He was a magnificently handsome man, broad muscular chest lightly furred, his belly flat.

He put his hand to his belt, jerked it open, and Emma rolled to face the wall.

"I'm assuming those other ladies did not require a barrier down the center of the bed," she said tartly, and he burst out laughing.

"No, my dear Mrs. Reynolds, they certainly did not. And they weren't even pretending to be my wife."

She felt him lower himself into the bed beside her. Soon abrupt snorts told her he slept.

"You're making the most despicable racket!" Emma sat up angrily in the darkness. "Please roll over on your side or your stomach."

"Madam, I'm tired and need my rest," he grunted. "Whatever racket I'm making I must have made on previous nights we've shared a room. It didn't disturb you then."

"Then you weren't cast up beside me!" She flounced around, pummeling her pillow. "Surely some of your 'ladies' must have informed you that you snore most abominably when you sleep on your back."

"My dear Mrs. Reynolds, when those other ladies shared my bed, I did very little sleeping, I can assure you."

"Argh!" She threw herself back beneath the covers, her back to him.

His deep, sensuous chuckle only served to rankle her further.

****

Emma awoke in the morning to find him gone from the cabin. On the table sat a coffeepot and a basket of breads. Feeling warm and comfortable and lazy, she stretched languidly. For a few moments she lay gazing up into the sunlight flooding through the skylight.

Admit it, Emma Prescott, you're enjoying this adventure. You're safe from that odious man under the protection of the handsomest man you've seen outside of those books on Greek gods. You may even be quite a wealthy lady once you get to America and sell a few of those gems.

She felt a shiver wash over her as another thought occurred. The last woman who'd possessed that necklace had come to a tragic end. Did it carry some sort of curse?

Don't be a goose! She scrambled out of bed and hurried to the wash basin to splash water over her face.

She was dressed and enjoying coffee brought by Edwards when he knocked at the door. "Mrs. Reynolds, are you up?"

"Yes, do come in, my dear." Emma patted her hair and arranged her skirts. "It appears to be a lovely morning," she said as he stepped into the cabin.

He wore his seaman's jacket, well-fitted breeches, and high leather boots. His shirt was open at the throat, adding to his virile appearance. Emma tried to distract herself from his attractive person and continued, "I'll go up on deck shortly. As you've said, we may have rough sailing ahead and must make the most of this fine weather."

"Aye, that we must, Mrs. Reynolds." He removed his jacket, hung it on a peg, and came to join her at the table. "Will you pour my coffee?"

"Certainly." *My, don't we make the perfect*

domestic pair. The tips of her lips quirked upward as she filled a cup.

"You smile." He looked over at her. "Do I amuse you?"

"We amuse me." Emma handed him his coffee and met his gaze. "We are becoming amazingly adept at playing a happily married couple. I'm sure we could fool most anyone."

"Well, good." He paused, took a sip. "We'll have to be excellent to fool my sister, Iona. She's a shrewd lass, not easily deceived."

"Then we must practice more diligently." Emma arose and reached for her bonnet. "Perhaps as we take a morning promenade around the deck?"

"Very well." He stood and crooked his arm. "Come along, my dear."

"Certainly, my darling." Emma cast him her most coquettish glance. Together they went out of the cabin and climbed the ladder to the deck.

****

Captain Morgan Reynolds couldn't sleep. Long into the night he lay on his back, long after Emma's regular breathing behind him told him she slept. Finally he rolled on his side to look at her beyond their blanket barrier. A deep sigh escaped his lips. The lass puzzled him no end.

He longed to question her about her past, yet she'd made it clear she'd have none of it. She hadn't denied she'd been some rich man's mistress, but neither had she out and out confessed to it. To further confuse him, she had the deportment of a lady, occasionally laced with a touch of minx, a combination he found altogether too appealing. He'd loved Vanessa with a passion. He could never forget or deny the fact, but this mysterious woman who'd come to him out of the night intrigued him to the bone.

She was beautiful enough to make any man's

blood run hot and hard. It rankled him to see the admiring and even lustful glances his crew cast upon her when they thought their captain wasn't looking. Demur and daring, bold and beautiful, if any woman could make him get over Vanessa Cameron, Emma Smith was definitely the one.

But how could he be so fickle? Only days ago he'd been convinced he could never love anyone aside from Vanessa. Now, here he lay, peering around a rolled-up blanket at the sleeping countenance he found himself likening to that of an angel.

A fallen angel. Annoyed, he rolled away from her, put his back against the barrier, and tried to will himself to sleep...without snoring.

Chapter Five

"What is it? What's wrong?" Emma pulled herself up against her pillows and blinked into the light of a lantern casting swaying shadows around the cabin. The bed beneath her tossed and rolled like a thing possessed. Captain Reynolds stood in the middle of the room, buttoning his vest.

"Storm." He reached for his seaman's jacket, hanging on a peg near the door. "Get dressed but stay in the cabin. Don't on any account try to move about the ship."

He strode across the cabin and out the door.

Emma started to sit, but the ship heaved violently and she was tossed against the backboard.

"Ouch!" She rubbed her head as she became aware of the roar of wind and water breaking over the *Ula*. *Get dressed, he's said. Probably good advice, in case of emergency, but first...* She ran her hand beneath the mattress at the back of the bed, where it met the wall, and extracted the necklace.

Clutching the jewelry in her hand, she clambered from the bed. Grasping the pieces of furniture bolted to the floor, she made her way to where her clothing hung in the press.

Ten minutes later, fully dressed, she secreted her booty in her bodice and decided she would not attempt to pin up her hair. Lurching about the cabin, she gathered up a few items she deemed essential if they were forced to abandon ship and, using the cloth from the table where they'd shared their evening meal, tied them into a neat bundle. Then she donned her warmest cloak and boots and seated herself on the bed, her hands gripping her cache of supplies.

She marveled that she didn't feel ill. Perhaps she was what she'd heard termed a born sailor. She hoped so. She couldn't imagine anything much worse than being ill in the present situation.

For what seemed like hours she sat in place, listening to the roar of wind and water. Sometimes, above it all, she heard Angus bellowing orders. What must it be like up on deck? What would the captain be doing? Was he safe?

Then she thought of the horses. Poor little Bonnie must be terrified. She staggered to her feet. She had to go to the little mare and try to reassure her. Lurching, tumbling, at times falling, she made her way out of the cabin to the ladder. Grasping it with every ounce of her strength, she began the ascent.

The ship bucked and lurched, and several times she believed she'd be thrown back into the bowels of the ship. When she finally reached the top, she pushed against the hatch. At first it felt as if she were pushing against a rock wall, but finally it yielded.

A mighty gust grasped it and sent it crashing wide open. Wind and water struck her like a giant wave. She gasped and staggered. Visions of being washed back into the ship flashed through her mind. When she managed to right herself, she lurched out onto the streaming deck, head bent against the storm. Clutching at ropes and rigging, she started forward toward the hold that contained the horses. As she drew near, she could hear their terrified screams.

"I'm coming, Bonnie!" she cried. "I'm coming!"

The next instant she was struck by a great wall of water. As her feet were swept from under her, she screamed. She was sent spinning across the deck on her stomach. Her head hit the bulwarks with a thump. Dazed, she lay where she'd come to rest.

Suddenly she was pulled to her feet and half-dragged, half-propelled back across the rolling, sea-swamped deck. Before she could comprehend what was happening, she was flung down the hatch from which she'd just emerged. She dropped on her knees at the bottom of the ladder with a dull thump. Still stunned from her ordeal, she remained where she'd landed.

"Dear God, woman!" Boots thumped beside her and she was being gathered up into the captain's arms. When she looked up into his face, she saw it was a hard mask of fury. He strode to the end of the short corridor, opened the door of their cabin, pulled her inside, and kicked it shut behind them. A moment later she was unceremoniously deposited on a chair.

"Have ye no common sense!" He stared at her, water streaming down his face from his drenched dark hair. "To go abroad on a night like this, especially after I gave ye clear orders not to leave this place."

"I was concerned about the horses' safety..." she began.

"The horses are fine," he snapped. "They are secured and cannot dash about the deck causing chaos and wasting the time of working sailors. Now I suggest you do as I say this time, or I'll be forced to fasten you in, as well."

"Fasten me in!" Emma tried to rise indignantly to her feet, but the ship pitched violently and she sat down abruptly.

"Aye, fasten you." He stared at her, eyes blazing. "I've no time to go chasing a feckless woman about my decks."

"Captain!" Angus yelled from the deck. "Captain, there's been an accident!"

"You stay here." He gave Emma one last, hard look before he strode out of the cabin, slamming the door behind him.

Drenched and breathless, Emma shoved wet strands from her face as she tried to calm her anger and shock. Before she could do either, Captain Reynolds was back, kicking the door open and bursting inside with Edwards, the young seaman who'd been fetching their meals, in his arms. Blood streamed from a gaping wound in his forearm.

Captain Reynolds carried the groaning young man to the bed and laid him gently on it.

"Mrs. Reynolds, have you anything to staunch the flow?" he said, looking at Emma.

"No...yes." Emma struggled to regain control of her roiling emotions. So much was happening so fast. "That is, if you'll remove his upper clothing, I can stitch up the wound."

"Stitch up...?" The captain stared at her. "What do you mean?"

"Mistress Mason supplied a small sewing kit with my new wardrobe," she said, staggering to her trunk. "I've seen wounds sewn. I'm confident I can do it. Do you have any laudanum to kill the pain?"

"Yes." He was staring at her. "Are you sure you know what you're doing?"

"Quite sure," Emma replied with much more confidence than she felt. "Now, please dose Edwards." Taking a needle from her sewing kit, she began to thread it.

"Very well." The captain went to a small medicine chest and removed a bottle, uncorked it, and held it to Edwards' lips, carefully administering two swigs.

Then, taking the flask of whiskey from the cupboard, he knelt beside her and the wounded man to splash some of its contents over the wound. Emma flinched when the man yelped. Drawing a deep breath, she bent over her task.

****

Later, Morgan would only be able to marvel at the way Emma soothed the frightened young sailor and, once the young man fell under the influence of the laudanum, the care and efficiency with which she stitched the torn flesh. Still in her drenched gown, she'd concentrated on her task, occasionally pushing a stray curl from her forehead, never pausing, although her complexion blanched, and once Morgan saw her slim shoulders shudder.

When she'd finished and wrapped Edwards' arm in a clean white cloth, she heaved a deep sigh, pulled a quilt over the young man, and slowly stood. Although the *Ula* no longer pitched and tossed, she staggered. Morgan slipped a supporting arm about her.

"Here, come, sit." He led her gently to the captain's chair behind his desk.

He returned to the cupboard, drew out another flask, and splashed some of its contents into a mug. "Drink this," he said. "It's good for the nerves."

"I'm quite all right." She looked up at him, emerald eyes appearing brighter than usual in a face blanched pale.

"Yes, of course you are, but oblige me." He thrust the container into hands that quivered. "Now rest. I'm going to take Edwards to Angus' cabin. He will send a seaman to watch over him there."

"But he'll need more care. He'll be frightened when he revives."

"Rest, Mrs. Reynolds." Morgan placed a restraining hand gently on Emma's shoulder as she started to rise. "You've done more than your share for one night."

Sinking back into the chair, she raised the mug to her lips, and took a sip. She coughed. He patted her on the back.

"That's my girl," he said. "One sip at a time. You'll be ready for sleep shortly, I promise.

****

When he returned to the cabin after settling Edwards in the mate's cabin, he found Emma nodding in the chair, the empty brandy mug beside her on his desk, her skirts leaving a small puddle about her feet.

With a muttered expletive, he strode to the bed to pull away the soiled covers. Once he had it re-made, he went to Emma and shook her gently.

"Mrs. Reynolds, you have to get out of that wet gown and into bed before you become ill." He drew her to her feet and began to unbutton the top of her gown.

"No." She raised her hands to stop him but her protest was a weak, weary one.

"Mrs. Reynolds, let me assure you, I have absolutely no dishonorable thoughts at this moment. I only want to get you out of those wet garments and into a warm bed as quickly as possible. I have one injured soul aboard. I don't need a sick one, as well. Now stand still."

Emma seemed to wilt in the face of exhaustion and his promise. She stood passively as he removed her gown. Only when he began to loosen the ribbons at the top of her chemise, did she protest again.

"Very well, very well." He caught her up in his arms and carried her to the bed.

"Get beneath the covers and remove those wet undergarments. I'll fetch your nightgown."

****

By the time he'd found the garment and returned, Emma was fast asleep, her wet underclothing in a heap on the floor. Gently he dropped the nightgown across the end of the bed, drew the covers more securely around her, and knew that this night he would sleep on the floor. There was no way he could sleep in the same bed with a naked Emma Smith.

****

Emma awoke to find the ship rolling gently beneath her and sunlight once again streaming in through the skylight. As she came fully awake and found herself naked, she suppressed a gasp. Good Lord, she'd never slept without a nightshift in her life. What had happened in the night?

Clutching the bedding to her throat, she lay back on her pillows and began to remember. Nearly swept overboard, rescued by Captain Reynolds, the wounded sailor, mending his arm, the captain giving her brandy, undressing her...

No, no, no! She buried her face in the pillows. Then she realized the blanket barrier was missing from the bed. *Oh, Emma Prescott, what have you done!*

The door opened and he entered, again looking handsome and earthy in his seaman's clothing, his shirt open well away from his throat. He carried a tray with a pot of coffee and breakfast. He set it on the table, then turned to grin at her.

"Awake at last, Mrs. Reynolds. Do you know you've slept most of this glorious spring morning away?"

"Captain Reynolds." Emma retreated into the farthest corner of the bed and pulled the covers more tightly to her chin. "Last night, did we...did you...did I...?"

"Definitely not." He turned away to pour himself a steaming cup of coffee. "I'm not a man who would take advantage of a woman suffering from exhaustion, shock, and..." He glanced back over his shoulder at her, eyes twinkling wickedly. "Brandy."

"Brandy? I was inebriated?" The words were a gasp of dismay.

"Certainly not." He stirred his coffee slowly, a

smile tipping his lips. "Just so exhausted a half-measure of brandy hit you very hard. And I'm glad. You needed a good rest. Now climb out of that bed, have some food, and I'll take you on deck to enjoy a breath of fresh air. It will put color back in your cheeks."

"Not unless you promise to face the door until I'm fittingly attired."

With a weary sigh, he sat down and turned his back to her. "But don't take too long over it, or I may have to move to ease my muscles."

Emma gave an exasperated sigh as she reached for her nightgown and heard him respond with a deep, throaty chuckle.

****

When Morgan returned Emma to their cabin an hour later and went back to his place on the quarterdeck, he leaned on the rail and found himself once more musing over the woman who was masquerading as his wife.

She had annoyed him to the quick the previous night with her foolish attempt to visit her mare in the midst of a storm. This morning, in the clear light of day, he saw her actions as they'd been intended: kindly if ill-planned attempts to comfort a frightened creature.

And within the hour she'd utterly amazed him as she cared for the young seaman. He'd never met a woman with her strength and courage when faced with such a gruesome accident. He felt consumed with admiration for her.

He had to force himself to remember that she'd been an English laird's whore, a woman who'd been paid a queen's ruby for her services. He stretched stiff shoulders, his brow furrowing as he gazed at the horizon. Was she perhaps more thief than courtesan? Which would he prefer? Neither held much attraction.

"Captain." Angus approached him. "It goes well, this voyage, thus far, don't you agree? Perhaps having your lady wife aboard is good luck."

"If you discount the storm last night, and young Edwards' accident."

"Ah, Morgan, lad, those things will happen on any voyage." The older man moved closer and spoke confidentially. "How did it go with the money lenders in London? Did they grant an extension on your loans?"

"A short one." He drew a deep breath. "A very short one, Angus. I will be able to quell them for a time once I sell this cargo, but after that I can see a solution that will work only if the Americans declare war on us."

"Ah, laddie, you can't mean..." Angus' weathered face fell.

"Aye, brother, I do. I'll turn the *Ula* into a privateer. A few rich prizes and I'll soon be free and clear from the mess I allowed that faithless woman to draw me into."

"I don't know what Iona will say about this, and that's a fact." The first mate wagged his head sadly. "What about your wife, lad?" He looked sharply at Morgan. "What will she say when she learns you've decided to turn pirate?"

"Nothing, if she's wise." Morgan strode off, leaving his brother-in-law to gape after him.

****

Three weeks later they sailed into the port of Halifax under clear skies and gentle breezes. Emma stood at the rail, watching the town and its hilly fortification loom larger and larger until finally the ship slid into a docking. Ropes were cast off amid shouts from the sailors, with a general bustle of activity. When all was secure, Captain Reynolds strode up to her and offered his arm.

"May I escort you into His Majesty's town of

Halifax, Nova Scotia?" He looked down at her, smiling.

"Certainly, my dear." Emma inclined her head. Together they crossed the deck and proceeded down the boarding plank.

****

"There's to be a ball tomorrow evening," he informed her two hours later when they were ensconced in rooms he'd rented in an elegant old house some distance from the bustling docks. "The governor and his lady are sponsoring it. We are invited. I hope the ball gown I ordered for you in London has survived the journey in decent repair."

"A ball at the governor's mansion?" Emma raised her eyebrows. "I had no idea you were so well connected, Captain."

"I'm not." He went to a window and drew aside the curtains to look out into the bustling street below. "My former fiancée was. The invitation was issued because of her father's wealth and position in the neighboring province of New Brunswick. James Cameron is a rich man, with a great deal of influence in the timber trade. Therefore, as his future son-in-law, I was issued an invitation with the unwritten supposition that Miss Vanessa Cameron would companion me to the event."

"You're assuming that the governor and his lady will welcome you with a stranger on your arm?"

"It would be damned awkward for them to question my choice of a lady." He swung back to face her, his expression darkening. "And I do plan to put in an appearance, not hide myself away because I was jilted."

"Very well." Emma drew herself up and stuck out her chin. "Put in an appearance we shall, Captain. Let me assure you, I will do all in my power to make it appear you've gotten much better in the bargain."

"Thank you, Mrs. Reynolds." His tone reflected his amazement. "I will be most grateful."

****

Emma swung first one way and then the other as she surveyed herself in the mirror. The gold ball gown overlaid with snow-white Italian lace was indeed a seamstress' masterpiece. It swept low over her breasts and, in the fashion of the day, gathered beneath them to drape gracefully to the floor. A matching lace shawl lay over a nearby chair. Bathed and smelling softly of the lavender with which her tub had been scented, Emma would have been thoroughly satisfied with her appearance if it had not been for her hair. She'd noted the ladies in the streets of Halifax were wearing their hair in a new upswept fashion. She'd struggled to copy it but failed. She lacked the correct pins and combs.

A knock sounded at the door. She frowned. She wasn't expecting the captain for another half hour. When she opened it, she found an attractive young woman standing outside, a covered basket on her arm.

"Good evening, Mrs. Reynolds. I'm Jenny Waters. The Captain hired me to dress your hair for the ball."

"Really?" Amazed, Emma stepped back to allow the young woman access. "When did my husband make this arrangement?"

"This morning, ma'am, but I was expecting his request." She crossed to the table and set her basket upon it. .

"You were?"

"Of course, ma'am. On the evenings of balls, I always arranged..." She stopped short, casting her gaze away from Emma.

"You always arranged Mistress Vanessa's hair?"

"Yes, ma'am. I'm sorry, ma'am." Jenny blushed and blinked.

"Don't worry, Mistress Waters." Emma smiled and took a seat before the mirror, careful to arrange her skirts to prevent wrinkling. "I know all about Mistress Vanessa, and I little care, now that she is a permanent part of my husband's past."

"Yes, ma'am. Thank you, ma'am." The young woman's hands, already busy in Emma's thick, soft hair, relaxed. "You have lovely hair, Mrs. Reynolds. Doing it up will be a treat."

****

When Morgan opened the door to his rooms, he stepped briskly inside—and stopped short as he saw Emma. In the gold-and-lace ball gown, with her hair piled about her head, glittering combs holding it in place, she was dazzling.

"You stare, Captain." She cast him a demur smile and fluttered her fan coquettishly. "Am I so appalling to look upon that I take away your words?"

"Mrs. Reynolds, false modesty isn't something I admire." He shut the door firmly behind him. "Your words are just that. If you've chanced to look in the mirror yonder, you know why I stare."

"Thank you, sir...I think." Carefully she seated herself at the table and gave her fan another superfluous flutter. "But you're late. We are due at the governor's mansion in less than a half hour and you've yet to dress."

"A man takes little time to arrange himself for such social activities." He pulled off his jacket and flung it over a chair as he crossed the room toward the bedroom. "I shall be ready within five minutes. You may time me."

As he was closing the door, he saw Emma arise and go to hang up his coat. She was becoming more and more wifely each day. As he headed toward the clothes press he wondered how he felt about the situation.

****

90

The June evening was warm and balmy as they drove in a hired carriage through the streets of the military town awash with uniforms and the raucous voices of soldiers and sailors enjoying a few hours of freedom from duty.

"Not a town in which a lady should be abroad alone," he remarked.

"At night," she finished.

"Night or day. Halifax is gearing up for probable conflict with the Americans. It's flooded with the military, the majority of whom are neither officers nor gentlemen."

"And you think this war unavoidable?" Emma smoothed her skirts and adjusted her white lace gloves. The small gold reticule hung from a golden cord at her wrist, and she couldn't help thinking she would not disgrace him at the ball.

"Most definitely. Now enough talk of wars and rumors of wars. Here we are. Driver, take us up to the door, if you please."

The three-story stone mansion seemed to blaze with lights. As the carriage stopped before the wide front steps, Emma could hear the sound of the new music she recognized as a waltz issuing from within. A liveried footman opened the door and offered a hand. Ignoring him, the captain swung to the ground and reached to assist his wife.

"Mrs. Reynolds?" He offered her his arm once she was by his side.

"My dear." She tilted her head and smiled conspiratorially up at him. "Let the evening begin."

****

An hour later Morgan ended a conversation with a rotund, balding gentleman. He let his gaze roam the room until he found his surrogate wife. Standing by a mantel chatting with the governor's lady, she appeared so charmingly at ease he felt pride flooding through him and a smug smile tugging at his lips.

Whatever Emma Smith had been before she'd come under his protection, she'd somehow, somewhere, mastered the deportment of a lady. She never ceased to amaze him. In fact, she was quite possibly the most amazing woman he'd ever met. He remembered her bravery on the night of the storm. Only his austere half-sister Iona might be able to rival her courage. But Iona couldn't best her in a ballroom.

"Captain Reynolds." A short, stout man, his face reddened from the heat, drew Morgan's attention from his lady in gold. He turned to the newcomer.

"Mr. Henderson." His gut knotted.

"Perhaps not a good time to bring up such matters, but I've learned you'll be sailing on the morning tide, and I fear I must make my employer's position perfectly clear before you do. You have missed several payments on your debt to Mr. Cotton, Captain, and he has asked me to impress upon you the necessity of bringing these up to date."

"I'm in the process of selling my cargo, Mr. Henderson. Even as we speak, my mate is finalizing a number of transactions."

"All well and good, Captain, but I fear your ship cannot hold enough to make good your arrears."

"Please do not distress yourself, sir."

Morgan turned to see Emma standing close behind him. She moved to his side and slipped her hand through his arm and smiled up at him like the besotted bride she was pretending to be.

"The captain will shortly be in possession of my dowry." She turned on the lawyer. Looking down at her Morgan saw her green eyes turn as hard as emeralds and just as cold. "My father is not a poor man. Once the final documents are returned to him in England, he will forward more than enough to cover your employer's paltry loan.

"Now, come, my dear. They've just struck up a waltz and, though some find it a scandalous dance, I think we may, as loving newlyweds, perform it without causing tongues to wag."

She inclined her head abruptly to Henderson and led Morgan toward the dance floor.

"Your father? A dowry! Lass, have you gone mad!" he hissed as she slipped her arms into position.

"No, just buying time. You can settle the debt once your cargo is sold, can't you?" Her eyes twinkled mischievously. "And anyway, I didn't like that man's attitude."

"You're a delightful little rogue." Chuckling, he whirled her out onto the floor until her skirts billowed and onlookers remarked on their flamboyant style.

****

"Ma'am? May I have the honor of the next dance?" Emma, who'd been in conversation with a lady glittering with jewels, was astonished to see Farand Thatcher, the young man she'd met briefly on the London dock weeks ago, smiling at her and offering his hand.

"Mr. Thatcher. I am surprised to see you here."

"Ah, so you remember me!" His tone reflected his delight. "When we met in London, I was, like yourself, about to embark for New Brunswick. My ship, traveling in ballast, arrived shortly before the *Ula*. Now, will you dance with me?"

Remembering her surrogate husband's reaction to the handsome young man on the dock, Emma hesitated. She didn't want to annoy Captain Reynolds. If he abandoned her, finding passage to the Caribbean would become much more difficult. She'd have to try to barter or sell another jewel on her own. Her transaction might be witnessed. She could become prey to thieves.

"Thank you, sir, but I fear my husband would not take kindly to my dancing with another man."

93

"Come, come, dear lady. An innocent prance about the floor, nothing nearly as daring as that waltz I saw you performing with him only moments ago. Surely he could not object."

Before she could protest further, Farand Thatcher grasped her hand and propelled her into the group of dancers taking up their positions on the floor. Without causing a scene, Emma realized she could not renege.

They were completing one of the patterns, her fingers lightly in Farand's, when she saw him. Glowering at her, Captain Morgan Reynolds stood near a mantelpiece, his face dark as a thundercloud. A cold shudder washed over her. She'd a deal of soothing to do, once the dance ended.

****

"We're leaving, Mrs. Reynolds." Captain Reynolds took her firmly by the arm the moment the dance ended and headed her toward the door.

"It was a pleasure, Mrs. Reynolds," Farand Thatcher had the temerity to call after them.

"Captain, really!" Emma felt his fingers clamping her arm like steel pins. "He gave me little chance to refuse, and once on the dance floor..."

"Spare me the excuses. My wife's cloak, if you please," he ordered a servant near the door. The man scuttled off to obey.

"I find your attitude highly objectionable." Emma decided to take a chance and drew herself up haughtily. She would not allow him to treat her as a possession. "Your jealously is not only unwarranted but deeply annoying."

"Oh, so you find me annoying!" The servant returned with Emma's cloak and Morgan slung it about her shoulders. As he guided her out of the mansion into the soft summer darkness, he leaned close to her ear and hissed, "You find it necessary to hide my indebtedness with a blatant lie and my deficiencies as a husband by dancing with the first good-looking young buck that smiles your way. You've already accused me of snoring abominably. Damnation, madam, what else can you do to unman me?"

He waved to a footman to bring up a carriage. As they waited, Emma suddenly felt herself shaking with laughter.

"Now I amuse you." He looked down at her, his lips quirking with annoyance.

"Yes, you do. Your charges are so ridiculous that the only one to which I can possibly give credence is the latter."

"Argh!" As the carriage arrived, Morgan herded her inside and snapped at the driver, "Number Fourteen Barrington Street, driver, and hurry. I've had quite enough of this evening."

The drive through the star-sprinkled spring night was a silent one. Emma became as conscious of a chill in the air as she was of the coldness emanating from the man by her side. Deciding it would be pointless to try to change his attitude, she settled down quietly.

A sudden cool breeze whipped through the carriage. Her thin cloak, more decorative than warm, offered scant protection. After the heat of the crowded ballroom, the small gust seemed doubly cold. She shivered.

"Come here, Mrs. Reynolds." His voice was gruff as she felt his arm go about her shoulders. "Let me protect you from the chill as you protected me from a debt collector's queries."

Startled, she glanced up at him and saw his mouth quirking into an amused grin.

"You're no longer annoyed?" She let him draw her inside his coat against the warmth of his body.

"About your false dowry? No. But about that young man..."

"A stranger I will never see again." She snuggled into the warmth and sighed. "If all my problems were as small as that..." She stopped herself abruptly.

"Tell me, Emma Smith-Reynolds." She was startled to feel his lips brush the hair above her ear. "Tell me all your troubles."

She looked up at him. For a moment green eyes met blue in a question. Then, slowly, he lowered his head until his lips met hers.

A small gasp escaped her but she didn't resist. Instead she felt a ripple sweep through her body, a ripple of a wonderful sensation she'd never before experienced. When his tongue probed her parted lips, she welcomed him, shyly at first, and then as her body reacted to the closeness of this handsome, virile man who masqueraded as her husband she returned his actions with a fervor she'd never have believed herself capable of.

"Emma, Emma," he breathed when he released her mouth. "You're a beguiling creature. I've never met the likes of you."

Then he was sliding her slowly down onto the carriage seat, covering her with his body, his hand sliding her dress from one shoulder, his mouth following it. A whirling giddiness overwhelmed Emma. As his mouth found her breast she gasped, her fingers burying themselves in his dark curls.

"Fourteen Barrington, sir." The driver drew to a halt. With a disgruntled mutter, Morgan pulled himself upright, bringing Emma with him and adjusting her gown.

Like someone emerging from a dream, Emma accepted his assistance from the carriage. She knew, the minute the cold evening air washed over her, that she had made a huge mistake.

****

"Emma." Inside his rooms, Morgan reached out

to take her back into his arms, plans to lead her to his bed swirling in his mind. But she stepped away.

"I'm sorry, Captain." She addressed him as formally as if they were strangers. "I believe I may have enjoyed too much excellent champagne this evening. Please forgive my behavior in the carriage. The chill in the night air has restored me to my senses."

She went into the bedroom, shutting the door firmly behind her.

For a moment Morgan stared at the closed panel. Then he slammed his fist into the palm of his other hand.

"Damnation!" he bellowed and believed he knew exactly how his stallion felt when he was forced away from a prancing mare. "Damn you, Emma Smith!"

There was no response from behind the closed panel. Frustrated beyond anything he could have believed possible, he tore off his cravat, jacket, and shirt and strode over to the sideboard to pour a tall glass of whiskey. As he swilled it down, he paced the room, kicking at various pieces of furniture until finally, his rage vented, he sank, bare-chested and sweating, into a chair.

The woman suggested she'd been some Englishman's doxy, yet when it came to satisfying him, her new protector, she made some ridiculous excuse about having imbibed too much champagne. Damn it, he'd never understand her. He'd leave for New Brunswick tomorrow. After allowing himself and Angus a brief visit with his sister, he'd head for the Caribbean, even if he had to go in ballast. He had to get rid of Emma Smith, and the sooner the better.

Chapter Six

Emma found him asleep in a chair the next morning, a glass with a whiskey spill spread out around it on the floor below his drooping arm. Snoring and the worse for a night of drinking, naked to the waist, a dark stubble covering his jaw and chin, still Captain Morgan Reynolds was a breathtakingly handsome creature. Yet she, Emma Prescott, had had the strength to resist his advances even though he'd made her senses reel, her entire body explode with the prospect of the erotic pleasure she felt certain he could offer.

You're quite a woman, Miss Emma, she complimented herself as she pulled the bell to summon the landlady with their breakfast. Judging from the housekeeper's preparations in London, apparently the wonderful Miss Vanessa Cameron had lacked that strength.

The thought sent an unpleasant sensation washing over Emma. For a moment she failed to recognize it for what it truly was.

Don't be insane! How could you possibly be jealous. You and this man have no future.

A knock at the door announced the arrival of Mrs. Roy with a tray of coffee and rolls. Morgan awoke. For a moment he blinked in the sunlight, then put the heels of his hands to his eyes and rubbed them.

"Damnation!" he muttered, once again facing the sunshine and scowling. "What time is it?"

"Nearly nine o'clock. Pull yourself together, Captain." Emma faced him squarely. "Mrs. Roy is here with our breakfast. I'd advise you to put on a shirt."

"Argh!" He struggled out of his chair. By the time Emma had opened the door for the landlady, he was thrusting his arms into the crumpled evening shirt he'd worn the previous night.

"Good morning, Mrs. Reynolds." Mrs. Roy placed the tray on the table and glanced from Emma to Morgan. "I trust you had a pleasant evening at the ball."

"Absolutely delightful, didn't we, my dear?" Emma turned to cast a sparkling smile in his direction.

"Yes, yes, absolutely delightful," he muttered. "That will be all for now, Mrs. Roy."

"Certainly, sir. Will you be requiring luncheon, sir?"

"No. We'll be sailing on the noon tide." His tone altered. "You must excuse my gruffness this morning, Mrs. Roy. I'm afraid I enjoyed myself a bit too much last evening."

"Ah, sir, a gentleman's prerogative, is it not?" Apparently satisfied by his explanation, Mrs. Roy smiled and left them alone.

"Coffee, my dear?" Emma, in a delicate tangerine gown, seated herself daintily at the table and picked up the pot.

"Yes. And you can stop the simpering little wife performance." He flung himself into the chair opposite her. "Since act is all you do intend."

"Captain, I'm afraid I do not understand." Emma filled his cup, then hers, talking all the time. "We have an arrangement, and nothing in that arrangement involves our becoming intimate. If you now wish to change the terms, we will have to discuss the situation at length and..."

"Damnation, woman, you know what I wanted last night. If you are what you profess, it wouldn't have been a great hardship to accommodate me."

"You're saying a lady who has been mistress to one man has no right to deny any other gentleman favors? Sir, how undemocratic!" She glanced coquettishly at him over the rim of her coffee cup.

"Undemocratic! Don't talk politically to me, madam! You've made it clear you're only averse to me, not handsome young blond men who shamelessly accost you on docks and in ballrooms!"

"Accost! Hardly a correct word, Captain. Even if Mr. Thatcher is interested in me, I hardly see where that concerns you. Ours is a business arrangement that will be successfully fulfilled within the next few weeks. Perhaps, after it is, I will welcome Mr. Thatcher's or some other young gentleman's attentions."

"Very well, mistress." He arose, scraping back his chair. "I have business in town this morning. While I'm gone, I'd appreciate it if you'd ready yourself for sailing. We will be leaving at noon. I promise you, this time I'm definitely in no mood to be kept waiting."

****

Emma had finished her packing when a knock sounded at her door.

"Come in, Mrs. Roy," she called, snapping the lock on her trunk.

The landlady entered with a large bouquet of roses in her arms. She held them out to Emma.

"For you, Mrs. Reynolds," she said, a smug smile crossing her face. "The captain must have had a lovely evening yesterday, to send such an offering."

"I hadn't thought..." Emma brought herself up short. It wouldn't do to tell Mrs. Roy their night had ended acrimoniously.

She carried them to a table. A small, white envelope was tucked among their leaves. Furtively she slid it into her hand. Keeping it away from the prying eyes of the landlady, she glanced down at the words. She barely managed to suppress a gasp.

"To the lovely woman with whom I had the pleasure of sharing but a single dance." It was signed "Farand Thatcher."

"You're a lucky woman, Mrs. Reynolds." Mrs. Roy was moving about the room, straightening furniture and bric-a-brac. "It's not every husband that's so thoughtful...or sentimental."

"Yes," Emma responded absently as she continued to stare down at the card. "Yes, I am most fortunate."

She was standing at the window, the card still in her hand, when a carriage drew up in the street. Her heart leapt as she saw the captain emerging.

"Mrs. Roy, would you like these?" she asked quickly. "I'll be leaving shortly, and they'll never withstand the voyage. It would be a shame to waste them."

"Oh, ma'am, are you quite sure?" The woman gazed at the flowers, longing in her faded features.

"Yes, of course. Only, please take them and go at once. I prefer to tease my husband about not receiving them."

"Oh, you are a minx, Mrs. Reynolds!" The landlady chuckled as she slipped out of the room, the roses clutched in her arms.

Emma glanced down at the card in her hand, then at the unlit fireplace. She had to find a place to dispose of it before Morgan returned.

His booted footsteps coming toward the door forced her to make a quick decision. Lifting a chair cushion, she thrust it beneath.

****

When Morgan entered the apartment a few minutes later, he paused and let his gaze roam around the room. Emma felt her heart pound. What was he looking for? Did he somehow suspect?

"Ah, good. I see you're all packed and ready." He indicated the trunks, and she felt relief engulf her. "Two of my men will be here momentarily to collect both our luggage and us. Time and tide wait for no one, Emma."

"Then let's be off, my dear." Gathering up her bonnet and gloves, she smiled up at him. She was glad he appeared to have recovered from their dispute of the previous evening.

At the door he paused and glanced back across the room.

"Mustn't leave the place in disarray," he said and strode back to straighten the chair cushion beneath which Emma had hastily hidden the card.

"Oh, do come along!" she cried. "Remember, time and tide wait for no one."

"Very well." He gave the cushion a hasty jerk and returned to Emma to offer his arm.

Emma felt the trickle of sweat beneath her breasts begin to dry as he led her out of the apartment. She was glad she was leaving Halifax and brash, handsome Farand Thatcher. Her life was complicated enough without his presence.

****

Morgan watched Emma standing by the bulwarks as the ship sailed smoothly up the coast of New Brunswick under clear skies and a fair breeze. He had wondered for more times than he could count about the woman and her past. At times she fascinated him, at others she frustrated him. Sometimes she delighted him, then almost immediately she'd do something to irritate him to the bone. Worst of all, she made him aware of his needs, basic needs Vanessa had always satisfied. Now she was gone and in her stead was Emma, who refused to deny that she'd been a rich man's fancy woman yet had the power to make his body lust night after night.

Was he so shallow that he could so quickly transfer his interest from one woman to another? No, definitely not. What he'd felt for Vanessa had been love; what he felt for Mistress Emma Smith was lust, pure and simple. He mustn't let it get the better of him. She was only a temporary presence.

Furthermore, how could he even consider a relationship with an Englishwoman? He'd been lucky she chose to rebuff him on the night of the ball. Too much champagne and just a tad of jealousy at seeing her dancing with that good-looking young lad had almost been his undoing.

He watched her, the ribbons of her bonnet flitting in the wind, stray curls dancing enticingly about her beautiful face, and felt disgusted as his body reacted.

"Mr. MacLeod, more canvas!" he bellowed to his first mate. "We're wasting a stiff breeze."

"Aye, sir." Angus turned to the sailors and roared out his captain's orders.

Damnation, Morgan thought as he watched his men racing aloft to do his bidding. He wished he'd never found her on the road that night.

****

Emma was at the rail again when a sailor high in the rigging shouted, "Land ho." She leaned forward, straining for her first sight of the province Captain Reynolds now called home.

"The Miramichi," he said, coming to join her as a ribbon of dark green appeared on the horizon. "The first habitations you'll see as we sail into the bay will be those of French fishermen, Acadians who managed either to escape the Deportation of 1755 or who returned when they deemed it safe."

"Deportation?" Emma looked up at him.

"Lord in heaven, girl, have you been living under a rock? Do you not know about the Deportation of the Acadians fifty-seven years ago?"

"News of events in the colonies is often slow to reach England, never mind that I have lived most of my life much removed from the centers of commerce and news." Emma tossed him a disdainful look. "Perhaps you'd care to enlighten me on this Deportation as you have on other world events."

"Very well." He leaned on the rail, keeping his gaze focused on the ever-thickening band of green before them. "In the 1750s the English began to suspect that the pastoral French who lived in this area were planning to unite with their brothers from France to help overthrow British rule. They never once paused to consider that these people thought of themselves as Acadians, citizens of this land they'd named Acadia, with little or no loyalty to a country many of them had never seen. Most of the families had been here for over a hundred years and felt this was their home, not some strange land across the ocean.

"In what the English justified as protecting themselves, they rounded up as many of these peaceful folk as they could. Some were shipped south to Louisiana, some back to France, and still others to England. Those who managed to slip through the British net hid in the woods until they thought it safe to return to their lands."

"Much as you and your people were driven from the Highlands," Emma said thoughtfully.

"A good deal the same." Captain Reynolds squinted into the sun. "Now the ban against them has been lifted, but many of those who chose to return have found their farms and lands taken over by British Loyalists who fled the revolution in the American states. They've had to start over again, often with little more than the clothes on their backs. But start over they have. They're a tough, resilient lot. I've no doubt they will prevail.

"I must return to the helm. Guiding the *Ula* into

the bay and up the river to our home is no task to leave to my crew."

A half hour later they were deep into Miramichi Bay, sailing smoothly past a few small islands and into the wide-open mouth of the river. Emma saw small, rude dwellings scattered in the forest along the shore, with small boats bobbing in the water in front of them. Here and there people stood watching the ship pass. She waved to them.

A few acknowledged her greeting, while others turned their backs and walked away. After what Captain Reynolds had told her, she believed she understood. The scars left by British atrocities must still lie heavily in their minds.

"This area, except for a few Acadians, was largely a wilderness when a Scotsman named William Davidson and his partner John Cort came here to set up a fishing industry," Angus MacLeod informed her as he joined her. "Then the revolution to the south broke out, and the river became infested with American privateers. They burned and looted. Davidson decided to take his people and move out of the area until things settled down."

"Privateers?"

"Pirates who act with government approval, provided they do harm to the enemy." Angus' jaw clenched and twitched.

"Then were there no English-speaking settlers again in this river valley until you, your wife, and the captain came to settle?" Emma looked at him in surprise.

"Nay, nay, lassie." The mate chuckled. "Davidson returned when it became safe. The war had cut off England's supply of lumber and masts from New England. The conflict with France had blocked the Baltic ports, where such necessities were once also obtained. He knew this valley abounded in timber perfect for those needs and saw it as his chance to become a rich man.

"He obtained permission from the Governor in Halifax to set up business. Bringing men and tools to the valley to do the harvesting, Davidson established a settlement far up river. Naturally, with news of his success, others soon followed. James Cameron, Vanessa's father, is one of them."

"And he also became rich?"

"Aye, lassie, and he also became rich." He heaved a deep breath as he turned away. "Now I've stood here jawin' long enough. I'd best get back to work or the captain, brother-in-law though he be, will be layin' into me."

So Vanessa's father was a wealthy man. She leaned her back against the bulwarks and stared up into the sails, some of which had been furled to slow the *Ula*'s progress in navigating the river channel. Perhaps there'd been more than one reason for Morgan's haste to marry her. Perhaps he saw her wealth as a way out of his financial problems. After all, the only reason he'd agreed to take her to safety had been because she'd been able to pay him handsomely.

She turned back to watch the shoreline. She must watch her steps very carefully around the handsome captain. Virile and charismatic, he could be a danger to her if her previous response to his kiss in the carriage was any indication.

****

As they rounded a bend in the river, the ship moving slowly to avoid a small island and sandbars, Emma saw it. A big, rectangular three-story house built of stone, with massive chimneys at either end, its windows glinting in the morning sun, stood on a rise overlooking the river. It looked as if it had been transplanted from a wealthy English estate.

"Who owns that massive house?" she asked, turning to the captain, who stood on the quarterdeck above her. "Is there a governor for this area? Is it his house?"

"No." He shook his head. "It's mine. Roberts, steady as she goes, man! If you're not careful, you'll have us aground."

"Aye, aye, sir." The helmsman straightened his course.

"Yours?" Emma stared at him, then back at the manor house. "How could you...?"

Realizing the inappropriateness of the time for her question, she turned away and focused on the small cluster of crude buildings, fronted by a long wharf, that had come into view. The community of Pine, she reckoned. This was where she would have to play her role as Captain Morgan's wife to perfection.

****

Pine was a bustling little community in spite of its isolated locale. The wharf at which the captain docked his ship was piled with timber of many sizes and shapes. Plank buildings as well as several older structures of log clustered near the water's edge. Others under construction along the forest's edge gave the impression their half-built frames were attempting to push back the wilderness, Emma thought, as she gazed down from the ship's deck.

Then two sailors led Bonnie and Lad up onto the deck. Although Morgan had had them taken ashore and exercised in Halifax, both animals were frisky and giving the men a difficult time, especially the stallion.

"Easy, my Lad." Morgan took the prancing animal by its halter. "You're home at last. No need to cause a scene." He chuckled as the great horse quieted and nuzzled him. "Now let Roberts take you quietly ashore. Shortly you'll be free to kick up your heels in the paddock behind my stables." He turned to the sweating sailor. "Go ahead, take him ashore.

He'll behave now."

"Aye, aye, sir." Roberts once again started for the newly lowered boarding plank, gingerly leading the quieted stallion.

Emma watched, amazed. It appeared her surrogate spouse had power over beasts as well as men...and women. She'd have to play her wifely role with great care.

****

Fine riding horses like the Lad and Bonnie must not yet be common in the community, Emma decided. As the pair was led ashore, a crowd assembled to admire them.

"Fine beasts, Captain," a big, burly man called out to Morgan, who'd come to join Emma at the rail.

"Thank you, Ben, but I can only claim ownership of the stallion. The little mare belongs to my wife."

"Ye have married Mistress Vanessa, Captain?" The man looked up at Morgan in surprise. "We thought ye would do us the courtesy of bein' wed here in Pine, so's we could have a fine ceilidh."

"Not Mistress Vanessa." Morgan drew Emma forward. "Mistress Emma Smith, now Mrs. Reynolds. I trust you'll all make her feel welcome."

Astonished faces gazed up at her. For a moment silence fell over the gathering. Emma forced a smile she hoped was sufficiently demure for a bride, but her heart was racing. When a murmur began among the spectators, she knew she'd never previously felt as uncomfortable.

"Greetings! My husband has told me so many wonderful things about Pine and yourselves, I'm most eager to become acquainted with each and every one of you." The lie made her wince inwardly, but lies would be her way of life from now until she arrived at her brother's mission in the Caribbean. She would have to become accustomed to telling them.

After a slight pause, a ripple of acceptance seemed to wash over the small crowd, and light applause broke out as they looked up at her, relaxed approbation mirrored in their countenances.

"Welcome, Mrs. Reynolds!" yelled the man Morgan had called Ben. "Faith, and it's time the man took himself a wife."

Laughter broke out, only to stop abruptly at the sound of an approaching conveyance. The assemblage turned as one to face the newcomer.

The elegant landau drove out onto the wharf. In the back sat a portly, well-dressed gentleman of past middle age. As the driver drew to a halt and jumped down to assist his passenger to the ground, the group of well-wishers began to scatter, looking furtively back at the new arrival, then up at Morgan and Emma standing at the ship's rail.

"Welcome, my boy." The gentlemen stepped heavily to the ground and waved up at Morgan. "I trust you've had a good voyage and that the holds of the *Ula* are stuffed with the manufactured goods we so desperately need?"

"Aye, James, and even a few luxuries...oranges, and a couple of cases of your favorite whiskey straight from the distillery in Edinburgh."

"Good, good. Well, come down here, that I might greet you properly. It's been months since you've set foot in Pine."

Emma repressed a wince as Morgan took her firmly by the arm and led her down the boarding plank toward the newcomer. He wasn't hurting her physically, but she realized this must be James Cameron, Vanessa's father, and wondered how he would react to the bride hastily taken by his recently prospective son-in-law.

As they reached the dock, the older man extended his hand and smiled. "Welcome home, my boy, welcome home."

"It's good to see you, James." Morgan accepted the greeting, then turned to indicate Emma. "James, this is my wife, Emma. Emma, this is James Cameron, a man who's been like a second father to me...after Angus."

"Your wife, lad?" A Scottish burr broke over the man's formerly proper English. "Your wife? Lad, I cannae countenance..."

"James, I assume you know by now what Vanessa has done." The captain met the older man's astonishment squarely. "Her marriage to another freed me to do as I please. And I was pleased to meet and marry Miss Emma Smith, now Mrs. Reynolds."

"Aye, free, lad, but so soon, so sudden." James Cameron clasped gloved hands together and rubbed them in his agitation. "Have ye known this lass long? Is she someone you met in your travels?" He paused, then a flicker of hopefulness came into his words. "Is she perhaps a Scottish lass?"

"No, I have not known Emma for long, and no, she is not a Scottish lass. I believe, however, that it's sufficient to say that I love her, she says she loves me, and we plan to be happy together. I'd be grateful if you'd welcome her, James."

The older man paused, looking first at Morgan and then at Emma at his side. Finally he drew a deep breath. "Mrs. Reynolds, welcome to Pine. I hope you will be happy in our little community."

"James, about Vanessa..." With the distant crowd now surrounding the two newly arrived horses, Morgan again approached the subject Emma guessed had been burning in his mind.

"I know, my boy, I know." The big man shook his head sadly. "I can't imagine what came over the girl. I know she always had a hankering to be a lady, a titled lady, that is, but I never thought she'd throw away all she had with you for some jackanapes of a British m'lord. You know I've always thought of you as a son. I'd hoped to be able to call you such as her husband. It will be difficult, but for my sake will you try to forgive her?"

He looked up at Morgan, his face taut with concern.

"I have already, James," the captain replied, although Emma doubted his words. "And a good deal of the credit goes to my Emma." He smiled down at her, and Emma, keeping to her supposed position, returned the expression, clinging to his arm.

"Then I'm happy for you both." Relief spread over James Cameron's face. "Now come along. I'll drive you to Angus' house, where I've been told Iona has a feast awaiting you. Angus!" The lumber baron turned and called to the mate, who was in the crowd around the horses. "Let Roberts take care of those beasts and join us in the landau. I'll drive you to your house, where your good lady awaits."

"Ye don't have to ask twice, James." Angus hastened to join them. "I've not seen my Iona in months. It will be a handsome reunion, I can tell you, even if..."

He glanced at Morgan as he stopped beside him.

"So you had no luck?" James looked at the captain, his forehead furrowing. "I'm sorry...for all of you. I know how much success in your quest meant to your family."

Emma glanced quickly from man to man to man, puzzled. What quest? How had Morgan failed in it? She'd wait until they were alone to question him, she decided, as he helped her into the fine landau. She sensed it was not a subject he was ready or willing to discuss at the moment.

Five minutes later, the landau drew up in front of a modest frame farmhouse downriver, within sight of the manor Morgan had told her was his. A tall, slender woman in a black dress, her dark hair streaked with gray, stood on the front steps. She started down the steps, her gaze fixed on the group in the carriage, the expectant expression she wore quickly dissolving as she perused their number.

Angus leaped to the ground and gathered her into a hearty embrace.

"Ah, lass, how I've missed ye!" Emma heard him breathe.

"But you've nae found him." She remained rigid in his arms as she stared up at the three in the carriage.

"No, sister, I did not." Morgan got out and offered his hand to Emma. "Luck wasn't with me, although I tried my best."

"I've no doubt you did." She looked bleakly at her brother. "It seems fate has decreed I'm never to see my son again."

Her son! Emma's eyes widened. Morgan had been looking for his nephew that night he'd rescued her on the road. Had he already admitted defeat, or had his getting involved with her curtailed his search? No, it couldn't have. Somehow, knowing the man as she now did, she doubted anything short of knowing that he absolutely couldn't be successful would have diverted him.

"Iona, I want you to meet Emma." Morgan drew her over to face his sister as Iona MacLeod stood by her husband's side, his arm draped around her slim shoulders. "Emma and I were married in England just before we sailed."

For a moment Iona MacLeod stared at Emma.

"Hello, Mrs. MacLeod." Emma put on her best smile. "I hope we'll be friends as well as sisters-in-law."

"An English woman, no less!" Iona's tone was cold and caustic. "James told me about Vanessa's treachery, but I never would have believed you'd grasp the first wench that crossed your path, never mind an English one, and wed her."

"Iona!" Angus dropped his arm and moved to confront her. "I'll not have you speak so of Morgan's wife. He's chosen her and she is making him happy. That is all that should concern us."

She hesitated, took a long, hard look at Emma, and drew a deep breath. "There's little I can do about it now. Come inside. I have a meal waiting."

"Aye, that's the ticket!" Angus proudly put his arm once more about his wife's shoulders and walked beside her into the house.

"After such a welcome, how can we refuse?" Morgan looked down at Emma, a sardonic grin twitching up the corners of his mouth.

"I'm ready, my dear." Emma slanted him a conspiratorial glance, then turned back to the businessman still sitting in the landau. "Mr. Cameron, won't you join us?"

"Thank you, Mrs. Reynolds, but this occasion is for family. Morgan, my lad, I'd appreciate it if you could meet with me later today or tomorrow morning to discuss the sale of your cargo."

"Of course, James. As soon as I've seen Emma safely settled in my...our home, I'll visit you."

"Very well. Vincent, you can take me home now." James Cameron touched his walking stick to the brim of his hat in farewell salute. The carriage swung about to return to the village.

"Come along, Mrs. Reynolds." Morgan led her toward the front steps. "I'm sure my sister has a sumptuous meal prepared. And," he leaned close and spoke softly into her ear, "if you wish to endear yourself to her, you'll be lavish in your praise."

"I fear it will take a great deal more than flattering Iona's bill of fare to put me into her good graces," Emma replied, lifting her skirts to ascend the first step.

****

The MacLeod kitchen was a big, sparsely

113

furnished room, but every surface from plank table to sideboards had been scrubbed to pristine cleanliness. Even the board floor looked freshly washed. Emma drew a deep breath as she gazed at the tidy hearth, where not a single ash had managed to escape the fervent cleaning of the lady of the house, and wondered how she'd live up to such standards of housekeeping.

"Come, sit." Iona MacLeod indicated places on benches on either side of the big table laid for dinner. The chairs at either end were apparently reserved for herself and her husband, Emma thought, lifting her skirts to slide into place as Morgan held out his sister's chair.

The meal laid before her made her eyes widen. There was freshly baked bread, a platter of a pink-fleshed fish bathed in a smooth, golden sauce, small boiled potatoes, a dish of melted butter, a plate of oatmeal, and a mixture of greens. At the center sat a bowl of strawberries and beside it a pitcher of thick cream.

"Ye'll say the blessing, husband." Iona bowed her head.

"Dear Lord, we give ye thanks for the bounty of this table and for the captain's and my own safe return from the sea. We ask that you will always keep us in your care. Amen."

"Well said." Iona reached for the fish and passed it to Emma. "Salmon from the river. It's reputed to be the best in the world. However, I'm not yet convinced it's any better than those from the streams and rivers of the Highlands."

"I'm sure it's very fine." Emma took a helping, then handed the platter to Angus as Iona extended the potatoes to her.

"From our own garden, the first of the season," she said proudly.

"They look delicious." Emma followed Morgan's

advice and praised the dinner.

Shortly they each had full plates, but as Emma began to eat her potatoes, she was surprised to see Morgan take up the bowl of oatmeal, roll his potatoes in it and then in the container of melted butter. Angus and Iona followed suit.

"A Highland treat." Morgan caught her amazed expression and grinned over at her. "If you don't already have a taste for oatmeal, you'll be well advised to acquire it if you're to live with a Scottish family."

"I'll certainly try." She took the oatmeal from Iona when it was passed to her, and began to coat her potatoes.

****

An hour later, Morgan and Emma left the farmhouse and headed on foot up the incline toward the manor house visible through the burgeoning leaves of birches and maples.

"The food was very good," Emma commented.

"If not the company." The corner of Morgan's mouth twitched upward in a sardonic grimace. "My sister can be a harsh, unrelenting woman. She is also a fair one. Given time, she'll come around."

"How did she come to be separated from her son? Was it many years ago? Were you returning from a futile search when you rescued me?"

"So many questions." He paused and looked down at her. "Yes, Iona lost her son many years ago, before we were driven from our home in the Highlands. The boy was only three years of age when he was taken from us by a band of English soldiers—taken to live with his father."

"His father is an Englishman?"

"Yes. He was the commander of an English regiment who commandeered our cottage as a headquarters when they were patrolling the Highlands. I was only a lad at the time, Iona in her late twenties. I was often away from home tending our sheep, and I didn't know until much later that the officer took those opportunities to rape Iona. He threatened to kill me if she rejected him. Eventually their reign of terror ended and they left us alone. After they'd gone, Iona discovered she was pregnant."

"How terrible!" Emma put a gloved hand on his arm. "The result was the son she sent you in search of. Why, after all these years? Why would she want the child of a man who treated her so brutally?"

Morgan wet his lips and looked up into the branches above them before replying.

"Iona has come to that age when a woman knows she will never be able to have a child," he replied finally. "Knowing Robbie will be her only offspring, she's become obsessed with seeing him again. In order to give her peace in her soul, I agreed to try to find him on my next voyage to England."

"How did you know where to look? Surely after all these years..."

"Surely after all these years Reginald Falkner has not changed his name so very much," Morgan said.

The trees and sky reeled as Emma's world staggered from the verbal blow. "That was the name of your nephew's father?" She heard her voice sounding as if far away. "Falkner?"

"Of recent years he'd taken to calling himself Squire Falkner. It makes little difference. A stench in any breeze is still a stench."

"And this...Squire Falkner...he did not have the boy at his home?" Emma felt her heart pounding so violently at her ribs she feared Morgan might hear.

"The boy, as you call him, is now in his early twenties. He'd gone to the continent with friends, no doubt gambling, drinking, and womanizing as young men of his wealth and social standing are prone to do at that age. Mrs. Reynolds, are you unwell? Your complexion has blanched."

"You judge him harshly," Emma forced out the words. *Please, God, let me not betray myself.* "After all, he is your nephew, your sister's son."

"Brought up by that despicable bit of British trash, how could he be otherwise than a wastrel? I wish my sister had never developed this insane desire to see him before she dies. He's no longer any more her son than any other male child on the face of this planet. He was lost to us eighteen years ago, and as far as I'm concerned he should stay that way. Now come along." He took her by the arm and started up the rise to the house, his long strides making her trot to keep up, her light head making her giddy and nauseous.

Chapter Seven

Emma's first impression, the moment Morgan shoved open the front door, was of emptiness. Not a single piece of furniture graced the foyer, the large parlor to her right, or the spacious dining room to her left. The latter two contained only stone fireplaces against outside walls. The echo of Morgan's booted footfalls on the plank floor echoed in the hollowness of the house.

"Welcome home, Mrs. Reynolds." Morgan waved a hand about, bitterness tainting his tone.

"It's very large...and bare." Emma moved slowly past him, trying not to shiver from a chill both physical and emotional. "But once it's furnished..."

"It will never be furnished." He walked to a window and stared out at the river. "I have no more money to sink into a house that will never see the wife and children I pictured living in it. Before we sail for the Caribbean, I'll put it up for sale."

"It could be a lovely home." Emma moved slowly about, admiring the fine mahogany trim and elegant wall covering. "You wouldn't have to spend a fortune to begin. A piece at a time..."

"I've already told you." His tone turned to a thunderous volume. "It goes for sale within the month. Don't start making plans."

"Whatever you say, my dear." Emma turned to him and bobbed a submissive curtsey.

"Argh!" He strode toward the back of the house. "Come along, then, if you're so all-fired anxious to nest here. The kitchen has a cooking hearth and table and chairs. I'm sure Iona has seen to the larder in anticipation of our arrival. You can satisfy your need for domesticity by making us some supper."

"Of course." Emma strode after him, head held defiantly high. "I'm sure I can manage something that will keep us both from starvation's door."

"While you're concocting a meal, I'll see to the horses. I don't trust Roberts to have stabled them properly. He's a fine sailor, but he's had little training in animal husbandry."

****

"That was surprisingly good, Mrs. Reynolds." Morgan pushed back from the table and drew a deep breath. "I had no idea you could cook."

"Only the simplest of fare, Captain." Emma stood and began to clear the table. "I'd hardly call eggs and ham an elegant repast."

"Still, well cooked and the tea nicely steeped. Now, if you'll permit, I'll enjoy a cigar and a drop of brandy. Will you join me in the latter?"

He got up and went to a sideboard where a humidor sat beside a full decanter and a pair of glasses.

"There are dishes to wash..." she began.

"Leave them." He chose a cigar, clamped it in his mouth, and carried the decanter and glasses to the table. "You can play housewife tomorrow."

"Very well." Emma removed their plates and utensils to the counter near the sink and resumed her seat on the straight-backed chair. "I think a small libation might help me sleep. It's been such an exciting day I fear I'd have trouble dropping off."

"Did you explore the upper stories?" he asked, pouring out the amber liquid.

"I was too involved in exploring the pantry and planning our meal." He handed her a glass. "Thank you, Captain."

"Allow me to take you on a tour," he said. "Bring your brandy. You may need a stiffener once you see

119

the remainder of this mausoleum of which you've become mistress."

****

When Morgan pushed open the door of the master bedroom, Emma suppressed a gasp. Unlike the rest of the mansion, it had been outfitted with taste and elegance. A massive fourposter bed, topped with a thick feather tick, rested its tall headboard against the left wall. Piled atop it was a collection of fresh linens. Between a pair of tall, bare windows a dressing table with a large mirror and bench held a collection of silver combs and brushes. A massive stone fireplace along the right wall held split wood and logs, ready for kindling. A door beside it stood open, revealing a dressing room complete with bathing tub. Their trunks had been stacked against the far wall.

"Oh, my!" Emma moved slowly inside and stood gazing about. "This is very elegant."

"I hope you will enjoy it, Mrs. Reynolds."

"I shall, but so shall you." Emma turned to face him. "Since this is the only bed in the house, we must share it as we did the one in your ship's cabin. I will not countenance your sleeping in less comfort than myself."

For a moment he stood staring at her in the gathering twilight.

"Emma Reynolds, you are a remarkable woman," he said finally. "Truly remarkable. And perhaps a tad too trusting. We'll be quite alone in this house. I'd have guessed you wiser to the ways of men and their desires."

"I believe I am, sir, very wise." She faced him squarely. "Therefore, I know what men to trust and what men not to trust."

"And you've decided you can trust me...even after what happened in the carriage after the ball?" He narrowed his eyes and stared at her.

"Especially after what happened." She walked slowly over to the bed and smoothed the tick cover. "You could easily have forced yourself on me, but you didn't. You were merely reacting to a romantic evening and too much champagne. And even under those conditions you behaved decently. So, my good captain..." She smiled at him. "We will share this wonderful featherbed. I shall do so with the greatest of confidence. Now, I see your men have brought our trunks, so if you will excuse me, I'll prepare for bed. Perhaps you'd like to bank the kitchen fire and bar the doors?"

****

Once again Captain Morgan Reynolds couldn't sleep. Behind a blanket roll, Emma slumbered peacefully, her golden-brown curls tumbling over the whiteness of the pillow cover, the gathers at the throat of her high-necked nightgown visible above the quilt. She looked like an angel, an innocent angel. Yet she couldn't possibly be. He wondered if he'd ever really know the truth about Emma Smith before they parted company in a few short weeks.

The realization hit him like an epiphany. Suddenly he knew he didn't want to part company with her...not now, not in a few short weeks, never. She'd become a part of his life; a beautiful, comfortable, reassuring part of his life.

But, as he rolled onto his back and clasped his hands behind his head, he knew he had to let her go. He couldn't offer her marriage. When he'd been about to wed Vanessa, he'd known her father approved the match and would see his loans secured until he could pay them. Now he wallowed alone in a sea of debt. He'd probably have to sell his ship to keep creditors from forcing him into debtor's prison.

He turned away from Emma and pounded his pillow. Only a miracle could save him and his beloved *Ula* now, never mind his being able to offer

Emma Smith marriage.

****

As he strode back up the hill toward his house the next morning after his visit to James Cameron, he stopped short and stared. Strung between two trees was a clothesline. Flapping gaily in the breeze was not only a lady's apparel but a full selection of his shirts and underwear.

Damnation! Now the woman was behaving like a scullery maid. He'd told her he would hire a village girl to do housework. Why couldn't she have waited? Furthermore, who had given her the right to go digging about in his personal effects, dragging out his underwear and setting it flapping in the breeze?

As he rounded the back corner of the house, he saw her, immersed in a wash tub to her elbows, vigorously scrubbing what looked like one of her undergarments on a board.

"What do you think you're doing?" He stopped abruptly and made no attempt to disguise his annoyance. "I've told you I'll get a girl from the village to handle the domestic chores. In fact, I've already found a likely one. Her young brother is to act as stable lad while I'm gone."

"I'm glad you've hired someone to care for the horses." She straightened and pushed a strand of curls back into place. "However, I have no need of a serving girl. I'm perfectly capable of handling the simple bit of housekeeping required for two people. And since money is at a premium..."

"Damnation, woman, I'll not have people thinking I'm such a pauper that my wife must become a drudge! Furthermore, what gives you the right to go pulling out my drawers and putting them on display?"

"Would you prefer to wear unclean ones? And how else am I to dry them? You're being unreasonable." She cast him a sly smile. "Why,

Captain Reynolds, I believe I've embarrassed you."

"Argh!" He turned and stomped up the steps to the back door. At the top he rounded on her. "Very well, be a housewife. But don't come complaining to me when your hands are red and raw and your back aches."

"Never fear." Emma turned back to her washing. "I'm made of much sterner stuff than you give me credit. There's a pot of oatmeal porridge warming on the hearth. I'll be in shortly to pour your tea."

****

That afternoon, as Emma hung clean clothing in the bedroom clothes press, she heard a carriage approaching. Glancing out of a window, she saw James Cameron's landau. She watched as Morgan went down the steps to greet the entrepreneur and, chatting companionably, led him into the house. The sound of their booted footsteps told her they made their way to the kitchen, the only room with chairs. She started to go downstairs to join them, then reconsidered. They might wish to talk business or discuss Vanessa. In either case, her presence wouldn't be necessary.

As she returned to her task, she tried not to wonder about their conversation, but curiosity regarding both possible subjects jabbed at her. Finally she could stand it no longer. On soft-slippered feet, she made her way downstairs. Easing herself into a small alcove near the kitchen, she settled back to listen.

"I'm sorry, lad," James Cameron said. "But if you'll not allow me to lend you money there's nothing I can do. Your creditors are not patient men. When they discover you're not to be my son-in-law..."

"Do ye not think I understand that?" Morgan's words resonated with the Scottish burr she'd come to recognize as reflecting his level of agitation.

"Look here, lad, I'm still willing to help you and

your wife in any way I can. You can't for a minute think I condone how my daughter treated you, do you? It was herself that was hankering after being a lady, not me. You're the son-in-law I've always wanted, you must understand."

"I know, James." His tone moderated into a sigh. "But I cannot be accepting your offer. My cargo's fetched a fair sum. Hopefully that will keep the sharks at bay a few more months."

"Hopefully."

Emma scurried back upstairs as she heard chairs scrape back, indicating the end of the interview. Her thoughts flew to the necklace still hidden among her clothing in one of the trunks. She wished she could use it to help Morgan, but making its presence known would only serve to raise the question of where she'd gotten it. She also knew she could not risk trying to sell even a single gem of it here in this small village. Such a move would fast become the talk of the town.

****

"You've been busy, Mrs. Reynolds."

Morgan stepped into the bedroom.

The bed, made up with fresh linens and pillows, had been moved to rest with its headboard between the two long windows now dressed in maroon velvet draperies and white lace undercurtains. The dressing table and bench were against the left wall. A small fire crackled on the hearth, dispelling the chill of the spring evening. Their trunks—unpacked, he assumed—had been banished. Vases on bedside tables held wildflowers that cast their seductive fragrance through the air.

"You approve?" She slanted a glance up at him in the lamplight.

"It looks...settled." He advanced farther into the room and perused it more fully. "Much as I imagined it would be, only..."

"With another woman in attendance." Emma headed into the adjoining bath and dressing room. She paused in the doorway and looked back at him over her shoulder.

He wanted to deny her words but found he couldn't. He couldn't deny he'd been dreaming of Vanessa sharing that bed with him, of making love with her as the fire on the hearth cast bewitching shadows over their writhing bodies.

"Yes," he said.

Emma turned away, shutting the door behind her with a distinctive bump.

****

They were at breakfast the next morning when Angus burst in the back door, out of the June sunshine.

"War!" he cried breathlessly. "The Americans have declared war on us!"

"I knew it wasn't far off." Morgan leaned back in his chair and drew a deep breath. "Come, sit, Angus. Now we can embark on those plans we discussed a month ago. When can you be ready to sail?"

"You still plan to...?" The mate glanced at Emma, then back at the captain.

"Aye, Mr. MacLeod." He stood. "I'd advise you to inform my sister of our plans before we start rounding up our crew. I don't fancy she'd be delighted to hear it from other lips than yours."

"Aye, lad." Angus heaved a sigh, then turned and left the house. He'd only gone a few yards from the door when he paused, raised fisted hands above his head, and let out a mighty whoop. Then he strode off toward his house with long, proud strides.

"What plans might those be, Captain?" Emma looked up at him. "Or will your own wife have to find out through village gossip?"

"First of all, you're not my true wife." He stretched back his arms and his shirt that hung

125

open over his powerful chest spread wider ajar. Once again Emma was taken by his blatant virility. Sometimes, at moments like this, she caught herself wondering what it would be like to truly be Mrs. Emma Reynolds.

"Very well." With an effort she brushed aside her errant thoughts and reached for her bonnet hanging on a peg near the door. "I'll go to the village. If I learn nothing of your proposed venture there, I shall call on Iona. By that time, I'm sure Mr. MacLeod will have told her the facts of your newest ventures."

"I'll not have my supposed wife wandering about the village asking about my plans and appearing to have been kept in ignorance." He caught her hands as they began to tie the bonnet ribbons. "I'll not have people speculating about our intimacy."

"Oh, you won't, will you?" She smiled sweetly up at him, knowing how his being apparently unable to ruffle her annoyed him. "Then suppose you tell me yourself."

Her hands encased in his large, scarred ones, she looked up at him. As their gazes met, she drew a sharp breath. If only he weren't still locked in his love for another woman...

So slowly, so sensuously she was mesmerized, his arms went about her, he lowered his head, and the next instant Emma felt his mouth on hers. At first it was a gentle caress, but as she made no move to pull away, it deepened. His tongue pushed inside her slowly opening lips. Emma felt herself become weightless, swirling, swirling into an exotic place full of magic sensations she'd never known existed.

"Emma, Emma," he breathed against her hair when he'd released her mouth and molded her into every swell and curve of his tall, lean body. "Whatever am I to do about you? You bring out urges...urges I have to deny. And now I'm about to leave for a war from which I may not return."

"War?" Emma jerked back in his arms. "You're going to war?"

"As a privateer. That is what Angus meant. We'll be leaving within a few days for Halifax. There I'll apply for a Letter of Marquee and Reprisal. That will make it legal for the *Ula* to prey on American shipping and profit from any prizes we're sufficiently fortunate to take. It will be my way out of debts."

"But a privateer!" Emma pulled free of his embrace and stared up at him. "That's just a polite name for pirate! Surely..."

"Surely I must." He stepped away from her into a ray of sunlight flooding in through the open doorway. "Emma, you know how much money I owe. If I'm to have any life in the future, I must clean these obligations away. If I'm ever to have a wife and a family..."

"I cannot imagine any woman wanting a home and children with a man who is a confessed pirate." She pulled free and drew herself up proudly. "I could never countenance finding happiness that has been the result of death and destruction."

For a moment he stood staring at her. Then he spoke.

"Ah, well, then, I guess that ends any hope I may have entertained for us, Mistress Smith." He turned away and strode out the back door. "I must honor my financial obligations. I'll be grateful if you'll have my clothes clean and ready by tomorrow evening. I've no doubt I'll be sailing on the tide," he flung back over his shoulder.

****

He was back within the hour, a box under his arm. "Mrs. Reynolds, I want you to accompany me to the woods behind the stable," he said as he stood in the doorway of the bedroom where she was laying out the clothing for his departure.

"I'm engaged at the moment, Captain." She ignored him as she carefully folded a snow-white shirt. "Your imminent departure has cast a number of duties my way."

"Perhaps you misunderstood, *wife*." His tone turned into the one he used with his crew, one that brooked no denial. "I am ordering you to come with me *now*."

"Very well." Emma heaved a sigh that she hoped sounded casual although her heart had upped its beat. What did he have in mind?

As she started to bypass him in the doorway, he grasped her arm. Together they swept down the stairs, out of the house, and along a path that led back of the stables. When they were some distance into the trees, he paused, placed the box on a tree stump, and opened it. Inside lay a pair of pistols. Emma felt her breath snag in her throat.

"Don't blanch, wife." He looked into her face, a sardonic smile quirking up a corner of his mouth. "I'm not going to murder you. I simply want to instruct you in their use before I leave. I will feel much better knowing you have a means of defending yourself, should the need arrive. Mind you, it shouldn't." He must have seen apprehension pass over her expression because he continued, "I have asked James to look out for both you and my sister. James is a powerful man, and while he has appeared only charming and gracious in your presence, he can be a dangerous enemy. No one familiar with the man would risk bothering any lady who came under his protection. Now, pay attention." He picked up one of the guns. "This is how you load."

****

Emma stood on the front steps of the house she'd shared for less than a week with Captain Morgan Reynolds and watched the sails catch the wind as the *Ula* gathered speed and sailed smoothly past, headed downriver. She could see him beside the helmsman, his gaze fixed on the ship's course. He didn't so much as glance shoreward as they passed his property. An overwhelming sense of loneliness and loss washed over her as his ship glided out of sight.

She turned and went slowly back inside. The house seemed vast and hollow as she stood in the foyer, the last rays of the evening sun making moving patterns of the shadows of the maples reflected on the bare plank floor. Loneliness overwhelmed her as she wandered to the kitchen and poured herself a cup of tea.

It had grown cold. With a sigh she set it aside as she sank down at the table. How long would she have to endure this solitary life? It was quiet, so quiet she could hear the soft soughing of the breeze in the pines beyond the open window above the sink, and the haunting call of a loon from the shore.

"Good evening." His voice, bright with cheerfulness, made her start. She glanced up to see Farand Thatcher smiling at her through the open window. "May I come in? I would enjoy a cup of tea, if you've any to spare."

"Mr. Thatcher." She arose and went to open the door for him, suddenly glad of company, any company that might dispel her sense of loss. "While you are not the last person I expected to see here, you are very near the top of the list. Do come in and join me in a cup of tea. It will just take a moment to reheat the pot. Would you care for a scone? My...sister-in-law sent over some very fine ones only this afternoon."

"Thank you." Removing his hat, he came in, a wide smile on his face. "I've only just arrived in the village and, aside from taking a room at the inn, I've had no time to see to any other needs. I'm told the food there is hearty but plain. I doubt scones will be on the menu."

"Please take a seat." Emma indicated a chair at the table and bustled about, stirring up the languishing fire on the hearth and swinging the teapot over it. "What brings you to the Miramichi, Mr. Thatcher?"

"Commerce." He looked up at her pleasantly as she placed butter and jam, also from Iona, with the scones before him. "I'm seeking out prospects for my father's business. He's hoping to expand into North America. He has sent me to investigate the possibilities of this valley, which he's been told is rich in the white pine essential in shipbuilding. With war closing the Baltic ports and most recently those of New England to Britain, New Brunswick lumber will be as precious as gold."

"Ah, yes, the war." Emma's tone became thoughtful and tinged with bitterness.

"I'm sorry." His gaze followed her as she arose to check the teapot. "I'm sure it's a sore point with you, what with your husband newly left to join in the fighting."

"You know?" Emma looked at him sharply.

"It's the talk of the village. The gallant Captain Morgan Reynolds sailing off to seek fame and fortune in the battle against the Americans. He's been the first from this province to volunteer, I understand. But there'll be more merchantmen joining the battle as soon as they realize what rich booty there is to be gained as privateers. Oh, they might claim they're defending this country that has as yet no official navy, but their purpose will soon become apparent as they fatten their purses under the guise of fighting for king and country. Forgive me, Mrs. Reynolds." He stopped abruptly. "I overstep the bounds of polite conversation. I meant no disrespect to your husband. I've been told he's a gallant seaman who'll treat captives fairly and with respect. None of this robbing women and cutting off fingers to get their rings for him, no, definitely not."

"Cutting off fingers..." Emma felt the blood draining from her face. Surely Morgan wouldn't, *couldn't*, do anything so heinous. Surely paying off his debts couldn't be worth inflicting such cruelty.

"I've distressed you." His brow furrowed. "I came here to offer you an enjoyable evening's companionship, not cause you discomfort. I do most humbly apologize."

"You haven't told me anything I wouldn't have learned in the village streets." Emma went to fetch the teapot from the hearth. "So let us forget it and proceed with the pleasant evening you suggest. Do you play cards, Mr. Thatcher? I believe I saw a deck in a drawer."

****

Emma tossed and turned. On her first night without Morgan, sleep was proving evasive. Now that he was gone, all she could think about was how safe she'd felt knowing he was in the same room every night since she'd fled that awful man.

She wondered what her surrogate husband was doing. Was he on the quarterdeck, the wind in his hair, his hands clasped behind his back, as he took his ship's bearings from the stars to guide the *Ula* southward? Southward toward Halifax and that license to pillage, rob, and maybe even kill.

Farand Thatcher's words returned to haunt her. *Robbing women, cutting off fingers...* She wouldn't believe it. She couldn't.

She turned on her side to stare at the moonlight streaming in through the lace curtains at the window, the curtains he'd bought with another woman in mind, and she clutched her pillow until her knuckles whitened. She'd never replace Vanessa Cameron in Morgan Reynolds' heart, so why torture herself with his memory. Another man, a younger man, a handsome man, a gentlemanly man had that very evening shown his interest in her. She remembered the roses he'd sent her in Halifax. Morgan had never sent her roses, had never courted her in any way, shape or form.

She burrowed into the feather mattress and tried to see only Farand Thatcher's face as she struggled toward sleep.

****

"Good morning, Mrs. Reynolds." James Cameron alighted from his landau and came toward her, smiling.

"Good morning, Mr. Cameron." She paused in brushing Bonnie. The mare stood tied to a tree near the stables. "A beautiful day, is it not?"

"Grand, grand." He stopped beside her, doffed his hat, and used his handkerchief to mop his face. "How are you faring without Morgan? Not too lonely up here, are you?"

"Not as yet." She gave the mare a pat and came to stand before the lumber baron. "I plan to visit my sister-in-law this afternoon. I hope we'll become friends and companions, now that our husbands are gone at sea."

"I don't wish to discourage you, my dear, but that might take a bit of doing." He heaved a deep breath. "Iona MacLeod is as stubborn as she is brave and beautiful. She's not pleased that Morgan chose to take an Englishwoman as wife. I fear that aversion will be difficult to overcome, even though it has nothing to do with you as a person."

"Ah, well, Mr. Cameron, you don't know me yet." Emma put her hands on her hips and cocked her head to one side. "I am just as determined that Iona MacLeod will be my friend."

"Well, good luck to you, lassie." He chuckled. Then he sobered. "Discussing Iona and her fads and fancies isn't why I've come. Morgan has told me you appear to have a bit of an education. How would you feel about starting a school for the village children? I would be willing to pay a fair wage for the service, and you could hold classes in the parlor and dining room of your big, barren house until such time as a decent schoolhouse can be constructed."

"A school?" Emma, momentarily surprised, quickly discovered she liked the idea. "Pine's first school. Yes, Mr. Cameron, I do believe I would enjoy such a challenge. And," she continued more cautiously, "as you know, the money will not go astray."

"Excellent!" The entrepreneur rubbed his hands together and beamed. "I'll spread the word. When do you think you'd be ready to commence?"

"When do you think I might get supplies? I'll need writing materials and slates and..."

"All things I purchased last year in anticipation of finding a teacher for our community. I'll have Vincent bring them up this very afternoon. You'll need a desk and a few chairs, benches, and a couple of tables. I'll send them, as well. Thank you, Mrs. Reynolds. You'll be making a great contribution to developing this area. You know, thanks to John Knox, Scotland had the best educated lower class in Europe. Following his example, I should like to have everyone in Pine literate by the end of the decade. With your help, I just may. Good day to you now."

He started toward his carriage, then turned back. "I'd not expected to find you engaged in stable chores, my dear. Is the stable lad Morgan hired not working out?"

"He does a passable job. He feeds the horses and shovels the stalls, but I'm afraid he's lax about grooming and exercising them. He's told me he longs to go to sea and is forever watching the arriving ships for a chance at a position."

"Ah, well, then, I'll keep my eyes open for

another likely lad, one who enjoys horses." He waved and continued on to his landau.

Emma watched him drive off. Excitement at the prospect of establishing the community's first school excited her.

****

"Iona." Emma knocked on the back door of the farmhouse. "It's Emma, come to thank you for the excellent scones."

As the door opened, the stern face of Iona MacLeod appeared. "They were for Morgan," she said coldly.

"Well, I do thank you. They were excellent." When Iona failed to respond, Emma continued, "May I come in? It's a very warm day. I would appreciate a glass of water."

Iona hesitated, then stepped aside.

"Thank you." Emma gathered up her skirts as she entered the hot, clean kitchen. "Goodness, it's warm in here. Are you baking?"

"Food must be prepared no matter what the weather." Iona went to the sink and began to pump water. "You'll have to toughen to housewifely chores if you're to make Morgan any kind of wife." She handed a full mug to Emma.

"Why don't you pump yourself a drink and we'll enjoy them outside?" Emma smiled as she accepted the offering. "I saw a couple of chairs beneath the trees. It should be pleasantly cool out there."

"I've work to do."

"Surely you can spare a few minutes. Iona, we do have to learn to get on together. Our men will be gone for God only knows how long. We can be of considerable help and comfort to each other, if you'll just give us a chance to be friends. It is what Morgan and Angus want."

Emma held her breath as Iona MacLeod hesitated.

"Very well," she said gruffly. "But just for a quarter hour. Then I must be back at work." She returned to the pump.

****

"Iona, I very much want us to be friends."

Seated beneath the gently rustling branches of an ancient maple tree, Emma faced the Scotswoman. "I know it would give both Morgan and Angus peace of mind to know we would look out for each other during their absence at sea."

For a few moments that seemed like an eternity to Emma, Iona remained silent, staring out at the river visible through a windbreak of spruce trees.

"You seem a decent sort...for an Englishwoman," she said finally, looking down into her mug. "And Morgan needs someone to help him over the deep hurt Vanessa has caused him. Are you prepared to stand by him as she never did?"

"For as long as I can." Emma drew a deep breath. She tried not to think about the duplicity in her words. "He's been kind and generous. I will do my best to repay him."

"Generous!" Iona guffawed. "Yes, indeed, that would be Morgan. It was his generosity to that Cameron woman that has landed him in his present unfortunate position."

"Yes." Emma fingered her mug thoughtfully. "Because of her he's turned to piracy."

"Piracy!" Iona jumped to her feet, eyes blazing as she glared down at the younger woman. "I'll thank you to modify your words, mistress! Morgan is requesting to become a privateer, a defender of this country, fully licensed by the government! Each ship he takes must be sailed into Halifax under one of his men, called a prize master, and part of his crew. There the Court of Vice Admiralty rules on its legality and arranges an exchange of its passengers and crew for our seamen held in American prisons.

If the Court rules the prize illegal, Morgan and his crew get nothing for their trouble except perhaps injuries, even death, and whatever damage their ship incurred in the process. And yet you dare to label my husband and brother as pirates!"

"Couched in those terms, their endeavors appear acceptable, perhaps even patriotic." Emma stood and handed her mug to Iona. "Still, I find the violence that must be required of such a venture abhorrent."

"Life is not all pretty bows and ribbons, lass." Iona heaved a heavy sigh as she looked out at the mighty river flowing past her property.

"No, of course it isn't." Emma remembered what Morgan had told her of the violence his sister had suffered at the hands of the British officer. "Still…"

"Enough of such talk." Iona changed the subject abruptly. "James told me you'll be setting up a schoolroom in the front of Morgan's house. I have some books that may be helpful. Come into the house and I'll give them to you."

"Thank you." Emma drew a deep breath and followed the straight-backed woman toward the house.

She might not have succeeded in winning Iona MacLeod over entirely, but she'd made the first step in that direction.

Chapter Eight

The children filed into the house, shyly glancing about the two big rooms where Emma had set up the tables, chairs, benches and desk James had sent. She'd arranged in the center of her desk the few books he and Iona had contributed and hung about the walls a few charcoal drawings, alphabet letters, numbers, and basic words she'd made on sheets of paper. The windows, open to the warmth of the summer day, allowed a July breeze to fill the room with fresh air and sunlight.

"Come in, children, and take seats." She smiled. "The younger ones can sit on the quilts I've placed on the floor, while you more mature students can take chairs and benches at the tables."

There were a dozen students, four little ones who flocked into the parlor and sat down on the quilts and eight older children who moved cautiously into the dining room where seats had been arranged around the tables. Most of them were barefoot.

"Now, we'll set about seeing just how much you already know." Emma stood in the foyer, from where she could see her young charges in both rooms. "Can any of you read the words or numbers on the wall?"

"If we could, we wouldn't be wastin' our time here." A tall, gangly boy of about twelve years of age, the oldest male in the group, sneered.

"No, I daresay you wouldn't." Emma smiled at him. "Very well, then let us begin...so that we won't be wasting any more time for Mister...?" She looked at the boy who'd spoken.

"Ellis, Charlie Ellis. I didn't want to come here.

137

Me dad said it was a waste of time. It was me ma that made me come. She has crazy ideas...like me bein' a business man someday."

"Perhaps not so crazy, Mr. Ellis. This is a new and exciting country, full of opportunities for those who are prepared to take them. Learning to read and write and manage numbers is the very best way that I know to get ready to take advantage of them."

He looked up at her, a sneer crossing his freckled face, and rubbed a hand across his nose. "Yeah, well, then start preparin', schoolteacher. I ain't got all day."

"Very well." Emma went to stand before the large letters she'd drawn on a large paper tacked to the wall. "This is the letter A."

She was about to dismiss the children for a mid-morning recess when Iona arrived with a pitcher of lemonade and a great platter of cookies.

"Have they been doing well, Sister?" the tall, austere woman surprised Emma with her form of address.

"Yes, very well, Sister," Emma replied and smiled, delight warming her heart.

"Then perhaps a wee drop of refreshment might be in order."

"I think that is a very good idea. I'll fetch mugs from the kitchen."

She saw delight registered in the faces of her students as she left the room. Iona MacLeod may not have had the opportunity to bring up her own son, but she certainly knew how to make children happy. Emma also strongly suspected that under the Scotswoman's crusty exterior lurked a kindly heart.

****

"Has it been a good morning?" Iona helped Emma wash the mugs and tidy the schoolroom after the last child had finished the food and gone outside to play.

"Very good." Emma paused in replacing mugs on the kitchen shelves. "But I'm afraid I'm deficient on one very important area where the girls are concerned. I've never been much of a hand at sewing and fancywork, and some of these girls I'm sure can barely thread a needle. I was wondering..."

Hoping her companion wouldn't comprehend that she was telling an untruth, she paused to look at the other woman.

"Yes, you were wondering?" Iona looked at her, eyes narrowing.

"I was wondering if you might help out in that area. It would only take a few hours each week," she hurried on as she saw Iona about to refuse. "You'd be doing the children a great service. Young women should be proficient with a needle, since most are destined to be wives and mothers."

"We'll see." Iona went back to her cleaning. Emma returned to her mug washing, a smug smile tipping her lips.

****

The following morning Charlie Ellis limped into the classroom and sat down sullenly. In passing the boy later in the morning, Emma chanced to look down and saw his big toe swollen and oozing a thick mucus.

"Charlie, will you remain for a moment?" she asked when the children filed out for their mid-morning recess.

"What'd I do now?" he muttered sullenly.

"Nothing wrong. Please come into the kitchen with me."

Shuffling and limping, he followed her.

"Sit." She indicated a chair by the hearth. She brought clean rags, a basin, soap, and a bottle of whiskey she'd discovered in a cupboard, placing them on the floor in front of the boy.

"What air ye goin' ta do?" He drew back,

clutching the arms of the chair.

"Simply clean your toe and bind it out of the dirt." She knelt in front of him. "Otherwise infection will set in and you could lose it, perhaps even your foot."

"No!" Terror blanched the defiant face, making his freckles stand out.

"That won't happen if you'll let me tend it now." She looked up at him.

He hesitated. "Will it hurt?"

"For a minute only. By tomorrow it should be feeling much better. I've found a pair of the captain's boots you can wear while it heals. They will be too large, but we'll stuff them with rags. What do you say?"

"Okay. Go ahead. But if I lose me toe..."

"You won't...not if you follow my instructions and let me change the dressings every morning when you come to school."

"Don't matter what ye do, Teacher, I'd still rather be tendin' me father's horses. Horses make a deal more sense to me than people..."

He broke off in a howl as she thrust his dirty foot into the basin of warm water.

****

A week later, after the last child had left for home and while Emma was setting her improvised schoolrooms to rights, Farand Thatcher tapped softly on the still-open front door. It was a hot day, and Emma had opened all the doors and windows to allow what little breezes there were to penetrate the house.

"Mrs. Reynolds, may I come in?"

She hesitated. Iona had left only minutes previous. She might even yet be in the yard of her farmhouse, able to view Emma's visitor. Even though she and Emma had become closer over the course of the last few days, Emma wasn't confident that she might not relish telling Morgan about his wife's handsome young male visitor.

"Allow me to assist you." Before she could protest, he strode into the schoolrooms and began to stack books and papers on the children's desks.

"There's really no need..." She hurried to his side, but he silenced her with a finger placed gently to her lips, a teasing twinkle in his eye. Struck by his forward gesture, she froze. Charged with sexual tension, the moment held her in its grip as she gazed up into twinkling brown eyes. Then he turned back to his chore.

"Actually..." He continued piling up books as if nothing untoward had happened. "I've come to offer my services. I'm a passable musician. I play guitar and sing. I thought I might offer some basic instruction to amuse your students."

"I had no idea you were talented in that area." Emma leaned back against a table to gaze at him in surprise as she willed her heartbeats to return to normal. "Of course, your assistance would be most welcome. However..."

"However, you're afraid your jealous husband might not approve." He crossed his arms over his well-tailored waistcoat and grinned. "Since I observed your sister-in-law leaving several times this past week, I can only surmise she is assisting you. Under such austere scrutiny, how could he possibly object? And be honest. Wouldn't a little music add a bit of fun to the often dry subjects of reading, writing, and needlework? I can play a fulsome jig as well as classical pieces."

"Well..." Emma weighed the matter for a moment, then brightened as she replied. "Very well. When can you begin?"

"Tomorrow." He spread his arms wide in acceptance. "Or will that be too soon?"

"I'll expect you at ten o'clock."

"Ten o'clock it is, then. Now." He rubbed his hands together in a satisfied manner. "Can we seal our agreement with a cup of tea?"

"I've a deal of work to do, Mr. Thatcher." After her reaction to his touch moments earlier, it wouldn't be prudent to allow the man to linger.

"And I shall help you...after refreshment." He smiled at her, and she felt her resolve melting.

"Perhaps just a quick cup," she relented.

He followed her into the kitchen. She felt him watching as she took mugs from the cupboard and swung the teapot over the hearth. His scrutiny made her uneasy, and she felt clumsy at the task.

"Please have a seat at the table." She placed two mugs before him. "The tea will be hot in a minute. Would you care for cookies? Iona makes them for the children, and I'm sure I have some left." She started to scurry toward the pantry, but he was suddenly in front of her, blocking her way.

"Emma." He caught her by the arms. "Don't you see? Three times now we've been thrown together. Fate has a plan for us."

"Sir, you overstep propriety." Emma jerked free and backed away from him. "I am a married woman."

"I think not, my dear." He strode over to the window and stood staring out toward the stables and the forest beyond. "You see, I did some checking at Somerset House in England before I sailed. Nowhere in London, where you profess to have been recently married, is there any record of the union."

"Why would you do such a thing?" Aghast, Emma could only stare at him, her mind racing to find a logical lie to cover her tracks.

"Is it so difficult to understand, my beautiful Emma? From the first moment I cast eyes on you, I was smitten. Then I was told you had been recently married to Captain Morgan Reynolds. Something about your manners toward each other, however, didn't support this idea. So I checked. And lo and behold, no record anywhere."

"We were married before we got to London." Emma stood her ground, although her heart was hammering against her ribs.

She would definitely be branded a woman of easy virtue if such gossip were set loose in the village. And somehow it mattered more to her what people would think of Morgan than of herself. Jilted by the local beauty, the daughter of a man who was probably the wealthiest in the valley, Morgan did not need to be held to more unsavory news. She must not allow this newcomer to besmirch his good name...or hers.

"Not likely, since the handsome Captain Reynolds was then on his way to wed another. Come, come, Emma, your secret is safe with me...for the time being."

"What does that mean?" Emma clutched the sideboard behind her back until her fingernails dug into it.

"Until you come to care enough for me to make a clean breast of it and leave this wilderness as my companion."

"How dare you suggest such a thing!" Emma's hands dropped to her sides, clenched into white-knuckled fists. "I will swear up and down that I am Morgan's wife. Few in this valley will have the time or resources to ferret out records in London."

"I agree, but will not such a tale make things most unpleasant between you and your newly befriended sister-in-law? I don't think Iona MacLeod takes kindly to gossip."

"Please leave my house this instant!" Emma strode to the back door and flung it open. "I'll have no more of your threats and slander voiced in Captain Morgan Reynolds' house."

"Very well." He sauntered across the room but paused in front of the door. "Beautiful Emma." He reached out and managed to run a finger sensuously down her cheek before she flinched away. "You may send me packing now, but after weeks, perhaps months, without that big, marauding brute you refer to as a husband, you may start to look at me differently. Remember, my darling, I'm ready, willing, and able to offer you a very real, very legal marriage with no blonde-haired vixen to haunt the joys of our conjugal bed."

"Go!" Emma pointed. "And you can forget about teaching music tomorrow."

With a final sly smile he obeyed.

The moment he was outside, she slammed the door and bolted it. For the first time in weeks, Emma Prescott was truly afraid.

****

The next morning Charlie Ellis arrived early for school, whistling. He carried Morgan's borrowed boots under his arm, a bunch of wild violets in his hand.

"'Mornin', Teacher." He walked up to her desk, dropped the boots on the floor beside it, and held out the flowers. "I brought these here fer ye...fer healin' me toe. Ma said it was the polite thing to do."

"Thank you, Charlie." Emma was startled to find tears spring to her eyes. "That's most thoughtful...both of you and your mother."

"Yeah, well, I didn't fancy losin' me great toe." He started to turn away, but an idea suddenly struck her.

"Charlie, do you think you might find time to care for my horses? There's just the two of them, but the lad who is currently tending them wants to be free to go to sea. There's pay in the job. You said you were good with horses."

"Tend the captain's horses?" His face lighted up.

144

"I seen 'em at the docks when ye arrived. They're beauties, and no doubt about it. It'd be an honor to care for 'em while the captain's off fightin' in the war."

"Then I'll relieve the other lad of his duties this evening and expect you tomorrow morning?"

"That you will, Teacher. That you will."

Whistling, he strode with manly strides from the house to wait until the other students arrived.

****

Morgan stood at the rail and watched Angus and his men sail into the distance with their third prize of the voyage. He'd put so many of his men aboard captured vessels, he was operating with a skeleton crew now and knew he'd have to follow his mate into Halifax. It was no longer wise to risk taking on enemy vessels with so few men, especially if it came to hand-to-hand combat when the ships were at broadsides.

He rubbed his forearm and felt pain shoot through his shoulder. The blow he'd taken from a belaying stick had come near breaking it. He needed a few days' rest in Halifax, as well.

Halifax. His thoughts flew back to the ball weeks before. And Emma. Emma waltzing in his arms, light as a feather, lovely as an angel. Emma fighting a raging storm to comfort a pair of horses, and sewing up a seaman's bloody arm. Emma lying charmingly to save face for him. Emma taking on the entire village of Pine and his formidable sister with the same untruth on her lips. Emma washing his drawers and cooking his meals without a single complaint. Emma, Emma, Emma.

Perhaps when this war was over and his debts paid he would pay serious attention to Miss Emma Smith. Perhaps he might convince her she need not go on to the Caribbean and her brother to find a home and safety. Perhaps he might convince her to remain at Pine and truly become his wife. Who or what she'd been before he met her was fast fading into a realm of no consequence.

"Land, ho!" A sailor high in the rigging broke in on his thoughts, and he turned to see a green line on the horizon. They'd be in Halifax by sundown.

****

A week later, as Emma taught sums to the four eldest children while the younger ones drew pictures, a knock sounded at the front door. Farand Thatcher poked his head in.

"Good afternoon, Mrs. Reynolds." He cast her his most charming smile as he entered, a guitar in hand. "I've come to offer some music instruction, if I'm allowed."

"It's really not a convenient time." Remembering the threats of their previous encounter, Emma stood and drew herself up proudly.

"Oh, come now, Mrs. Reynolds." He cast his beguiling smile over the children. "I'm sure your students have worked diligently all day and deserve the reward of a little music. What would you say to hearing a few jigs and reels, children?"

Seeking her consent, all eyes turned on Emma.

"Please, miss?" It was Charlie Ellis, his freckled face imploring her.

"Very well." Emma heaved a sigh. She couldn't refuse the lad who'd come so far from the belligerent boy she'd first encountered. "Children, gather around."

There was an eager shuffling as the children scurried to surround Farand Thatcher where he had settled on a chair in the middle of the foyer.

"First a couple of lively tunes some of you may have already heard." He strummed the guitar. Expressions of rapt delight appeared on the faces of most of the children. Emma suddenly realized that for most this would be their first exposure to good music.

The moment Farand Thatcher began to play she was further amazed. The man played easily and beautifully, often glancing up at Emma with a smile that had probably charmed many a young lady in his past.

At first he played gentle melodies like "Greensleeves." Then he burst into a rollicking tune that had the children clapping their hands in time. He began to sing and, after repeating the chorus a couple of times, invited them to join. They vigorously if not always tunefully obliged.

Finally Emma brought the concert to a close. Parents would be looking for their children. She must not make them tardy for chores or evening meals.

"Dismissal time." She clapped her hands. "Please thank Mr. Thatcher before you leave. I will see you all promptly at nine a.m. tomorrow morning."

Reluctantly they gathered up their belongings and headed for the door. Some mumbled their thanks as they passed the musician, but Charlie Ellis paused and held out his hand.

"That was a right fine lot of pickin', sir," he nodded, his changing voice cracking over the words. "Thank ye."

"The pleasure was all mine, young man." Farand arose and accepted the boy's work-hardened hand. "I'll come another day and we'll sing together again...if your teacher will permit." He looked inquiringly at Emma.

"What do you say, Teacher?" Charlie looked at Emma with an eagerness she'd only dreamed of seeing in his expression a short time previous. She knew she couldn't refuse. These children needed joy and happiness as much as they needed book learning.

"Very well. Mr. Thatcher may come again...provided you work diligently at your other studies."

"Thank ye, Teacher." Charlie touched his forelock, then turned and strode out of the classroom on dirty, bare feet.

Well." Farand laid aside his guitar and arose. "That went well, did it not, Mrs. Reynolds?"

Emma closed the door after the last child and turned to face him, crossing her arms on her chest. "Yes, it did. But what is the real reason for this unannounced visit? Have you come to threaten me again? I promise you, I will not be treated in such a manner. You may tell all the tales you wish in the village, but I think you'll be hard pressed to have anyone believe a newcomer like you over the wife of one of their most respected citizens."

"You may have a point." He looked at her, brown eyes twinkling. "I also admit I was out of line in making those statements. It's only because I know you are not legally married to that brute and I so passionately desire to court you."

Emma felt her breath come into her body in an unexpected deep inhale.

"Court me? Mr. Thatcher, you must be mad!"

"Mad with love, Mrs. Reynolds. But your supposed husband is engaged in a hazardous profession. Any day now you may be receiving the news that he's been lost at sea or killed in fighting. When such an event occurs, rest assured that, after a decent period of mourning, I will be waiting to pay my respects and seek the hand of the lovely Widow Reynolds."

"Leave this house at once, sir! I'll not tolerate such blasphemous statements to be made under my husband's roof!"

"Very well, madam, but the day will come when you'll welcome my presence and be happy I was diligent in my suit. I will never believe that a woman as fine and decent as yourself can love a pirate."

Picking up his guitar, Farand Thatcher opened the door and strode out of the house. Emma watched him swinging jauntily down the path past her sister-in-law's house. She hoped Iona wasn't at a window. Farand Thatcher's appearance was that of a contented, happy man. She didn't need Morgan's sister surmising things that were far from true.

Abruptly she slammed the door on the scenario. Why should she waste time worrying about that strict old prude? What if she did tell Morgan a story about Farand's visit? Emma and Morgan weren't truly married. All that could annoy him was the fact that she, Emma, might cause gossip in the village.

She drew a deep breath and tried to turn her undivided attention to tidying the schoolrooms. Her mind, however, drifted back to Farand's dire predictions about Morgan's future. Her supposed husband was at sea in a war, albeit a war some had termed a gentleman's war with little actual animosity on either side, whether British Maritimers or New Englanders. As far as she could discern, the battle between them consisted mainly of blockading coastlines and preying on commerce. She'd even heard that some merchants in New Brunswick continued to carry on a highly lucrative trade with their neighbors in Maine and vice versa.

Still, there had to be some bloodletting in those battles for prizes. Surely no one gave up their ship's cargo without at least some sort of struggle. And Morgan wasn't a man to back down from a fight. With a shudder, she stacked the last pile of books neatly on the corner of the table and went into the kitchen to prepare her solitary supper.

****

The evening smelled of fresh leaves and wildflowers and the river. A full moon rose over the water, reflecting down onto its still surface as Emma sat gazing out the window. The bedroom was stifling and she'd gotten up to sit by the open window, hoping to catch even the faintest of breezes. Her thin chemise clung to her as she brushed a damp curl from her forehead. Outside all appeared quiet.

She took a lighted candle from the dressing table and made her way downstairs. At the front door, she placed it on the floor and raised the bar. Seconds later she was outside, shaking her damp nightshirt free of her perspiring body and throwing back her head to let a breeze from the river caress her throat. The air felt wonderfully cool and soothing on her hot flesh as she sank down on the plank steps.

Gazing at the moon's reflection, she wasn't aware of his approach until he spoke.

"Mrs. Reynolds. What a delightful surprise."

"Mr. Thatcher!" Emma jumped to her feet and wrapped her arms protectively about her scantily clad body. "What are you doing here?"

"I've taken to making a nightly patrol around your house and that of your sister-in-law," he said, placing emphasis on the last words. "You are two ladies living quite alone. I feel it my duty as a gentleman to care for both of you since your husbands," again the emphasis on the final word, "are off fighting a cruel war."

"That is thoughtful of you, sir, but I doubt that anyone, knowing the characters of our husbands, would dare to trouble us. Also, my husband has left me two fully loaded pistols. It's fortunate you have made your patrols known to me, or I might have shot you as a prowler."

"Emma, Emma." He came up the steps and grasped her hands in his. She tried to pull away, but he held so tightly she flinched and gave up the struggle. "Can you not interpret my haunting your grounds at night for any other purpose? Do you not know you've rendered me sleepless with the vision of your beauty? Can you not understand how distressing it is to long for the unattainable? Emma, have you never yearned for an unattainable love?"

The word sent a spear of utter surprise through her being. Love! This handsome, charming young man loved her? Surely not!

"Mr. Thatcher, you must not speak such words. I am, as I've told you innumerable times previously, a married woman, loyal to my husband. I cannot and will not dishonor him through a pointless affair with you."

"Ah, but my beautiful Emma, I'm not proposing a pointless affair." She saw his eyes bright in the moonlight. "I am offering you the honorable state of matrimony. A real marriage, a legal marriage, a tender, loving marriage."

He leaned forward to kiss her gently on the forehead while Emma stood mesmerized by his words. Slowly he released her hands and backed carefully down the steps, his gaze holding hers locked on his.

"Think on it, my lovely Emma," he called back softly as he dissolved into the shadowy trees. "That is all I ask for now. Just think on it."

****

After the children had been dismissed the following day, Emma felt an overwhelming desire to get away from the house, to breath air untainted by either her husband's or Farand Thatcher's presence. She dressed in riding habit and asked Charlie Ellis to saddle her mare.

"I've been exercisin' like you asked, Teacher, so she'll make easy ridin'." The lad pulled off his cap and scratched his thatch of amber curls. "But the stallion, now he's another matter entirely."

"I understand. He is a spirited creature. I don't

want you risking injury by attempting to ride him. Do you think you could find a gentleman in the village sufficiently experienced with horses to exercise the captain's horse?"

"Never in a hundred thousand years, missus." Charlie grinned ruefully. "That big black devil only allows the captain on his back. Anyone else who tries ridin' him will be takin' their life in their hands."

"Ah, well, then, the Lad will just have to be content with racing around the paddock."

****

A half hour later, Emma halted the mare a mile downriver from her house and sat gazing out over the water. A wind had arisen. Black clouds were pushing in from the horizon to coat the blue of a warm summer's day in a darkening shroud. There'll be a storm tonight, she thought, and shivered in spite of the heat. She hated the idea of being alone in the big, empty house when thunder boomed and lightning flashed.

Lost in those thoughts, she was startled when another horse and rider appeared out of the trees on the trail behind her.

"Good afternoon, Mrs. Reynolds." Farand Thatcher touched his quirt to his hat brim. "A lovely evening for a ride, is it not?"

"What are you doing here?"

"Why, pursuing you, my lovely Emma, as I will continue to pursue you, to the ends of the earth, if necessary." He halted his chestnut gelding close beside Bonnie, brown eyes twinkling.

"This is entirely inappropriate!" She made a move to turn her mare away from him, but he caught the animal by the bridle.

"No, Emma, it is not." His words brooked no denial. For a moment she paused, unnerved yet intrigued. This handsome young man was apparently infatuated with her. Furthermore, she was not a married woman, nor had Captain Morgan Reynolds expressed any intention of making her one. There was no reason for her to spurn Farand Thatcher's advances.

He was leaning toward her, ready to kiss her, she fancied, when hoofbeats from the forest made them both turn toward the trail.

Morgan Reynolds, riding the Lad, burst out of the trees and galloped up to them. As the stallion came to a sliding stop beside Emma, Bonnie shied, unseating Emma. Only Morgan's arm sweeping out to encircle her waist and hoisting her into his saddle saved her from being thrown to the ground.

"Mr. Thatcher, is it?" He held his prancing horse in check with one arm and Emma in place with the other. "I'd advise you to hie yourself back to the village at once, sir, and leave my wife alone. Do I make myself clear?"

"As you wish." Farand carefully backed his horse away. He paused to touch his quirt to his hat. "Good evening, Mrs. Reynolds." Swinging his gelding about, he put his heels to the animal's sides and galloped back down the trail.

"You may put me down, sir." Emma felt his saddle digging into her lower extremities. "I'm not about to run away."

"Is that a fact?" He eased her to the ground and swung down beside her. "Gossip in the village says Mr. Thatcher has been a most attentive guest in our home on more than one occasion."

"He has been assisting me by instructing the children in music." Emma smoothed her riding habit and tried to sound cool and calm. At the first sight of the captain bursting out of the trees, however, her heart had begun to pound, her stomach filled with butterflies.

"Ah, yes, the school. Where you labor for wages.

Well, you can put all that behind you." He stood before her, tall, broad-shouldered and handsome, hands on his belt buckle, feet astride. "I've been fortunate in taking some excellent prizes. I've managed to pay off many of my debts. Soon I'll be able to furnish our home in a style befitting such a manor. Therefore, there is absolutely no need for you to work for the pittance James is paying you to operate schoolrooms in our house."

"But I enjoy the children, seeing them learn, hoping I'm leading them to a better future!" Emma stepped close to him, eyes bright with enthusiasm. "And it fills the empty hours while you're away," she finished, shyly lowering her gaze.

"I thought Mr. Thatcher did that." He scowled down at her.

"How you do underestimate me." She narrowed her eyes angrily, looking up at him. "You have been kind to me, saved my life, in fact. Do you think I'd embarrass you by taking a lover while I am posing as your wife? Really, Captain, you infuriate me!"

She swung away from him and made a stumbling attempt to mount Bonnie. Failing, she took up the reins and started to lead the mare back down the trail up which she'd come.

"Emma, wait." He strode after her and caught her by the arm. "I spoke out of turn." His tone moderated, became gentle. "I don't believe you'd dishonor me. Still, it's hard to trust a woman whose past has been such as yours."

"You mean a former harlot?" She looked up at him. "Well, let me clear up that matter. I never was and never will be any man's mistress. I let you believe it because I could not tell you the truth about my past, about how I came to be on that road that night in the storm. To share it with you would be to make you an accomplice in protecting a woman sought not only by a man who seeks her ruin but also by the authorities."

"Good God, woman! You're a criminal? What have you done? Surely not murder?" His expression mirrored the shock her confession had inspired.

"No, definitely not murder. My crime does not involve bodily harm to anyone. But that is all I am prepared to tell you at this point. It should be enough to put your mind at rest for the present. At least you know I'll neither take a lover nor murder you in your bed!"

She started to walk indignantly away, but he caught her arm again. Turning back to him, she saw a twinkle had come into his wonderful blue eyes, a smile starting on his lips.

"Emma, Emma, what am I to do about you? You drive me wild, you haunt my thoughts day and night. Emma Smith or whoever you are, I believe I must ask you to marry me, legally and forever."

Emma stared at him dumbfounded. She had not expected this, not at all, yet the idea set her pulse racing, her solar plexus spinning. Married, really married to this handsome, swashbuckling creature who had the power to take her breath away with just one suggestive look? Yet how could she marry him? She, Emma Prescott, a thief who'd run away from one of the most powerful men in England, who'd stolen a priceless necklace and sold a piece of it for her own purposes...

"That's not possible, sir." Mustering every bit of her strength, she faced him as she refused the offer she fervently wanted to accept. "I will not see you wed to a criminal. You deserve better."

Turning, she started again down the trail leading her mare, her heart plummeting. In those few moments she'd realized she loved Captain Morgan Reynolds. She would probably never love another man in the same way again.

"Wait." He caught up to her and once again

stopped her with a hand on her arm. "Let me help you back onto your mare. It's a long walk back to our house, and there's a storm brewing. We'll have to hurry to get the horses stabled before it breaks. Once we're safe and sound inside, we'll discuss this further."

She hesitated, then placed her booted foot into the stirrup he made with his hands to hoist her back into the saddle.

"Thank you," she said, looking down at him, her eyes filling with tears. "But our discussion is finished. You've done me a great honor in asking me to become your wife. I only wish I had sufficient honor left in me to accept."

She clucked to the mare and headed off down the trail at a trot, a stabbing, fiery pain infecting her breast. He followed her, remaining a few paces behind her all the way to the house.

She was relieved. She didn't want him to see that her heart was breaking.

****

In the stable yard he helped her from the saddle as the first rumbles of thunder announced the arrival of the storm.

"Go up to the house," he said as he led the horses into the barn. "I'll be along directly."

Glad for the opportunity to be alone to compose herself, Emma nodded and hurried away. Once in the darkening kitchen, she removed her gloves and hat with shaking hands, then hurried upstairs to change into a plain gown of blue cotton. By the time he entered, she was making tea at the hearth as the fat raindrops spattered against the windows.

"No tea this evening, Emma." He carried a bottle. "Champagne. Even if we cannot toast impending nuptials we can celebrate my safe return."

He went to the sideboard for a corkscrew. A

moment later, bubbling wine frothed into two mugs he'd taken from the cupboard.

"Are you sure this is wise?" Emma, seated at the table, accepted the cup and looked up at him apprehensively. "You do remember what happened the last time you drank champagne?"

"Ah, yes, *too much* champagne." He sat down opposite her and grinned. "Tonight I promise I will be more circumspect. Now..." He extended his mug across the table. "Here's to paying off debts and a brighter future."

She touched her mug to his. "To paying off debts and a brighter future, Captain."

"I'd be obliged if you'd call me Morgan in our home."

"Of course...Morgan." Emma took a sip, then cried out as a bolt of lightning lit up the room and the house shook with rolling thunder. The mug dropped as she covered her face with her hands.

Morgan rounded the table in a single stride to kneel beside her chair and gather her into his arms. She swung to cling to him, burying her face against his shoulder.

"Emma, Emma, it's only a summer storm." He rocked her gently. "I'll keep you safe, I promise."

It astonished him that this woman who'd braved a North Atlantic storm, doctored an injured sailor, and managed to live alone in a wilderness during his absence was cowed by an act of nature.

He had to admit that he wasn't sorry. He wanted her to stay in his arms, to feel her soft, warm body pressed against his.

"Morgan, when I was a child I was caught alone on the moors in a lightning storm," she breathed, her voice a trembling whisper. "I was terrified. I've never forgotten..."

"Hush." He gathered her up in his arms and started for the stairs. "I'll put you to bed and stay with you until the storm ends."

****

After he'd laid her in the big featherbed, he removed his shirt. For a moment, naked to the waist he hesitated, looking down at her.

"Morgan." She held her arms open to him, green eyes wide and frightened.

"Emma," he muttered as he lowered himself to lie beside her. He felt his body react as she snuggled into him. *Control, control.* "I need you so, my darling girl. Will you not reconsider my offer?"

"No." The word was a shaky whisper. "No."

Chapter Nine

"Once again I broach the question." Morgan, finished with the breakfast she'd prepared, pushed away from the table. "Will you, Emma Smith, do me the honor of becoming my wife? Will you make an honest man of me?" His eyes twinkled as he spoke, but his mouth was set in a deadly serious line.

"Morgan, I've already told you I cannot become your wife." She began to gather up the dishes.

"And what have you done that is so terrible, my sweet Emma?" As she reached for his plate, he caught her by the wrist. "You've told me it involves neither murder or bodily harm. The next worst thing I can think is that you've stolen the crown jewels and..."

His jesting tone died away as the London jeweler's suspicions concerning the ruby she'd given to him burst over him in an astounding epiphany. "Dear God, that's it, isn't it? You stole crown jewels...not the English crown jewels, but the crown jewels of France, of the dead Queen."

"Yes." She met his gaze steadily. "But it was not as you might imagine."

"Not as I imagine! Sweet Jesus, woman, you had a pack of hounds pursuing you when we met! I'm sure half of England and perhaps even a fair number of Frenchmen would like to know your whereabouts. What did you do with them?" He stopped as another realization came upon him. "Dear God in heaven! They're here in this house, aren't they? That's why you won't marry me, why you want me to take you to the Caribbean. There you'll be beyond the law, and you can live in luxury for the rest of your days with your English lover."

"No, Morgan, it's not like that!" Her eyes grew wide and pleading. "I didn't take the gems out of greed. I stole them from a man who was trying to force me to marry him. I took them only as a means of escaping him!"

"And that's supposed to make me feel better, the fact that you stole from another man who wanted to marry you?"

"Morgan, please, you don't understand..."

He kicked aside his chair and strode toward the door.

"I'll be sailing with the tide. It's high time I returned to the sea."

****

What had he gotten himself into, he wondered, as he strode down the hill toward his sister's farm. The woman had stolen a king's ransom from another man fool enough to fall under her spell, and now that fortune lay hidden somewhere in his house. This beautiful, astonishingly sensuous woman who'd only last night come to his bed a virgin...

He felt his body stir and knew that despite what he'd just learned he could easily take her back to their bed and make love to her for the rest of the day, for the rest of the week, for the rest of his life. Had he no sense when it came to women? It had been mere weeks since one had made a cuckold of him. Now this one, this Emma Smith, had made him lover to an international criminal.

He had to get away, back to his ship, back to the sea. He had to get into a good, running fight and take as many prizes as his skill and strength could manage. He had to take his chagrin and anger out on a faceless enemy for whom he held no personal animosity.

****

Emma shivered and pulled her shawl more closely about her as she sat by the hearth. Morgan had been gone a scant twelve hours, yet her heart ached and yearned as if he'd been out of her sight for months. She should have told him her entire story. Surely he would have understood. Surely he would have appreciated that she couldn't let Squire Falkner reveal to the entire village and the bishop the disgraceful fact of her father's gambling addiction.

Her father, a village vicar, had always prided himself on his high moral character—until he'd fallen into the Squire's clutches. The despicable creature had learned of Rev. Prescott's youthful weakness for cards and revived it with the devil's own skill and cunning. Finally he'd reduced the clergyman to penury with nothing more to gamble but one lovely daughter, who'd been the real prize Squire Falkner had sought.

There'd been a last, final, desperate game. The vicar had lost. He could not face the consequences of his actions. In the small hours of the following morning he'd taken a pistol and shot himself in the mouth. Emma still choked when she remembered how she'd found her beloved father draped over his desk, his blood soaking the next Sunday's sermon.

He'd barely been placed in his grave when the squire arrived with two of his men to lay claim to the vicarage and Emma. She remembered the sudden, all-encompassing despair and panic that had sent her heart plummeting when he'd shown her the paper signed in her father's familiar script—script that gave him claim not only to the contents of their home but also to his daughter's hand in marriage.

Emma had protested. England was a free country. No one could force anyone into a marriage they abhorred.

Then he'd made his threat. His corpulent face

gleaming with sweat, he'd informed her that if she failed to make good her father's promises, he'd tell everyone, including the bishop, of the vicar's gambling, of how he'd become so desperate at cards that he'd wagered his daughter's virginity.

Broken and heartsick, Emma realized she had no choice. All she had left was the family honor. If Squire Falkner did as he threatened (and she had no doubt he would) her father's good name would forever be destroyed.

But on the night of their engagement ball, when he'd demanded she wear that garish crimson gown, she knew she could not, even for her beloved father, go through with the marriage. As he ran his big, sweating hands over her arms and cupped her face between them, she knew she had to get away or die.

An hour earlier he'd shown her the necklace. He'd told her that once she was safely married to him, had spent their wedding night in his bed, it would be hers. She stared at the sparkling circle of jewels, recognizing a slight, desperate opportunity of escape.

When he returned to his guests, she stole into his bedroom, took the jewelry from its box by his bed, stuffed it down the bosom of that disgusting dress, and fled into the night. She'd hoped to be a good distance away before he discovered her missing, but that hadn't happened. If it had not been for Morgan... She drew her shawl more tightly around her and shuddered.

Now Morgan, her protector, the man she'd grown to love, was gone back to a war from which he might not return. Gone back hating her, regretting he'd ever made love to her. She buried her face in her hands, but tears would not come. Her pain was too deep for tears.

****

Morgan stood on the quarterdeck and watched

the third prize of the voyage being sailed off toward Halifax. He had a nasty cutlass cut on his forearm and a bruise was spreading up his right cheek, but he'd managed to avoid serious injury. It had been a miracle, he knew. Whenever physical combat had become necessary, he'd been in the thick of it, fighting like a madman. Smashing his fist into an enemy sailor's jaw or slashing a sword from a rival's hand helped in his effort to relieve the anger and tension he hadn't been able to shed since parting with Emma.

Two women had used him and then thrown their deception in his face. Well, no more. Once this war was over, he was making for the brothels of the Caribbean. At least there a man knew exactly what he was getting.

****

Emma faced the children and smiled. If it weren't for the school and her students, she didn't know how she would have managed, missing Morgan as she did. But each morning they appeared, becoming more and more eager to learn, brightening her day with their cheerful faces and inquiring minds.

During the first weeks of Morgan's absence she'd counted the days, fearing at one moment, longing at others, for signs of a pregnancy. But time passed and she knew such was not the case. She wondered if Morgan ever thought of the possibility but then decided against it. After all, they'd only had one night...and morning...of lovemaking. It would have been the greatest of luck—or misfortune—if anything had come of it. As a man of the world, he would have considered the possibility and dismissed it as highly unlikely.

One November morning the children were enjoying a morning break, playing in the yard, when she heard booted footsteps in her kitchen. Morgan!

Her heart leaped and she nearly tripped over her skirts in her haste to get to the back of the house.

"Good morning, Mrs. Reynolds." Farand Thatcher, impeccably dressed in tan breeches and vest, snow-white shirt and cravat, and highly polished riding boots, touched his quirt to his hat and cast her a dazzling smile. "I've come to offer the children a music lesson."

"Your lessons are most irregular, Mr. Thatcher," she said feeling her heart plummet. "You have not been about for several weeks."

"I've been traveling. I understand the captain has absented himself these past days, as well. No marital troubles, I trust?"

"Of course not." Emma swung the kettle over the embers and reached for the poker. "He's at sea, defending this country against the American menace."

"Ah, yes, ever the gallant seaman." Farand crossed the room, removing his hat. He threw it with his quirt onto the table and sat down. "I think you have a very faulty image of his role, my dearest Emma. Allow me to enlighten you."

"I don't wish to hear false tales of my husband's work." Emma stirred the dying fire and placed another log on it. The autumn day had grown cold and a cloud, drifting across the sun, darkened the kitchen.

"But you should know." He stretched out long legs and settled himself comfortably. "Your beloved spouse has become the most dreaded pirate on the eastern seaboard. He's taken more vessels than any other commander, and with such force and brutality that New Englanders have taken to calling him the Sea Wolf. Each day they lay traps for him, and each day he manages to elude them. But mind my words, sweet Emma, the snare is tightening, and soon the Bostonians will be parading him through their streets in irons while the good citizens hurl rotten fruit and eggs at him. Soon he'll be languishing in a New England jail and there won't be enough ransom in all of British North America to secure his release."

"I don't believe you!" Emma swung to face him, her heart pounding. "Captain Morgan Reynolds is an honorable man, a decent man, a—"

"A picaroon, a pirate of the first water. Emma, you've been sleeping with a cold-blooded murderer and you've been too blind to realize it."

"Get out!" Emma swung on him, eyes blazing. "I will not have such tales told about the master of this house!"

With a shrug, Farand arose and gathered up his hat and quirt. "Very well, my lovely girl. But my reports are true. I've just come from Halifax, where your esteemed captain is being hailed as the biggest rogue seaman this country has ever seen."

****

Emma hoped and prayed Morgan would return before the river froze, but such was not to be. In his stead, three letters from him arrived on the last ship to dock at Pine before the winter's permanent freeze. One was addressed to Iona, another to James Cameron, and the third to Mrs. Morgan Reynolds.

Emma couldn't bear to open it when one of James Cameron's men brought it to the house. Instead she offered the man tea and waited in a wildly nervous state while the man, cold from a blustery November afternoon, drank a cup and ate one of the scones she'd made. As soon as she'd bade him farewell, she closed the door on the inhospitable day. For a few moments she stood staring down at her supposed name scrawled across the envelope.

She walked slowly to the window, her skirts whispering over the bare boards in the silent house. There she paused in the dim light of the short, fading day and turned it over and over. Her hands trembled, but finally she found the courage to open it and remove the single sheet it contained.

"Mrs. Reynolds," it began. Its formality tore at Emma's heart. "This is to let you know I am well and prospering financially. I have sent a sum of money to James to see to your care. I do, however, request that you move in with my sister for the winter months. It will save the cost of maintaining two households and provide companionship for Iona.

"I will not return to Pine before April. I wish you a safe and healthy winter and promise that as soon as this war is over I will deliver you safely into the hands of your protector in the Caribbean.

I remain,

Your husband,

Captain Morgan Reynolds."

The hoarfrost forming on the window panes could not have been colder than his words. Emma sank down onto a chair at the kitchen table and crumpled the paper in her hands.

For a few minutes she sat lost in feelings of pain and rejection. Then the spirit that was the essence of Emma Prescott awoke. She took a deep breath and squared her shoulders. She loved the man. She would not give him up without a fight. She would write him a letter revealing to him the truth about her past. And then she would tell him she loved him.

She hurried into the parlor schoolroom, took a seat at her desk, and began to write.

****

A half hour later, bundled in her bonnet and shawl against the raw wind that blustered down the river, Emma headed for the wharf in Pine. She had to get to the ship that had brought Morgan's letters before it once more sailed. It was her last chance to send her revelations to Morgan before spring.

She was running, stumbling, as she came into view of the ship and saw seaman beginning to cast off lines.

"No, wait!" she cried, waving the letter above her head. "Please wait!"

Her voice was swept away on the wind as they drew up the boarding plank.

Caught by waves and tide, the ship bucked out into the river. Emma's hand holding the message from her heart dropped to her side. She watched the ship, buffeted by the gale, heading downriver. Then, with her heart feeling like lead, she started back to the big, echoing house in the forest.

****

Scottish Highlanders weren't people to celebrate Christmas, Emma learned, as she sat by the hearth in Iona's kitchen mending a stocking. It was December twenty-fifth, and to all appearances it was as any other day in the village. Emma had moved in with Iona as Morgan had requested and generally was satisfied with the arrangement. She'd cancelled her school for the three coldest months. Without the children to brighten her days, her time alone in the manor would have been lonely and purposeless. Here, with Iona, she was kept busy with knitting, sewing, mending, and cooking. They also looked after the four cows and dozen chickens that were part of the small farm.

Emma had had Bonnie and the Lad moved to Iona's stable. It made a lesser journey for Charlie to tend them and removed the necessity of keeping a trail open to Morgan's homestead.

Often at night Emma looked out her bedroom window toward the big, empty manor, standing dark and alone on the hill above the farm, and felt its loneliness. Later, when she'd lie sleepless in her narrow cot, she'd wonder about Morgan, about where he was and what he was doing. She couldn't believe Farand Thatcher's description of his undertaking to be the truth. Captain Morgan

Reynolds wouldn't resort to violence to fill his coffers.

Yet he was at war. At times he must be forced to resort to physical confrontation with the enemy. She remembered his confrontations with Farand Thatcher and knew he was capable, that he could be as bold and intimidating as a situation warranted.

Tossing and turning, she decided she had to talk to someone who could tell her the truth. Tomorrow she would visit James Cameron. She would ask him point blank exactly how Captain Morgan Reynolds comported himself in war.

*****

"Emma, my dear, come in, come in." James Cameron welcomed Emma with alacrity when she arrived at his house the following morning. "It's a pleasure to see you. I was just about to ride down to Iona's to invite you to my annual ceilidh on New Year's Eve. We Scots may not celebrate Christmas, but we do love to see each new year in with a bit of a party. Will you come? Iona always attends."

"If Iona will be coming, then of course I shall be pleased to attend." Emma let him take her cloak, which he handed on to a serving girl.

"Come, sit by the fire. You look half-frozen." James drew a chair up to the blazing hearth and turned to the serving girl. "Rose, fetch us some strong, hot tea and bring along lots of cream and sugar. Oh, and a few of those oatcakes Cook was making when I came through the kitchen a few minutes ago."

"Yes, sir." The girl scurried off as James seated himself opposite Emma.

"Now, my dear, I can tell by your expression you've not come simply to pay a visit to an old man. What can I do for you? Morgan has left you under my guardianship. Therefore, I'll be happy to serve you in any way I can."

"Mr. Cameron..."

"James," he corrected her gently. "Please call me James."

"James." Emma looked into the entrepreneur's kindly face and found it difficult to voice the questions she was about to ask. "I've come...to ask you about Morgan, about his new...profession."

"Ah, so you've been hearing rumors about the conduct of some of our less than honorable privateers, have you?" He drew a deep breath and stuck his thumbs into his waistcoat pockets. "Unfortunately, my dear, some are all too true. Women and children robbed, men beaten, on-shore communities looted and burned. War is a coarse and brutal business, there's no way around it."

"And does Morgan...my husband...participate in such unpleasantness?"

"To some extent, he must." James arose and went to a humidor to extract a cigar. "Do you mind if I smoke?"

"No." She shook her head. "But women and children..."

"Ah, now there I've led you astray. No, of course he doesn't molest women and children. Nor does he loot and pillage communities on shore." James took a faggot, stuck it into the fire, and used it to light his cigar before continuing. "Morgan conducts his business at sea, with all the gallantry befitting an officer of the British navy. You can feel proud to be wed to such a man, Emma."

"Thank you, James. I had to know the truth."

"I believe you already knew it...in your heart." He looked down at her, his blue-eyed gaze direct and soul-searching. "You only needed reassurance."

****

An hour later, Emma left James Cameron's house and allowed his groom to help her onto Bonnie. It was beginning to snow as she rode out of the drive and headed down the trail to Pine and Iona's farmhouse. She pulled her cloak more closely about her and was glad when she entered the shelter of a stand of spruce.

"Emma." A man mounted on a bay horse was blocking the trail as she rounded a turn. The trees and storm clouds had darkened the day. She felt a shiver wash over her at being caught alone in this isolated place as she recognized Farand Thatcher.

"Please move aside." Emma halted Bonnie and drew herself up imperiously. "I'm eager to get home before the storm breaks."

"Certainly. Let me provide escort." He turned his mount and brought it up beside her. "We can talk as we ride."

"We have little to discuss." Emma clucked to Bonnie, sending her forward at a sedate trot.

"Ah, but I think we have, my lovely Emma." He shot a mocking glance in her direction as he urged his mount to keep pace. "You went to see James Cameron to question him about your husband. You've seen how quickly he can be moved to violence. You've seen..."

"I do not wish to discuss my husband with you." Emma urged Bonnie to a faster pace, but once again he nudged his horse to keep up.

"You forget that I know he's not really your husband," he continued. "As for questioning James Cameron about Captain Reynolds' conduct, you went to the wrong man. James Cameron has every reason to protect the Captain's reputation. You see, he's his partner in this privateering venture. Who do you think bought the guns, the muskets, the cutlasses, the boarding pikes, and the powder to set your paramour up in his pirating trade?"

Shocked, Emma halted Bonnie and turned to stare at Farand Thatcher.

"You look startled, my dear Emma." Farand

Thatcher cast her a sardonic smile. "Think on it. And when next I call upon you, perhaps you'll be more receptive to my words and intentions."

He turned his horse, put his heels to its sides, and galloped off up the trail in the direction from which Emma had come.

Nonplussed, Emma barely notice when her mare once again began to trot homeward. Why hadn't she guessed? Morgan had had no money with which to equip the *Ula* for war. James Cameron would have been his obvious backer. The entrepreneur would not denounce the man with whom he was a business partner. Therefore, his words concerning Morgan's conduct were moot.

****

It snowed heavily on the last day of 1812. By midmorning, Emma decided she and Iona would not be able to attend the ceilidh at James Cameron's. Just as she was putting away the gown she'd planned to wear that evening, a messenger arrived to say Mr. Cameron would be sending his sleigh to collect them, and they were to bring whatever they might need to spend the night if it became impossible for them to return to the farmhouse.

"Shall we still go?" Emma looked at the austere woman, wondering if she would think a party worth the risk of being from their farm overnight.

"Of course," she surprised and delighted Emma by declaring firmly. "It would be rude not to attend a ceilidh, especially on the eve of the New Year. We'll feed the animals and see them safe and sound. That's all that is required. We'll be back here tomorrow noon, at the latest."

****

By evening the snow had stopped. Emma and Iona bundled themselves into the sleigh James sent for them. As they came within sight of the entrepreneur's mansion, they could see it ablaze with lights both inside and out. Emma repressed a shudder as she remembered the last similarly lighted manor house of her acquaintance. To dispel the memory, she noted the differences here. In the clear cold weather members of the local Indian tribes had set up their camps around fires in the dooryard and were sharing in the bounty.

She and Iona were welcomed into the lumber baron's house, festive and warm, with hearth fires, lamps, and candles driving back the chill and darkness of the winter's night. Although it was still early, the large rooms were filling up with guests, and food and drink were circulating freely. In the spacious parlor, a fiddler was striking up jigs and reels.

"Come in, come in, ladies," James greeted them with alacrity. "Let Violet take your wraps. Will you have a cup of mulled cider to chase away the chill?"

"Thank ye, James." Iona relinquished her black cloak to the serving girl and allowed a bit of a smile to tip her prim lips. "I see Mrs. Sutherland has seen fit to grace you with her presence. I'll just be havin' a wee word with her. Perhaps tonight she'll give me the recipe for her cordial. I'd like to have a batch settin' when Angus comes home. He's right partial to it."

She moved away into the milling crowd as a well-dressed gentleman, another lumber baron, Emma guessed, moved in to take James' attention. For a moment she stood alone, gazing about at the crowd. She wondered how many of them were parents of her students. She must invite them to the school when it re-opened in March. She should get to know them.

"Good evening, Mrs. Reynolds." The voice startled her out of her thoughts. She turned to find Farand Thatcher smiling at her. Impeccably dressed in formal black attire, he appeared every inch the gentleman.

"Good evening, Mr. Thatcher." She granted him a small, tight smile. "I thought you would have left this valley before winter closed us in."

"I'd considered it." He stood with his hands clasped behind his back looking down at her. "But then I decided what I wanted most was right here." The expression in his brown eyes left no doubt as to his meaning.

"I believe I will get a mug of that cider Mr. Cameron mentioned," she said, turning away.

"Allow me to fetch one for you." He caught her lightly by the arm and led her to a chair in a corner, away from the crowd. "Wait here. I will be back directly."

Emma watched as he made his way through James' guests, tall, broad of shoulder, slim of waist and hips, a handsome and self-assured young man. A young man who had no qualms telling her exactly how he felt about her. She could do worse, she was startled to catch herself thinking.

Then she realized that perhaps she was only being realistic. She wasn't married to Morgan Reynolds and never would be. He'd left either hating or at the very least disdaining her. Their relationship had come to a bitter and acrimonious end. She had to move on. She would like to be married someday. Why not to an enterprising young entrepreneur like Farand Thatcher?

You don't love him, a small voice reproved. *You love Morgan Reynolds, and no matter what has come between you, you always will.*

"Mrs. Reynolds...Emma." Farand was back, holding down a mug to her.

She accepted it and felt its warmth seeping into her cold fingers. Raising it to her lips, she took a sip and sighed. It wasn't the champagne Morgan fancied and she herself had come to enjoy, but it chased away the cold.

"Emma." He smiled down at her and held out his hand as the fiddler struck up a lively reel. "Will you dance with me?"

"Yes." She placed her cider on an end table, stood, and smiled at him. "Yes, Mr. Thatcher, thank you, I will."

"Your sister-in-law seems to be enjoying herself," James Cameron commented to Iona as the pair stood in the parlor archway watching Emma and Farand Thatcher laughing and dancing.

"Aye, perhaps a wee bit too much, James." Iona drew her lips into a pucker of disapproval. "With her husband away fighting in a cruel war, she should show a little more restraint."

"Come, come, Iona. She's a young lady who's spending her first winter in a strange land. It's proving to be a good deal more lonely than she'd anticipated, I'll wager." James Cameron took a puff on his cigar. "When she agreed to marry Morgan and come out to New Brunswick, she never in her wildest dreams expected to lose him so soon and completely. Be patient with her."

"I'll do more than that, if you please." Iona's expression hardened with each swirl Emma and Farand Thatcher made around the room. "I'll keep a sharp eye on that lassie. If she does anything to dishonor my brother's good name, I'll see he sends her packing the moment he sets foot back in Pine."

****

"Ladies and gentlemen, may I have your attention."

Emma glanced up from her supper plate to see Farand Thatcher at the musicians' platform at the end of the room, guitar in hand.

"While our talented musicians are enjoying a well-deserved respite and our host's sumptuous repast, I'd like to entertain you with a special song.

And," he continued, looking directly at Emma and smiling, "dedicate it to a certain lady."

Ignoring the fact that people followed his gaze to Emma, he strummed a chorus, then launched into song.

"My love is like a red, red rose
That's newly sprung in spring
Oh, my love is like a melody
That's sweetly sung in tune."

The words and music fell soft and sensuous on Emma's ears, his rapt expression leaving no doubt for whom his song was intended. She felt a blush warming her cheeks and wished she had the power to stop it.

"Disgraceful!" Emma heard the word hissed. She glanced up to see a matronly woman who'd been introduced to her earlier that evening as Mrs. Sutherland, who "makes a most excellent cordial," glaring at the young man. "Has he no decency?"

"Come now, Martha," James Cameron, ever the genial host, spoke softly. "The lad's only singing a harmless little tune."

"Serenading a married woman, more like! A married woman whose man is off at war defending this land! Disgraceful. Absolutely disgraceful!"

Emma bent her head over her food. Wrong though it must appear to be, she was flattered to be serenaded by the handsomest young gentleman in the room. Morgan would never have done such a thing.

****

"Good night, Mrs. Reynolds." Farand Thatcher raised her fingers to his lips as dawn was about to break and the party was disbanding. "It's been a night I won't soon forget."

"Nor I, Mr. Thatcher." Emma, flushed from dancing the night away in hot, stuffy rooms, smiled at him.

"Farand, I've asked you to call me Farand." He leaned close to whisper the words into her ear. "You look incredibly lovely at this moment. I can barely restrain myself from taking you into my arms and..."

"You must be eager to get on your way, Mr. Thatcher." Iona MacLeod appeared beside the couple, her tone colder than the icicles hanging from the mansion's eves. "It's a fair ride to your cabin in Pine. We'd not be wantin' ye to freeze along the way."

"I thank you for your concern, Mrs. MacLeod." Farand backed away from Emma and smiled at the woman who stood drawn up to her full height beside Emma, chin stuck out defiantly. "Good night, or perhaps I should more accurately say good morning, ladies. I hope to see you both again soon."

"Humph!" Iona watched him collect his hat, coat, and gloves from a footman near the door, then touch his forehead in final farewell to them before stepping out into the first rays of dawn. "Come, Emma. We'll be returnin' home directly. The roads are passable clear. There's no need for us to linger. We've work to do at the farm."

****

"I will countenance no more of that kind of behavior, Sister." Iona's words shook with anger as she addressed Emma the moment they were once more alone in their farm house. "Ye be my brother's wife. I'll not have tongues waggin' about your attentions to that Thatcher fellow while Morgan's away at war."

"I'm sure I don't know what you're talking about." Emma removed her wrap and pretended she didn't understand.

"Don't play coy with me, missy." Iona caught her by the arm and spun her to face her. "You and him talkin', and laughin', and dancin' like lovers. Then hisself havin' the temerity to sing that love song to you. I'll have none of it, do you hear!"

"I was simply enjoying the party." Emma shrugged free, but her heart was pounding. Alone in the shadows of the winter's dawn with the tall, austere woman she felt suddenly afraid.

"Nay, nay, lass, it was much more than that." Iona glowered down at her. "I'm no fool. But there will be no more. You'll no further disgrace my brother, a man who has been only kind to ye, who has provided ye with food and shelter, and most importantly, given ye his good name."

"I would never disgrace Morgan." Emma drew herself up proudly to face the Scotswoman. "He has been generous to me and I am grateful, no matter what you think. Mr. Thatcher provided me with a willing dancing partner this evening, that is all. As school is now closed for the winter, he won't be tutoring my pupils in music. Therefore it is doubtful I'll be seeing him again at any time in the near future."

"Good." Iona MacLeod began to build up the fire from embers languishing on the hearth. "Morgan will be returning a hero when the river opens up again. I want you waiting for him honorably and proudly."

Chapter Ten

An hour later Emma sat alone in the small gable room that was her bedchamber and gazed out at the snowy landscape and dark, brooding forest. She'd enjoyed the evening. She'd never been courted and that is definitely what Farand Thatcher had been attempting to do.

She removed the pins from her hair and let it fall about her shoulders, the memory of Farand Thatcher's song sliding back across her mind. She remembered the roses he'd sent her in Halifax, his bold move to meet her on the London dock. She felt a smile tilting her lips. He cut a dashing, romantic figure: young, vital, and unscarred by sordid affairs.

With a sigh she stood to remove her gown. She felt bone-weary, tired of the charade of a marriage she shared with Captain Morgan Reynolds. He'd left her in a wave of anger. By now he could well have taken up with some other woman. Certainly he'd wasted no time courting her. She couldn't imagine him sending her flowers or singing love songs in her honor.

Emma slipped into her flannel nightshift and slid into her cold bed as the rays of a frosty winter's morning beamed into her room. Shivering, she snuggled down beneath the quilts. She knew she wanted to be married, to be safe once and for all from the odious man back in England who wanted nothing more or less than her absolute ruin. Farand Thatcher seemed to be the answer.

****

"Good morning," Emma greeted the stable lad,

Charlie, later that day when she went to the barn to collect eggs for breakfast.

"G' mornin', Teacher." He paused in shoveling manure from the Lad's stall and turned to look pointedly at Emma. "Big doin's in the village early today, I hear."

"What has happened?" Emma paused, her hand on the latch of the henhouse. Something in the lad's outlook told her it wasn't good and it concerned her.

"A bunch of the lads got together and beat the daylights out of Mr. Thatcher." His freckled face twisted.

"What? Why?" Emma felt a wave of nausea wash over her.

"Folks don't take kindly to a man who goes sniffin' around another man's wife...especially when that man's away at war. Bet he won't do it again."

Emma walked back to the house in a sickened quandary. She longed to go to Farand, to see the extent of his injuries, and, if necessary, nurse him back to health.

She also knew it would be the most imprudent move she could make.

****

Yes, it was imprudent; still she felt impelled to do it. Her Christian upbringing required no less, she told herself, although she knew that wasn't the sole reason. As darkness fell and she was certain Iona slept, Emma Prescott slipped out of the farmhouse and headed toward Farand Thatcher's cabin on the edge of the village.

"Mr. Thatcher, it's Emma Reynolds." She knocked on the plank door. "Are you all right?"

Shuffling noises moved toward the door. It swung open to reveal a man Emma barely recognized.

Farand Thatcher's once handsome face was bruised black and blue, one eye swollen nearly shut.

His shirt hung out over his pants, revealing nasty welts on his chest. He held himself half upright with the aid of a stick.

"Come in," he rasped, then turned to limp back to a disheveled bed against the far wall.

Horrified, Emma advanced into the cabin and shut the door behind her. The condition of the single-room dwelling appalled her. Dirty dishes and clothing lay strewn about. It was cold, bitterly cold.

"What happened?" she breathed staring at the man climbing back into the tangle of covers that was his bed.

"Your so-called husband has friends as vicious as himself," he groaned as he rolled beneath the quilts. "They took exception to my interest in his wife."

"I'm so sorry." Emma breathed the words as she removed her gloves and threw her shawl over a chair. "You didn't deserve such treatment."

She moved to the hearth and threw a log into the fire languishing there. "Rest. I've brought soup and biscuits. As soon as I get this fire blazing, I'll heat up a decent meal for you. Then I'll clean this place."

****

At dawn the next day Emma awoke, poured ice-cold water from the ewer into her basin, and washed hastily before donning a housedress. Wrapping a woolen shawl about her shoulders, she headed downstairs. She'd been fortunate last night, she thought. She'd been able to return to the farmhouse undetected.

The remembrance of the condition in which she'd found Farand Thatcher still made her stomach lurch. She felt no remorse for what she'd done to make him more comfortable in his agony.

In the kitchen she found Iona sitting near the hearth fire, hunched over in her chair, her face ashen.

"Are you unwell?" Emma moved quickly to the woman's side and put a hand on her shoulder.

"A chill, nothing more." She started to rise but staggered and would have fallen if Emma hadn't caught her.

"You're ill. Stay by the fire. I'll fix you a hot rum drink."

"Nay, nay! I'm not a drinkin' woman," she tried to protest. "And if I were, it would be good Scottish whiskey, not the English demon rum."

"You can't make hot buttered rum with whiskey." Emma crossed the room and opened a cupboard. "There are some things English you will have to learn to accept, Sister."

****

An hour later Emma headed toward the barn, one of Morgan's pistols weighing like lead in her hand. Iona lay in a makeshift bed near the hearth, muffled in quilts, lulled to sleep by a large mug of buttered rum.

Tears coursed down Emma's cold cheeks as she struggled to stifle the sobs that were rising in her chest. She was on her way to kill one of God's own creatures, one of their precious laying hens. She had no choice. Iona MacLeod's life could well depend upon it.

****

"Chicken soup?" Iona looked up from the cup Emma held to her lips as the younger woman supported her into an upright position. "Where...ye didnae kill one of our hens, did ye, lass?" Even in the depths of her illness Iona MacLeod remained the frugal Scot.

"Your health is more important than a hen." Emma held the cup back to Iona's mouth. "Mrs. Littleworth cured me of such maladies as yours many times with chicken soup."

"Mrs. Littleworth?" Even before Iona asked the question Emma realized her faux pas.

"Our housekeeper at the vicarage," she replied honestly, deciding it was the best course to take. "My father was a vicar."

"Ye're from a God-fearin' family?" The woman's feverish eyes stared up at her. "Morgan has wed a decent lass after all, English though ye be. The fact gives me peace, Emma." She closed her eyes as Emma eased her back onto her pillows.

"Rest," she said softly. "You'll feel better soon."

****

Later that night Emma's confidence in her reassurance flagged. As a vicious January wind howled around the farmhouse, Iona tossed and raved, her face awash with sweat. Emma bathed her with snow from the dooryard and struggled to remain calm as the flickering flames on the hearth cast tall, weaving shadows about the room.

"Please, please, don't die," she whispered as she placed another snow pack on Iona's burning forehead. "Angus loves you, Morgan loves you, and I...care."

As dawn began to seep into the farmhouse kitchen, Iona MacLeod stirred and slowly opened her eyes. With an effort, she turned her face toward the fire burning low on the hearth and saw, on the floor beside her bed, wrapped in a quilt, her head on a pillow, Emma, her face pale, dark smudges under her eyes. She slept.

"Emma, child." She put her hand on the younger woman's tangled curls. "Emma."

At her touch, Emma's eyes flew open. She struggled up on one elbow to blink at her patient.

"Iona, you're awake!" she breathed, pulling herself to her knees and putting her fingers to the woman's forehead. "And you're cool. Oh, thank God! Your fever's broken."

"Aye, lassie, that it has." The Scotswoman struggled to a sitting position. "I'll just be gettin' us a wee bit of breakfast..."

"You'll do nothing of the kind!" Emma pushed her gently back onto her pillows. "You're still recovering from a nasty illness. You need rest."

"I am a tad wobbly," she admitted, submitting with a weary sigh.

"I'll make us some oatmeal." Emma got stiffly to her feet and brushed the creases from her crumpled dress. "I think some strong, sweet tea is also in order, for the pair of us."

As she went to the hearth and began to rebuild the languishing fire, Iona rolled her head to watch her.

"Thank ye, lass," she said, her voice a low, ragged croak. "Morgan chose well."

****

"The hen you killed for the soup...it wasn't the great white one, was it, lass?" Iona asked later that morning as Emma tidied the kitchen. "She was my...our best egg-layin' bird."

"I know." Emma paused and rubbed her hands down her apron. "That is why I chose the small gray one. Iona, I'd never killed a living thing before that hen." Suddenly tears spilled down her cheeks. "It grieves me to think of what I did to an innocent creature."

"Come here, child." Propped up on pillows, Iona held out her arms. "Come here, lassie. Grieve if you must," she said softly as she gathered the younger woman to her. "But if you hadn't sacrificed the small fowl, I'd likely not be here. Sometimes, for the greater good, we must do distasteful things. Like your husband fightin' a war to preserve our country's independence."

****

The first ship Emma saw arriving that spring

made her heart leap with the hope it was the *Ula*. Her spirits plummeted with disappointment when she saw it was not.

Slowly she turned away from the window and would have gone back to her sewing had not Iona appeared in the parlor doorway, their cloaks and bonnets in hand.

"Come along, lass." She handed Emma's to her. "Let us not miss the great event."

Her tone was light, congenial. Over the winter they'd become friends. In order to maintain this position, Emma had made no more clandestine visits to Farand Thatcher. Furthermore, when they chanced to meet in the village she acknowledged him with a curt nod and tried to ignore the warm suggestiveness in his twinkling brown eyes.

"It's not the *Ula*." Emma laid her cloak aside and resumed her needlework. "I see no point..."

"Dear heavens, lass!" Iona puffed out her cheeks in dismay. "Are you no curious as to what this ship brings? Letters from our men, perhaps?"

"I had not thought..." Emma thrust aside her sewing and arose, picking up her cloak. "Of course! How clever of you, Iona!" She gathered up her cloak, wondering why the thought of news from Morgan should excite her so. Certainly the last letter had been far from caring.

"Not clever at all, lassie." Iona replied gruffly. "Just experienced in the hopes and ways of a sailor's wife. You'll learn."

As she threw her cloak about her shoulders and followed the Scotswoman from the house, Emma thought of the unintentional irony of her last sentence. Little did Iona MacLeod know that Emma Prescott would never have the opportunity or need to learn.

****

When the ship drew alongside, its crew making

preparations for docking, the two women were standing on the wharf, cloaks and bonnet ribbons whipping in the wind. It appeared everyone in the community had come to greet this first visitor of the year, Emma thought, glancing around at the crowd as it waved and cheered. James Cameron in his landau sat to one side, watching the festivities. He probably had a vested interest in the ship's cargo, Emma mused, as Morgan had told her he did in most vessels arriving in Pine.

"Dear God in heaven, what is she doing back here?" Emma saw her almost in the same instant Iona breathed the words.

Standing at the rail, her emerald green satin cloak as bright as the gem its color copied, was a tall, slender woman, a few golden curls escaping from under an elegant bonnet. Its ribbons matched her wrap and fluttered with her ringlets in the cold April wind. Without any introduction or explanation, Emma knew she was Vanessa Cameron, Lady Whatley, the love of Morgan's life.

"Papa." The beautiful creature scuttled daintily down the gangplank and into the arms of a totally bewildered-looking James Cameron.

"Daughter." He held her for a moment, then drew her out to look into her face in surprise. "What are you doing here? Is Lord Peter with you?"

"He preferred to remain on our estate in England," she dismissed her father's query with a wave of a lace-gloved hand. She turned to Iona and Emma. "Good morning, Iona. And this must be Morgan's little wife. I heard he'd suddenly wed an English girl. Emma, is it not?"

Her tone and choice of words made Emma feel small and plain and insignificant. She swallowed hard. She would not be cowed by this imperious beauty. She was, in the eyes of this village, Morgan's wife.

"Good morning, Lady Whatley." She dropped a brief curtsy. "Yes, I am indeed Captain Reynolds' wife. It is interesting," she chose the word carefully, "to make your acquaintance."

"Ah, ha!" Lady Whatley drew back like a snake preparing to strike. "A clever little creature. I can see how you might fascinate Morgan...briefly."

"Vanessa!" James Cameron took his daughter's arm in a quick, hard grip. "That's quite enough! Come along home. We have much to discuss that does not involve Emma."

As he drew his daughter toward his landau, he threw an apologetic glance back over his shoulder at Iona and Emma. The former waved aside his unspoken apology and turned back toward the farmhouse.

"Come along, Emma," she said gruffly. "Let James deal with that elegant piece of baggage."

****

The news spread throughout the village: the *Ula* had been seen downriver. Iona immediately set about laying a huge supper, with Emma as her assistant. That done, she turned to the younger woman.

"Go, put on your best riding habit," she said. "I'll have the boy saddle your mare. You must arrive at the dock to meet Morgan fittingly decked out as his lady."

"But..." Emma began to protest.

"Go!" she said shortly. "You'll see the wisdom of my decision when we arrive at the dock."

****

Twenty minutes later they headed for the wharf, Iona leading Bonnie, Emma in her best deep blue riding habit in the sidesaddle on her back. Emma had to repress a chuckle as they walked sedately along, her companion's back as rigid and straight as if she were leading the mount of the Queen.

"Iona, I don't need to ride. It's but a short distance and..."

"Surely you do, and you will see why, shortly." Iona kept steadily onward.

Emma's attention was diverted as the *Ula* came into view on the river, sailing majestically toward a docking in Pine. By the time she and Iona arrived at the wharf, a crowd had assembled. Among them she saw James Cameron in his landau, and beside him Vanessa, resplendent in a low-cut spring gown of a vibrant peach color, with a matching bonnet and spencer.

Emma suddenly realized why Iona had insisted she dress in her best habit and ride Bonnie. Mounted, she was head and shoulders above the other woman and would most likely be noticed by Morgan first.

"Thank you, Iona," she said softly leaning forward over Bonnie's neck. "Now I understand."

"Good. Now draw yourself up like Morgan's lady and look as proud and haughty as ye can, that's a good lass."

****

Bone-weary, Captain Morgan Reynolds stood on his quarterdeck as the *Ula* approached Pine. He'd been at sea for the better part of nine months. He'd taken over a dozen prizes, some as the result of hard-fought battles. He wanted nothing more than to moor his ship and head for home for a much-needed rest.

Home. He wondered what he'd face there. He'd left under the cloud of incriminations he'd flung at Emma. He could hardly expect her to welcome him with open arms.

"Captain, we're about to dock." Angus MacLeod brought him out of his thoughts. "We'll be needing your orders."

"Aye, Mr. MacLeod. Bring her in gently, furl the

last sails. We're home."

****

Docking duties kept him too involved to scrutinize the cheering crowd assembled on the dock until the last ropes were being cast ashore. Then, as he paused at the rail and raised a hand to acknowledge the boisterous welcome, he looked down and felt an emotional wallop as mighty as any of the physical ones he'd received in battle.

There, brilliant as any butterfly that was her namesake, sat the former object of his passion. Vanessa nee Cameron, now Lady Whatley, highlighted like a rainbow in her peach-colored gown and bonnet, had lost none of her golden appeal. When she raised a daintily lace-gloved hand in his direction, he felt such an intense mix of emotions that he had to catch at the rail to keep from staggering. "Brother!" Iona's strong Scottish voice caught his attention. He turned in the other direction and saw Emma, mounted on her chestnut mare, demure and composed in her royal blue riding habit. Standing beside her, ramrod stiff as a sentinel as she held Bonnie's bridle, was his sister. She looked like the bellwether of some great and noble personage.

Something must have happened during his absence to change his sister's stance concerning his surrogate bride. He'd be facing a pair of females in opposition to the imperious lady seated in the landau, a smug smile on her lips.

His gaze returned to the beauty in the landau. She inclined her head and smiled coyly at him in a way he knew only too well, in a way that sent messages and memories coursing through his body. He swallowed hard and cursed himself for a fool.

He turned back to look at Emma sitting proud and straight on her little brown mare. She showed no evidence of being cowed by the presence of his former lover. Typical. He'd never known her to relent even when the odds were stacked against her.

The moment the gangplank touched the pier he strode down its length. Pausing only briefly when it was unavoidable to shake hands and accept congratulations and ignoring his basic instinct, he shouldered his way to his sister and Emma.

"Iona." He greeted his sister with a kiss on the cheek.

"Brother, you're looking well, considering what you've been through." Iona accepted his greeting with dignity. "I've brought your wife." She turned to indicate Emma.

"Yes." He rounded his sister quickly, lifted Emma from the saddle, into his arms, and amidst a rousing roar of approval from the crowd, kissed her passionately. He hoped Vanessa could see him, hoped she'd be driven to regret what she'd casually thrown away.

"Three cheers for the captain and his missus!" someone yelled and the crowd obliged.

"Come along, my girl." Morgan took her by the hand and started off toward their house at such a pace Emma had to trot to keep up with him. "Angus," he called back over his shoulder. "Rum for everyone! See to it, will you."

****

"You're looking well, Captain." Emma leaned against the kitchen wall as she tried to catch her breath and thought how cold their house, uninhabited all winter, felt.

"You lie as convincingly as ever." He turned away from her, strode over to the hearth, and knelt to build a fire. Her presence irked him, held him captive. "I've been twice wounded and haven't had a decent night's sleep in weeks. I've been drinking too much whiskey, eating too little food, and lusting after a wife that is no wife. Don't, I pray, don't tell

189

me I look well."

As he stood and turned to her, Emma saw the truth in his words. His weather-bronzed face had grown lean, his hair so long it curled about his neck and ears. His shoulders appeared broader than she remember, his chest revealed through a half open shirt front more muscular, his hips and thighs in fitted breeches taut. He looked every inch the sea wolf he'd been branded.

"Wounded?" she said, as the fire leaped into flame behind him. In the dancing shadows of the bitterly cold kitchen he looked satanically handsome and dangerously virile.

"Aye." He stripped off his jerkin and shirt, and she saw the scars on his chest and left shoulder. "Can you still say with truth that I look well?"

"Oh, Morgan." The words escaped Emma's lips in a thick whisper. "Are you fully recovered?"

"I'd be a fool to continue to command a privateering vessel if I weren't." He picked up his duffel bag and headed out of the kitchen. "Now I plan to sleep in my own featherbed for a couple of hours. I'd appreciate a meal when I arise."

****

As he divested himself of the rest of his clothes and fell into the soft cleanliness of their bed, he cursed himself again. He'd thought he was over her, free from the devastating spell Vanessa Cameron could cast over him at her slightest desire. Today on the wharf he'd discovered that was far from true.

What is she doing here? She was with her father. Has her husband perhaps met with an accident? Is she once again available to be mine?

He groaned as he remembered the way she'd looked in that peach-colored dress, the way her golden curls had framed her perfect face. As their moments of intimacy in his rooms in Halifax and London returned, he moaned and clutched his pillow. *Vanessa, Vanessa, Vanessa!*

"Captain, are you unwell?" Emma's voice from outside the closed bedroom brought him back to reality.

"Yes, yes," he snapped. "See to my meal."

"Of course." He heard the rustle of her dress as she returned downstairs and immediately hated his nasty words. Emma had been good to him. She'd agreed to this sham of a marriage, charmed his creditors, doctored his crew, and even washed his drawers. On one memorable occasion she'd shared his bed with a warmth and delight he'd found highly pleasurable.

But she wasn't Vanessa. She wasn't a beautiful, intoxicating, bewitching butterfly.

****

"May I have some bread and butter, and perhaps some ham and cheese?" Emma stood in the farmhouse doorway and addressed Iona. "Morgan wants a meal after he's rested. I have nothing in the larder save a bit of tea."

She stopped short, astonished as Morgan's sister turned from putting potatoes into a pot on the counter. Her dark hair, usually contained in a neat bun, hung in a loose tangle about her shoulders. Her cheeks were flushed a soft pink.

"What's wrong, lass?" Iona's words softened with compassion. "Was it because she came to the wharf? Surely he can't still be besotted with that faithless creature?"

"Nothing is amiss." Emma drew herself up proudly and tried to ignore Iona's appearance of a woman who'd just made love. "Morgan is weary and..."

"Lass, don't try to deceive me." Iona faced her squarely. "I've been a sailor's wife too long not to understand the first thing your man needs when he reaches his home port isn't bread and cheese. Now, sit ye down and tell me what is wrong. Angus is dead asleep at the moment. We won't be interrupted."

****

"It's still Vanessa." Emma looked down at her hands folded in her lap and drew a deep breath that sounded somewhat like a sob. "I thought after the way she betrayed him that he'd never want to see her again. But you saw what happened at the wharf. He couldn't take his eyes off her. Iona, he will never love me. Not while Vanessa Cameron, or Lady Whatley, or whatever name she's called by, lives."

"My brother has been a fool for that vixen since he was a boy." Iona squared her shoulders angrily. "Angus and I have warned him repeatedly about her, but he was deaf to our words and blind to her true character. He drove himself into debt for her. Oh, he doesn't know that I'm aware of his financial state, but there can be no secrets between husband and wife. Angus informed me months ago.

"And now, just when these devil-may-care adventures are once more putting him on the road to solvency, she returns to once again wreak havoc in his life. Och, I will nae allow it to happen. Ye're my sister-in-law. Ye saved my life. Now I'll save yer marriage."

She picked up her shawl and headed for the door.

"Come. I've a few words to say to my foolish brother, and they're best spoken in the privacy of his bedroom. Take bread and cheese from the counter yonder and come with me. You can prepare his repast while he and I talk privately."

****

"My sister tells me you saved her life." Morgan stood in the kitchen doorway, naked to the waist, sinewy arms crossed on his chest. "She also told me how you ministered to a village lad, saving his toe and quite possibly his foot."

"She exaggerates. I only did what anyone would have done." Emma stifled her reaction to his earthy, virile appearance and returned her attention to placing his supper on the table.

"She said you butchered a hen to make soup for her." He let his arms fall to his sides as he advanced into the room. "She also said you stayed by her side for hours...until her fever broke. She said you were...remarkable."

He stepped between her and the hearth, blocking her way as she moved between table and fire. Forced to stop, she looked up at him. He loomed over her, lean, hard, and determined, a pirate in the flesh.

"One must set priorities," she said, struggling to keep her tone even and unemotional. "Iona is a human being, and my friend, I believe." She tried to ignore her hammering heart, her racing desire for this wildly arousing man, as she gazed up into his cold blue eyes.

"It was not the behavior I'd expect of a thief, of a liar, or of a whore." He stood solidly before her and she saw a softening in his expression. "Mrs. Reynolds, I apologize for my bad temper earlier."

"Apology accepted. Now, come, sit. I have your supper ready."

"One more thing." He reached for the shirt he'd left hanging on the back of a chair. "My sister has convinced me I must behave as a proper husband. The fact that my former intended has returned to the community must in no way taint our relationship. I intend to do as she recommends."

"I expected no less of an officer and a gentleman," she said primly, cutting bread.

"That's remarkable." Sarcasm tinged his words. "I didn't expect it of myself."

****

Emma donned her finest white nightgown and brushed her hair until it shone. Then she climbed into bed and waited expectantly. Morgan was below, barring the doors and banking the fires for the night. A tremor of anticipation ran through her. He'd said he intended to behave as a proper husband. If that meant in the bedroom as well, she was willing, even eager.

When she heard his booted footsteps on the stairs, she drew a deep breath and adjusted her nightshift.

"Is the house secured?" she asked when he entered the room. She could think of nothing else to say.

"Aye." He stood inside the door gazing at her. A chill suddenly swept through her. "I'll be sleeping in the guest room. I had blankets and pillows brought from the *Ula*. I won't discommode you by intruding on your privacy."

"Very well." Somehow Emma managed a cool, calm reply over the lump of disappointment welling in her throat. "I wish you good night, Captain."

"And to you as well, Mrs. Reynolds. No need to rise early to prepare breakfast. I'll be riding over to James' early. I'll eat there."

He went out, closing the door softly behind him. When Emma heard the door to the room across the hall shut, she let two fat tears trickle down her cheeks. She'd lost him. Or perhaps she'd never truly had him.

****

Morgan galloped through Pine and on upriver toward James Cameron's manor house. Every nerve in his body seemed tensed, poised for the moment he'd see her once again, when he could seduce her into seclusion where he might have her all to himself.

He knew it was wrong, even though he'd learned

she'd left her husband behind in England. She was still a married woman. But then, when had the rules of decency and decorum ever given her pause when she wanted to do something.

His mind roiled as he recalled their many assignations. He had to admit it had come as a shock to discover on their first intimacy that she, at sixteen, was no longer a virgin. He'd filled with fury when she'd laughingly told him she'd allowed one of her father's grooms the honor of her first experience.

"Oh, Morgan, don't be such a prude!" She'd run her hands down his body, her eyes dancing wickedly. "I knew it wouldn't be a pleasant experience. I wanted to spare you."

He'd tried to retain his anger but she was kissing him, fondling him, making his senses reel, and he'd forgiven her as he'd always forgive her.

Now he wondered how he could arrange for them to be alone. It had to be soon. He couldn't bear to wait much longer.

****

"Morgan, my lad, there you are!" James Cameron arose from where he'd been sitting on his front verandah and came to the rail to greet his younger business partner. "A drop of whiskey, lad? I'm sure we have much to toast."

"Just a small drop, James." Morgan swung to the ground and tied the stallion to a hitching post. "I've a young bride, you know. It won't do for me to go returning to her in less than a sober state." The lie stung, but he could do nothing less. He ached and burned for the blonde woman inside his partner's house.

"Aye, aye, laddie, that it wouldn't. Come inside to my office, and we'll get down to business."

****

It was early evening by the time they concluded their accounting and Morgan stepped out onto the

195

verandah. His stallion stood tied to the hitching post, saddled and ready for his return to his house. Frustration irked him like a hair shirt. He hadn't seen Vanessa all day. Her father had told him she was visiting friends and wasn't expected back until after supper. Now he stared down the trail, smoking one of her father's fine cigars, barely tasting it in his anxiety. He'd have to leave soon. He could find no legitimate excuse for tarrying longer.

When the landau finally came into view, he flung his cigar aside and leaped the verandah railing to be ready to assist her to alight. His heart hammered, and he felt a strange lightheadedness he wished he could attribute to the strong cigar.

"Morgan, this is a surprise." She favored him with one of her radiant smiles. "Goodness, you look positively agitated. Has Father been playing the tyrant with you?"

"Drive on," he snapped to her driver the moment her feet touched the ground. The man, after a quick glance at the captain's expression, flapped the reins and obeyed.

"My, my." She snapped open her fan and gave it a few flutters between them. "Captain, you really must learn to contain your emotions, especially when they're of frustration and annoyance. I can't think what my father could have done to upset you so." She batted her eyelashes, glancing up at him from beneath them.

"You know perfectly well it isn't your father who's incensed me, who's driven me half mad these past months." He still held her arm by which he'd helped her from the carriage. "You know…"

"And you know I'm now a married woman, Lady Whatley, in fact. Therefore I can see no reason for your unbecoming demeanor." She shrugged free and strutted toward the steps.

"Don't play coy with me!" He strode ahead and

rounded on her to block her way. "You jilted me, would have made a laughingstock of me if I hadn't found another woman ready and willing to immediately take your place."

"Ah, yes, the demure little Emma." She gave him a belittling curl of her lips. "Tell me, how did Iona enjoy finding herself sister-in-law to an English whore?"

"Emma is no whore!" he bellowed.

"That's not what I've heard." Undeterred by his fury, she smirked up at him. "There's a gentleman in Pine by the name of Farand Thatcher who will swear on a Bible that he's searched diligently and found no record of your so-called marriage in London. He's also told me darling Emma has been most receptive to his advances during your absence."

"Both lies, bold-faced lies!" Morgan's jaw clenched so tightly he thought he heard a tooth snap. "You always did enjoy malicious gossip! Now you're collecting it at my wife's expense."

"You mean your whore's." She pushed past him and headed up the steps. At the top she swung back. "Go back to her. She must suit you well."

Then he saw the tears in her eyes. In an instant he was up the steps and gathering her into his arms.

"Oh, Morgan, my marriage was a disastrous mistake." Vanessa melted into his embrace. He smelled the familiar scent of lavender and remembered so many things. "Lord Peter Whatley is a cold, miserable excuse for a man. I believed him to be a wealthy lord of the realm. Only after we were wed did I discover he was deeply in debt because of his gambling and carousing. He married me only to get at my father's money. What am I to do?"

"You must seek a divorce." Morgan's lips stole toward her temple; he longed to let them slide lower to caress her slender neck. He hated himself but, God help him, he was once more falling under her

197

spell. He didn't want to hear about her mess of a marriage. He didn't want to lose his outrage toward her. The woman had all but ruined him, emotionally and financially. "I'm sure your father will welcome you back into his home."

"And live in this filthy backwater for the rest of my life? Oh, Morgan, we both know I can't do that!" She looked up at him, brown eyes pleading, as she placed a soft, gloved hand on his cheek. "Take me away, Morgan, to the Caribbean. I hear there are tropic islands down there where one can live like royalty on much less than the fortune I know you've made privateering for my father."

"Must I remind you we're both now married persons...married to other people?" He managed to push her away, out to arm's length.

"Oh, come now!" She swung away and strode angrily over to clutch the verandah rail in both hands. "My marriage has proven a farce, and your arrangement with that child you're calling a wife is anything but correct and legal."

He jerked her back to face him, a foul taste invading his mouth. "That bastard Thatcher only thinks he knows the truth. I'd put nothing past him. He's been plaguing Emma for months."

"Plaguing? Is that what she's led you to believe?" She cast him a sly glance. "Perhaps since you're newly arrived you haven't yet heard how some of the village lads, admirers of yours, I believe, took it upon themselves to administer a sound thrashing to Mr. Thatcher after he'd had the temerity to serenade and outright court your wife at the New Year's ceilidh in this very house!"

"You lie! Emma would never invite the advances of another man!" Morgan felt a sick, bilious sensation in his gut.

"Apparently Mr. Thatcher was not of that opinion. Rumor has it your sweet little Emma was later seen taking food—and, I assume, comfort—to him as he lay recovering in his cabin." She looked up at him, meeting the fire in his eyes with flames of her own. "Morgan, be sensible. She can never satisfy you the way I can, and you know it."

She slipped her arms about his neck. Her mouth covered his, her tongue probing between his surprised lips.

A slight noise made them break apart. They turned to see Emma mounted on Bonnie at the bottom of the porch steps. Staring up at them, her face was as white as death. The soft grass of the mansion's front lawn had masked the sound of her mare's hooves. With a soft cry, she whirled her mount about and sent her galloping back down the trail into the forest.

"Emma, wait!" Morgan shoved Vanessa aside and vaulted over the railing. He leaped into the Lad's saddle. "For God's sake, wait! You can't ride like that!"

"Morgan, let her go." Vanessa grasped the verandah, a vision in pale yellow silk and Italian lace. "Let her go." The last sentence was a breathed invitation.

He looked up at her for a moment as he held the cavorting, eager horse in check. Then he whirled the animal about and raced after the woman who'd vanished into the trees.

Lady Vanessa Whatley drew a deep breath, then, with a smug smile tipping her lips, she sauntered back into her father's manor. He'd be back. She'd known Morgan Reynolds since he was a boy. He'd be back.

****

"Emma!" he bellowed as he'd never bellowed to his men, even in the heat of battle. "Emma, stop! You can't ride well enough for this! Emma!"

He clapped his heels against the stallion's sides,

and the great horse flattened into a run. Within seconds he and his rider were abreast of the woman and her mare.

"Emma!" Morgan tried once more to stop her with words, then gave up. Sweeping out an arm, he pulled her from her mount and into his arms before him on the big black horse.

With an effort he halted the hot-blooded stallion. When he'd succeeded, he let Emma slide gently to the ground. Her knees buckled, and she would have fallen if he hadn't at that moment leaped down beside her to catch her in his arms.

"What do you think you're doing?" he asked as the Lad trotted off up the road, then lowered his head to graze. "You could have been killed, riding at that speed with your lack of skill."

"Well, there's one area in which you apparently don't lack skill!" She wrenched free and stood glaring up at him with such hatred he fancied he saw green fire flashing out at him. "Unfortunately, such talents are best kept for one special person, not spread thoughtlessly about! Or perhaps you did give it thought. A great deal of lewd, colorful thought!"

"Emma, that's enough!" He caught her by the shoulders and shook her gently. "What you saw, just now..."

"Was a vision, a product of a diseased mind? Don't insult my intelligence!"

"And don't you insult mine!" His control cracked. "Did you think I'd never learn of your dalliance with that bastard Thatcher? Did you plan to make a fool of me...again? You promised to behave as my wife until I delivered you to your brother. What happened to that vow?" He glared down at her, struggling to contain the roiling anger in his belly.

"And I did. I have." Her eyes became very wide and very green. He thought he glimpsed apprehension, even fear in them, and perhaps guilt?

"I've heard stories to the contrary." His grip on her arm tightened.

"Morgan, you're hurting me!" She tried unsuccessfully to shrug free. He wasn't about to let her go...not yet.

"Not as much as you've hurt me and my family, not as much as you've sullied my good name with your attentions to another man!" He felt his words come like a snarl, Vanessa's accusations burning hot and cruel in his soul.

"Oh, and what you were doing just now on the Camerons' verandah wasn't too disgraceful for a supposedly married man?"

Pain was fast overwhelming anger in the jade of her eyes. Morgan felt a disgusting upheaval rising from his gut to his chest.

"If I ask the lads at the tavern as to why they suddenly took it into their heads to thrash that young popinjay, what would they tell me, Emma? My sister may have been overwhelmed by your caring for her during her illness, but the fact cannot erase your shaming me before the village I choose to call home!"

"Oh, so a single dance with a gentleman in a crowded room is a disgrace, but a sly assignation alone in the shadows is not! Really, Captain, your logic escapes me!"

Emma wrenched herself free, whirled away from him, and ran up the dark trail into the forest. Bonnie raised her head, whinnied, and trotted after her mistress, trailing her reins.

For a moment he stared after her, but as she disappeared around a turn in the path, he swung up onto the Lad, put his heels to the stallion's sides, and with a war whoop headed the horse at full gallop after her. As he passed Bonnie, the little mare threw up her head and shied violently out of his path.

Seconds later Captain Morgan Reynolds, for the third time in his life, scooped Emma up onto his horse and carried her with him while he reined his stallion to a halt. Incensed, he dropped her to the ground less carefully than previously. She stumbled, failed to regain her balance, and ended up sitting down hard on her bottom.

"Brute!" She looked up at him and, although he couldn't see her clearly in the darkness, he guessed anger flared from every inch of her features. "Great, marauding pirate! Go back to your battle ship and leave me in peace!"

"Not before I see you back to my house," he said swinging to the ground. "I'm not monster enough to leave a woman alone on the road in the dark...as I'm sure you'll remember."

"I remember very well, Captain." Ignoring his proffered hand, she scrambled to her feet. "You may catch up my mare, if you've a mind, and take me back to your house. But I would ask from now until you sail again that you absent yourself as much as possible from my company. I no longer feel comfortable in your proximity."

****

Morgan dismounted and slung the Lad's reins about a hitching rail in front of the village tavern. He'd slept little the previous night, alone in his big featherbed. Thoughts of Vanessa lying in all her nightly radiance only a few miles away and soft, warm Emma in the next room had kept him in a hot quandary. One not in a position to do so had offered herself to him; the other although a free woman had made it clear she would not. How could a man get himself into such a mess?

In the small hours the thought of blustering into the adjoining room to roust his surrogate wife awake and demand she become his indeed fluttered through his mind. After all, by God, this was his house and she was, in the eyes of the village, his wife.

Then sanity had returned in all its cold, demeaning light. He wasn't some marauding barbarian. Emma must come to him on her own terms and because she wanted to.

When he finally drifted off to sleep, he dreamed of Vanessa in a seductive white nightshift ensconced in the bed in their London rooms, her hair forming a golden cloud about her shoulders. He was just about to join her when two people appeared. First, Emma in her prim little riding habit, hat perched jauntily on her curls, her eyes hard and accusatory. Beside her was an elegantly dressed gentleman, a prime example of British aristocracy. Lord Peter Whatley "tsked" dismissively and took Emma's arm to guide her from the room. As she glanced back over her shoulder at the door, Morgan saw her eyes had filled with tears.

"Emma!" He tried to go after her, but Vanessa had seized him, was holding him to her in a vise-like grip from which he couldn't escape. The next instant Emma and her escort had vanished. He'd awakened wet with sweat.

"Morgan, it's good to see you, lad." The landlord greeted the captain as he stepped into the tavern. "Look, lads, it's the captain hisself come to share a wee dram with us."

A cheer went up as the men surrounded Morgan. Slapping him on the back, they demanded stories of his exploits. Chafing as he was to speak privately with Andrew the barkeep, he nevertheless obliged for a few minutes, then begged off, declaring he wanted to share a drink and a private word with his old friend.

As the men returned to their tables, Morgan threw his second drink down his throat, then turned to Andrew Kenny.

"What's this I've been hearing about a bunch of the lads beating the tar out of the young lad who lives in the cabin at the edge of the village?" he asked trying to sound casual.

"Ah, Morgan, it was nothing. A bunch of the laddies had a little too much of the ceilidh spirit in them and took exception to a London dandy in their midst." He tried to turn away, but Morgan caught his arm in an iron grip.

"Do nae lie to me, Andrew," he hissed, the Scottish sibilance gushing over his words. "I've heard it had something to do with my wife. I want the truth, man!"

"Sure, sure, lad. Only loosen your hold before you break my arm."

"Tell me." Morgan released him.

"Ah, well, it seems that after that Thatcher chap danced with your missus, he preceded to serenade her. Then, on his leave-taking at dawn, he kissed her. Just a wee peck on the cheek, mind," the barkeep hastened to add as he saw dark fury descending over his friend's features. "But you know how fond the local lads are of you, Morgan, what a hero you are to them. Liquored up as they were, they decided to teach Thatcher a lesson about staying away from your wife."

"And how did Mrs. Reynolds react to Thatcher's attentions? Don't lie to me, Andrew. I can always tell when you're lying."

"She was polite...as becomes a lady." Andrew looked apprehensively at Morgan.

"You mean she did not openly spurn his attentions...perhaps she even 'politely' acknowledged them?"

"Now, Morgan..." the barkeep tried to divert him, but the captain swallowed the contents of the mug Andrew had replenished in the course of their conversation and strode out of the tavern.

He vaulted into his saddle and, putting his heels to the Lad's sides, whirled him about and galloped down the dusty village street.

****

At Farand Thatcher's cabin, he leaped to the ground.

"Thatcher!" he bellowed. He strode to the door, yelled again, then kicked it open. Silence. He paused a moment, then advanced inside.

Flies buzzed over dirty dishes left on the table, the unmade bed was a tangle of blankets and pillows, the floor lay filthy for lack of sweeping. All personal items had been removed.

"If you're looking for the young lad who rented this place, he's gone."

Morgan turned to see Jamie MacPherson, the cabin's owner, peering in the open doorway at him.

"Gone? Gone where?"

"Back to England, I'll wager." The landlord shrugged. "He weren't suited for this country, Morgan, and we both know it. A London dandy if ever I saw one. And not much of a tenant, judgin' from this mess."

"Aye." Morgan kicked an overturned stool aside and drew a deep breath. He didn't know if he was glad Farand had gone or sorry he'd missed the opportunity of confronting the man concerning Emma.

Chapter Eleven

"Why did you come to James' house last night?" Morgan confronted Emma when he returned to the house. Prickling with repressed anger and sexual tension, he could barely bring himself to speak civilly to her.

"A messenger arrived from the ship newly docked in Pine." Emma turned from fixing breakfast and faced him with equal spleen. "He said he had a message for you from the governor in Halifax. You're needed back there immediately to transport messages of great importance to His Majesty's Government since you own the fastest ship and are most adept at avoiding the French and Americans at sea. He said the governor would deem it a great favor if you came at once, and that there'd be no question about the renewal of your Letters of Marquee and Reprisal...which I can only assume are your licenses to piracy."

"I am no the pirate! I am an honorable privateersman!" He struggled to keep outrage from overwhelming him as greatly as did his Scottish accent at her accusation. What had Farand Thatcher told her?

"As you are an honorable husband in the eyes of this community? Eat your breakfast. I will gladly assist you to pack for your departure as soon as you've finished."

"We were never truly wed!" he bellowed.

"You expected me to keep up the pretense although you optioned to abandon appearances when it fit your fancy. How hypocritical! Don't call yourself an honorable anything in my presence!"

Emma slammed his plate down on the table and flounced out.

****

Emma's head ached and she felt ill. Morgan had left two hours earlier. She'd managed to remain cold and aloof during his packing and leave-taking, but the moment he strode out of sight down the hill, his duffel bag over his shoulder, tears had trickled down her face. She loved Captain Morgan Reynolds with every bit of her body and soul. He'd proven, however, his love to be as fickle as the winds that powered his ship. She could never commit herself to such a man.

Staring out the front window of the mansion now, she watched as the *Ula* glided downriver through a veil of mist. Her heart ached like an ulcerated tooth.

"Sister?" She turned to see Iona in the kitchen doorway removing a damp shawl from about her head and shoulders.

"Iona, I'm glad you've come."

"You're watching our lads leave." The woman came to join her at the window, a wistful little smile on her lips. "We must keep them in our hearts and pray for their safe return."

"Yes." As the *Ula* slid out of sight, Emma turned to her. "Yes, of course." Her words sounded as flat and lifeless as the big house suddenly seemed. "Come into the kitchen. I'll make tea."

"Emma." Iona caught the younger woman by the arm. "Morgan told me what you witnessed between him and Vanessa. He then ordered me to get our Bible. With his hand upon it, he swore it had been none of his doing, that she'd initiated the embrace. He made me promise to come and tell you after the *Ula* had sailed."

"Morgan swore upon the Bible...?" Confusion prevented her continuing.

"Come, child." Iona put a gentle arm about Emma's trembling shoulders. "Morgan is a good, brave man, strong and clever, the best privateersman in the fleet. He'll be back safe and sound, I've no doubt. You can settle your differences then. Let me make you a cup of tea with lots of cream and sugar...and perhaps just a drop of your English rum."

****

The shocking news arrived six weeks later. Squire Reginald Falkner had been murdered at his estate in England. Captain Morgan Reynolds was the prime suspect.

"Lies, all lies!" Iona paced the floor of the farmhouse while Emma sat by the fire, hands clenched on her lap. "Morgan would never do murder, no matter how he hated the man. He would call him out for a fight or a duel, but stab the man while he lay sleeping in his bed? Never! At any rate," she continued, pausing to look at Emma, "we must take comfort in the fact that he hasn't been caught and never will be. Morgan is as wily as a fox and twice as hard to trap. We may not be seeing him for a while, but believe me, he won't be rotting in an English prison or swinging at the end of an English rope!"

"A rope?" Emma felt her head swim, her stomach heave.

"Lass, lass!" Iona was instantly beside her, her hand on her shoulder. "They'll never catch him. You mustn't worry."

Two weeks later, another ship brought more shocking news. Lord Peter Whatley had been found murdered in his bed two days after the Falkner killing. Both men had been brutally slaughtered while they slept. Once again, Captain Morgan Reynolds was named as the culprit. Emma's hands shook as she struggled to brew tea for herself and

Iona who sat slumped in a chair by the fire.

"They'll never catch him," the older woman murmured. "Not until he's been able to clear his good name and bring the real murderer to the law. Morgan is too canny a lad to let anyone take him prisoner before he's ready."

Emma suspected Iona kept repeating the words now only to try to reassure herself.

The next news concerning Morgan proved his sister wrong. Captain Morgan Reynolds had been captured by the Americans. Presently he was incarcerated in a Boston jail, the center of negotiations between the British government and the Congress of the United States.

"The Americans are willing to strike a deal with British authorities," James Cameron said, his face creased with lines of deep concern. "They say they'll hand Morgan over in return for six of their ships Morgan captured, ships that are now riding at anchor in Halifax harbor. This would also include releasing their crewmen currently being held in Halifax detention centers."

"Surely that's a king's ransom!" Iona breathed, sitting down heavily in a chair by the fire. "Surely there's no way the British will countenance such a deal."

"I'm afraid there is." James drew a deep breath and shifted his hat in his hands. "Those murders are the talk of England. British authorities are eager to hang someone and put an end to it. The Americans are equally anxious to hold up your brother, Iona, as a much-sought trophy. He was the terror of American shipping. They've no reason to be forgiving or ask anything less than a king's ransom for such a prized prisoner. I've heard rumors they've already paraded him through the streets of Boston in chains while the good citizens threw rotten fruit and vegetables at him."

"No!" Emma's hand flew over her mouth and she swayed on her feet. Not wanting either Iona or James to see her weakness, she sat down abruptly opposite Morgan's sister.

"Have they no respect for a naval officer!" Iona exploded. "Morgan has been nothing but honorable in his dealings with them. James, can you not do anything for the lad?"

For the first time since meeting the Scotswoman Emma saw pleading in Iona's blue eyes.

"Lass, lass, can you think I've not already tried? The man's like a son to me, but he has gotten himself into a terrible fix. I'm afraid only God can help him now."

The door suddenly opened and Angus MacLeod, dirty and disheveled, stood silhouetted against the fading light.

"I have escaped," he explained. "I have come back for help in freeing the captain. I have a plan, but I will be needing the assistance of his guid wife. If she's willing."

"More than willing." Emma came to her feet as Iona rushed into her husband's arms. "What is your plan?"

****

The jailer awoke from his drunken stupor to see a woman standing before him. A small, pretty woman with golden brown curls escaping from beneath a shabby blue bonnet, a woman obviously very pregnant.

"Ma'am." He straggled to his feet and doffed his cap. "Excuse me, ma'am, but this isn't a fittin' place for a lady. And," he continued as he came more to his senses, "How did you manage to get this far into the jail? This prisoner is not allowed visitors."

"I am his wife." She faced him squarely, drawing herself up to her full height. "Since I am to bear his child within the next few days, your governor has granted me leave to visit him. Here, read this." She swept a paper from her reticule and extended it toward him. "There are four little ones at home, as well, missing their father and seeking news of him." She drew out a handkerchief, lowered her head, and dabbed at her eyes. "Surely, surely you will not deny me the opportunity to see him just one last time."

In the gloom, the jailer bent forward, squinting to see the words. That was the last he would remember for some time. Angus MacLeod had brought a belaying stick down on his head. He crumpled to the floor with a dull thump.

"Quickly!" Emma grabbed the ring of keys hanging on the wall and handed them to Angus. "Unlock the cell! It won't be long before someone in authority realizes that the captain's pregnant wife and her father shouldn't have been allowed in here!"

"Aye, aye, lass." Angus scrambled to obey. "Dear God in heaven, if this plan fails we may all three hang, and I'll be responsible!"

"This is no time for self-recriminations, Angus. I welcome the opportunity to try to free Morgan."

He wrestled with the key in the rusty lock until it grated open. Emma stepped inside the wet, vile-smelling cell. In the scant light from a single barred window high in the wall, as her eyes adjusted to the gloom, she saw him squatted against a far wall, his shoulders stooped, a ragged white shirt hanging from them.

"Emma!" His voice was a hoarse rasp as he recognized her. "How in God's name...?"

"You once said I was not without charm." She cocked her head to one side as she looked down at him. "Well, I'm also not without guile. But there's no time for discussion. Quickly, on your feet! We've not a second to spare!"

****

Two hours later, safely aboard a British ship,

they sailed out of Boston harbor.

In the cabin beneath the deck, Morgan sat on the edge of the bed and looked up at Emma, his bloodshot eyes wide with questions. Bearded and filthy, he was a far cry from the swashbuckling man who'd once swept her up onto his great horse and ridden with her to safety.

"Emma, what's all this?" He spoke finally, gesturing to her extended belly. "If you tell me it's as a result of anything that Thatcher bastard has done, I swear I'll confess to both murders and let them hang me."

"No." She reached beneath her dress and pulled out a pillow.

"Ah." He lowered his head into his filthy hands. "Thank God."

"Morgan." She knelt before him and grasped them in hers. "After you'd gone, after Iona told me about your swearing on the Bible..."

"So you undertook this mad adventure to free me, an adventure that could have seen you in irons, in the shadow of the gallows?"

"Not so mad." She stood and removed her bonnet, a contented little smile tipping her lips. "We planned and plotted most efficiently. We chose the change of guard that would be most susceptible to a desperate, pregnant woman and her aged father. And what better person to enact the part of a British official than James? Surely his deportment and vigor could seduce anyone on that score. He got us into Boston by posing as a negotiator from England ready to bargain for your return to England."

"Emma, Emma, Emma, what have I ever done to be blessed with the likes of you?" He looked up at her, a wry grin twisting his dirty face. "I'd take you into my arms this moment but I fear I'd infest you with lice. Will you see if there's any chance of my getting a bath and clean clothes?"

"You'll be needing more than a bath and a change of clothes." Emma slanted him a sly, coquettish smile. "You'll need a decent meal in your belly if you're to fittingly thank me, because, you see, my darling, we're on our way to the Caribbean to be married by my brother."

"Married?" He couldn't believe what she'd said.

"Yes, Captain Reynolds, married." She looked down her nose at him. "I'm tired of playing house for you. Furthermore, that incident with Lady Whatley back in Pine convinced me you need to be settled once and for all. No chasing after married women, no more expecting fidelity from this woman without just cause. Now I'll send a sailor to see to your needs."

With a swirl of her skirts, Emma Prescott left the cabin.

For a moment he sat as she'd left him. "Married!" he repeated. "Really married to Emma."

Then, as the idea settled over him, Captain Morgan Reynolds felt a smile kinking his lips. Dirty, emaciated, and infested with lice, he was on his way to be married to the most devious, most enchanting woman he'd ever met. He grunted as he pulled himself to his feet and shambled to the cabin door.

"You there!" he yelled to a passing sailor.

"Aye, Captain, what can I do for ye?"

"Bring me water, towels, soap, and a razor," he said leaning against the door frame. "I will also need a change of clothes. Apparently I'm soon to be a bridegroom."

****

The Shanna trimmed her sails and glided into the natural harbor of Eden Island in the glassy heat of a tropic morning. Morgan stood beside Emma at the rail and watched the tropical island coming ever closer.

"Today, Emma, my darling," he muttered,

leaning on the rail so that he was near her ear. "Today you will truly become my wife."

"Most definitely, Captain." She gave him a glance that made his heart rate quicken. "Gladly. Joyfully, in fact." She removed her bonnet and shook her mass of golden brown hair free. "As soon as my brother says the words."

"I hope the man is standing on the beach at this moment," Morgan muttered. "I hope he's got his Bible in his hands." He didn't think he could bear much more of Emma's tempting presence without resorting to conduct unbecoming a gentleman. They'd been sailing for over a week, and each day since her declaration of her intention to marry him had been fraught with a tension he could barely stand. Now, now at last...

The ship dropped anchor. A boat was lowered to carry the first landing party to shore, Morgan and Emma among them. Morgan took a seat in the stern and pulled Emma shamelessly onto his lap. His hand caressed the section of her dress that covered her thigh, his lips found her temple.

"Emma, Emma," he muttered, his desire pressing against her.

"Captain," she whispered leaning back against his chest and bracing herself against the motion of the boat with a hand on his knee. "Control yourself."

"While you continue to tease me in the most diligent manner? Ah, my sweet Emma, you'll soon get your just deserts."

"I sincerely hope so, sir. Otherwise I wasted my breath in naming you as my intended." She slanted him a coy glance under lowered lashes that was almost more than he could stand.

"Emma, Emma." He drew her close and buried his face against her neck.

As they neared the shore Emma arose with a little cry, pointing to a young man on the shore.

"Colin!" she called out waving. "Colin, it's Emma!"

"Emma?" For a moment he stood frozen in place, a tall, slender figure in a shabby shirt and pants on a strip of white sand, a forest of lush green jungle as his backdrop. He suddenly appeared oblivious to the small crowd of natives and white people coming to the shore to meet the newcomers.

"Emma, what are you doing here?" He began to move toward the boat, wading out, fully clothed, to meet it. When he was waist deep, he caught the bow and stared at the young woman standing near the stern. "God in heaven, Emma, what are you doing here?"

"I've come because I need your help," she said.

As the boat moved shoreward, she knelt and caught at her brother's hand as she drew abreast of him. She continued to hold it as the boat was pushed ashore. Then she fell into the arms he held out to her.

"How I've missed you!" Morgan heard her choke and realized how lonely she must have been.

"What is the news of Father? I've not heard from him in months. Emma..." He broke off as he held her out at arm's length and looked down into her face.

"We have much to talk about, Colin," she said softly. "Later, at your mission."

****

Two hours later Morgan and Emma left Colin's jungle mission, newly married, and walked toward the village a mile distant. Sharing a thatched hut with his new brother-in-law wasn't Morgan's idea of a honeymoon. After waiting so long, he wanted to be fully alone with his bride

When they reached the settlement, Morgan drew Emma hurriedly down its dusty, single street to an inn near its end.

"A room, landlord," he ordered brusquely,

clutching Emma's hand in a grip so strong she could barely keep from grimacing. "And quickly."

The wizened little man, cowed by the tall, authoritative figure, hastily directed the couple to what he declared was "his finest," at the end of the upper story.

Once inside Morgan drew the shades against the heat and dust and began to strip off his shirt. "Come here, my beautiful wife," he breathed. "I've waited long enough for this moment."

Emma slowly untied the ribbons on her bonnet and cast it onto the bed, a sly smile on her lips. "What of me? Don't you think a woman has needs and desires as well, my darling? Don't you believe you've good and truly whetted my appetite?" She unbuttoned the few fastenings on the top of her dress and the cotton garment floated to the floor about her feet.

"Emma." Her name was an exhale, full of longing and accomplishment and anticipation.

She loosened the pins from her hair and let it cascade about her bare shoulders, over the thin straps holding her chemise in place. Then she turned and walked with slow, sauntering, seductive steps toward the bed.

"Sweet Jesus!" He was following her when a knocking sounded at the door.

"What is it?" he roared, and Emma was reminded of a bull she'd once heard on a neighbor's farm when the cows were taken from him.

"Champagne for the happy couple," came the reply.

"I ordered no wine. Take it away." Morgan was loosening his belt.

"Oh, but sir, the landlord will whip me if I don't deliver it," came the quavering reply. "Please, sir, just open the door."

"Damnation!" Morgan tightened his belt as

Emma scuttled beneath the sheets. He strode to the door and wrenched it open.

Emma gasped as he flew back into the room and landed on his back near its middle.

"Morgan!" she cried, leaping from the bed as he struggled to pull himself to a sitting position, a bloody wound on his left temple.

Farand Thatcher advanced into the room, a belaying stick in one hand, a pistol in the other, as Emma knelt by her husband's side. His face bore an expression of vicious triumph.

"So you're finally, truly married," he snarled. "Emma, you're most fetching in that attire. You make me almost sorry I didn't succeed in marrying you myself. Almost, but not quite. You see, I plan to wed another now...a lady of means, a lady of title, who'll honor me by being mistress of our newly acquired estates and wealth...while you two rot in hell!"

"You're mad, Thatcher." Morgan drew himself up on one elbow. "What titled lady, what estates and wealth?"

"Why, Lady Whatley, of course. "The estate she inherits from Lord Peter Whatley will make us powerful and respected. Furthermore, our union will not be without its romantic rewards. I understand my intended is most skilled in wifely practices, thanks to her many years with you."

"Bastard!" Morgan struggled to rise, but Farand lunged and thrust the pistol against Emma's temple.

"Take care, my good captain, take care. I shouldn't like to blow your bride's head off her lovely shoulders."

"Vanessa Cameron would never marry another pauper," Emma breathed as the cold barrel of the gun brought terror to her heart. She knew she had to keep him talking, bragging, until either she or Morgan found some way to save themselves.

"Ah, but have you not heard? I've come into a mighty inheritance of my own since the death of my beloved father...Squire Reginald Falkner. He disinherited me some years ago, because he found my behavior unacceptable. Recently, however, I managed to convince him to revoke that decision."

"Falkner?" The name was a grating mutter from deep inside Morgan's throat. "Sweet Jesus! You're Robert Reynolds? My nephew, my sister's son?"

"Aye, laddie." Farand aped Morgan's Highland burr and grinned sadistically down at his uncle. "Originally I came after Emma. I planned to marry her to thwart my father's hope of espousing her. It was incredible luck, my stumbling across you in that ramshackle inn on the night the pair of you were running from my father."

"You were the drunkard in the corner!" Emma gasped at the memory.

"Yes, my dear Emma, I was the drunkard. Only I was not as drunk as you believed. I recognized you, having seen you at my father's soirée earlier that evening. He didn't bother to introduce me, but I saw you. How could any man with eyes in his head miss you, in that becoming scarlet gown? That was when I decided I'd take you away from him, soil you so he'd never want you again.

"Later that evening, however, I learned of your theft. At first I thought it a great lark. Foiled by the woman he'd thought to own!

"Then I saw possibilities in his predicament. I told him I would bring both it and you back to him if he'd reinstate me as his heir. I said he must revise the will before I collected the spoils I was promising. Greedy and desperate for revenge, he agreed.

"I hadn't thought to begin my quest until the following morning. I found a likely wench and together we enjoyed a rather pleasant, if crude, roll in the hay of a barn near my father's estate. On my way home, I found myself in need of more drink. I remembered that dreary but accommodating inn was not far off. And you know the rest."

"Why did you not simply accost us there and take me back?" Emma gazed at him, astonished at his tale.

"You were with a man I could see was no stranger to violence." He smirked. "Furthermore, the prospect of cuckolding my miserable wretch of a father by marrying or at least bedding his virgin bride intrigued me no end. Now that I'd been reinstated heir to his estate, I was in no hurry. He'd given me a generous allowance to use in my pursuit of his errant intended.

"I followed you to London, where I discovered you were living as man and wife. I couldn't bring myself to believe a lady with Emma's background would so quickly have been wooed into bed. Therefore I made a search at Somerset House and discovered your marriage did not exist. The possibilities intrigued me. I accosted you both in London by way of introducing myself to the lovely Emma. Then I followed you to America.

"I tried to seduce you, Emma, and I would have succeeded if not for your pirate lover. Then I met Vanessa. She wanted free of her unfortunate choice of spouse but wasn't willing to give up either her title or his estate. I wanted a lady of her beauty...and talents. Together we devised a plan to suit both of us."

Morgan stirred again. Falkner pressed the pistol more firmly against Emma's temple and adjusted his finger on the trigger. Morgan fell back and he continued.

"On May seventeenth, my illustrious father's birthday, as he lay upon his bed in a stupor after hours of drinking and carousing, I killed him. Two days later, I rode to Surrey and got rid of Lord Peter

Whatley. I knew you," he addressed Morgan, "were in England and that you'd be the logical suspect in both cases. You had powerful motives for seeing both of them dead."

"May seventeenth and nineteenth? Those were the actual dates on which you killed them?" Morgan stared at him as if transfixed.

"I thought it fitting the old reprobate should die on a day he generally celebrated with great debauchery. Think, Emma. Wasn't that the date on which he tried to take you to his bed? The date on which you fled into the night and were picked up by this Highland bastard?"

"Morgan, what is it?" Emma, seeing a glazed expression in her husband's eyes, clutched his arm.

"This miserable cur has just cleared me of charges for both murders," he breathed. With a grimace he struggled to a sitting position. "I sailed from Portsmouth on May twelfth, fully five days before the killings. The harbormaster's records, my insurance documents, and my ship's log all will confirm I was not in England on those dates."

"Little good it will do you now, Captain," Falkner sneered. "No one's going to investigate further once you're found dead, killed by the son of the man you brutally murdered."

"How did you find us?" Emma struggled for words to buy time.

"Why, my betrothed, of course." His booted foot shot out and kicked Morgan in the groin. Morgan doubled up, clutching himself. Only the increased pressure of the pistol against her skull kept Emma from taking him into her arms. "Captain Reynolds' former paramour. Her father unwisely shared with her the details of your plans to free him from prison and sail to an island called Eden in the Caribbean."

"You have little respect for your future wife." Emma was devising a plan, but she had to keep him bragging, so sure of his victory over them that he'd grow careless.

"She will dress up my estate," he said. "We've both agreed that ours will be a marriage of convenience, enacted only when it's convenient or necessary. So you see, my charming Emma, it suits perfectly. At this moment she's waiting for me in a room down the hall."

"Ah." Emma moved a bit, her breath catching in her throat lest he choose to shoot her. "So you both have talked it through. How very convenient."

"Yes, we have." He drew the pistol from her temple and stepped back a pace. "Now get up, Emma. I plan to bind your husband while he's still writhing in pain. Then you and I shall have a long-awaited rendezvous in the bed yonder."

In the shadows of the room with the shades drawn against the sweltering tropic heat, Emma Reynolds made a sudden, desperate decision. Without rising she lunged at Falkner's knees. Taken by surprise, he toppled backward, the pistol discharging into the beams overhead. There was a dull thud as his head struck the mantelpiece.

Gasping, Morgan staggered to his feet to fall on the man, who didn't move.

Morgan felt for a pulse and found none. Turning to look up at Emma, he shook his head. "He's gone."

"Oh, dear God, I've killed him!" Emma, on her knees, covered her face with her hands. "I've done murder!"

"Emma, no, no, no!" Morgan drew himself to her on his knees. "You saved our lives. Emma, you've saved my life twice. Now," he held her by the shoulders and looked deep into her eyes. "Now I pledge it to you."

"Morgan." She melted into his arms, weak with relief and joy. Finally, finally she thought, they were both truly free.

****

"I swear I didn't know he killed Peter!" Vanessa Cameron-Whatley looked up at Morgan in the room she'd been sharing with Farand Thatcher, her eyes wide, her face ashen.

"And his father? Did you know about him?" he glared down at her, his shirt hanging loose over his trousers, his chest bare. He'd wasted no time in confronting Lady Whatley as soon as he felt certain Emma could be left alone. "His death made Thatcher—or Falkner, or whatever name he chose to use—a very wealthy man." Morgan glared at her and could feel no pity for the woman cowering before him.

"No, I swear! I knew nothing of his vicious acts! Morgan, as God is my witness, I would never countenance murder! You know I couldn't!"

"I'm not certain about physical murder." The words gushed out of him in an exhausted exhale. "But I do know you think nothing of assassination of the soul."

"Morgan." She ventured closer to him, brown eyes wide and appealing. "It was always you, it will always be you. Farand Thatcher was just a diversion, a source of information about your Emma and you. Surely you cannot have forgotten those days we shared in London and Halifax...and the nights, surely not the nights."

She slipped her arms about one of his, ran long, slender fingers over his bare chest and looked up at him with that suggestive gaze he remembered all too well. His breath rushed into his lungs as he looked down at her.

"Morgan!"

He wrenched himself free at the sound of Emma's voice. She stood in the doorway, her stricken expression making his heart slam into his ribs.

"Emma..." He started toward her, but she'd already fled down the corridor.

"Damnation!" He took off running after her.

"Morgan, come back, my darling!" Vanessa rushed into the hallway and called after him, but he was deaf to her siren wails.

****

He caught up to Emma at the top of the stairs. Grasping her by an arm, he spun her to face him.

"I know what you saw and how it looked," he muttered. "But like that evening on James' verandah, it means nothing. No, that's true. Now it means less than nothing."

"I saw your expression just now, Captain." Emma's face, pale with outrage, glared up at him. "I recognize lust when I see it. You're still lusting after a woman who betrayed you with not one but two men!"

"You couldn't be more wrong. Maybe once, but not any more. Never again! Emma, listen to me!"

"No, you listen, Captain Reynolds. With all my enemies dead except the voluptuous Vanessa, I no longer need your protection. So please oblige me by releasing my arm and removing yourself from my life...forever!"

223

Chapter Twelve

Emma looked down at her students in the new schoolhouse James had built for the village of Pine and smiled. It was December of 1814. She'd returned to New Brunswick nearly eighteen months earlier and once again moved in with Iona. Living in Morgan's house was out of the question, given their status as a separated couple, and Iona had been only too glad to have her back. Morgan and Angus had gone back to the war. When the captain returned to Pine, Emma assumed he'd live in the manor house either alone or with some new woman of his choosing.

Emma sighed at the latter thought but realized it was inevitable. Morgan enjoyed women and was not a man to live a celibate life. When she'd left the Caribbean a year and a half previous, he'd embarked on a ship bound for England, where he planned to clear himself of murder charges. That accomplished, Iona had informed her, he'd returned to the war to retake his beloved *Ula*. His ship had been sailed the past months as a privateer by the Americans under the name of The Black Joke.

Since there'd been no hard evidence tying Vanessa to Falkner's nefarious schemes, she'd also left for England aboard another ship to reinstate herself as Lady Whatley at her dead husband's estate. How long she'd be able to maintain her position was difficult to calculate. Already there were male heirs seeking to displace her and become lord of the manor.

Perhaps, thought Emma, she'd manage to marry

one of them and thus maintain her position. It little mattered to her. The woman had done all the damage she could do in Emma's life, and now she was out of it forever.

His daughter's heartless schemes and behavior had left James Cameron a sad, lonely man. Emma and Iona tried to relieve his suffering, but there had been little they could do. Instead of accepting their sympathy and concern, the entrepreneur had thrown himself into his business, working long hours in an effort to keep the memory of his only child's infamy at bay.

As Emma set about the day's instruction, she realized she was doing much the same. She sought to drown the memory of Morgan looking down at Vanessa, his gaze hot and hard, in her work with the children and in helping Iona run the farm.

She was tidying the schoolhouse at the end of the day when she heard a commotion at the wharf. As a cheer went up, she felt her heart lurch. Such a show of excitement could indicate only one event. The village's celebrated privateering vessel had returned from the war.

She started toward the door, then paused. She would not now go rushing out to meet him. She, Emma Prescott-Reynolds, had her pride. She would not so easily capitulate. She forced herself back to her desk on the raised platform at the front of the room and tried to focus her attention on grading papers.

****

"Mrs. Reynolds." His voice startled her and she looked up to see him silhouetted against a brilliant sunset in the doorway.

"Captain." Battling to appear calm and composed, she arose and ran her hands down the front of her gray skirts.

"You're looking well," he said advancing into the

225

room. She felt her innards flutter at the approach of his blatant virility.

"Thank you, sir. As are you."

"Have you found another man?" With characteristic bluntness he came immediately to the point.

"No." She lowered her gaze and tried to look involved in sorting books and papers. "What of yourself? Have you found a special lady?"

For a moment he didn't reply, and Emma felt her world plummet. He'd been gone for months. He was a healthy, virile man who enjoyed women. Of course he hadn't remained unattached.

"Aye," he said finally, the Highland accent dragging on his words. "Aye, lassie, that I have. She's standing right before me."

Her breath caught in a painful hiccup as she looked up. He strode forward, but when he tried to take her into his arms, she shrugged away. The initial joy at his declaration had quickly turned to anger at his presumption.

"And just what makes you think I'll have you!" she exploded. "You've been gone nearly two years without so much as a single letter! Angus came home to visit Iona, but you never once showed your face in Pine! Do you think you can now breeze in here and expect me to fall into your arms? Did it take you nearly twenty-four months to decide you'll never be able to have Vanessa and to settle for me?"

"Nay, lass. I was waiting for the war to end...as indeed it has, this past month. I could not honorably quit my obligations before that time. And I know how you feel about my privateering."

"Yet after such an absence I'm supposed to be ready and waiting on your first day in port?" Her hands clenched into white-knuckled balls at her sides, Emma faced him, green eyes flashing emerald fire. "Well, think again, Captain!"

"Lass, I love you. I swear I'll never take to privateering again as long as I live, if that's what you want. I also swear there's been no woman in my bed since I met you that night in the storm. If it's wealth you want, I have it aplenty now. All that I have is yours. My house, even my ship...I'll sign them all over to you, lassie. What more can you ask?"

Emma met his distressed gaze squarely, put her hands on her hips, and said, calmly but decidedly, "I want to be courted."

****

"Damnation, woman, I've sworn to be faithful to you for the rest of my life, I've offered my every worldly possession to you. What more can I do?" Morgan stood in the kitchen doorway of his sister's farmhouse that evening, his hands on his hips, his expression a testament to frustration and exasperation.

"I've told you." Emma didn't pause in laying the table for supper while Iona and Angus watched the drama. "I want to be courted, properly courted. If you're sincere in your desires, you should find it no hardship."

"The lass is right." Iona turned to swing a pot of stew out from the fire and looked sternly at her brother. She'd accepted the fact that Emma and Morgan had only become properly wed in the Caribbean with a great deal more calm than Emma had expected, and she remained Emma's staunch supporter. "It's a woman's right...especially if she's contemplating taking on the likes of you, my lad."

"The lass is already my legal wife." The words were a heaved gush of Highland sibilance. "Furthermore, I haven't the vaguest notion of how to woo a lady."

"Because you've spent most of your life lusting after the wrong woman and behaving shamefully

227

with her." His sister's reply was quick and acidic.

"Don't go sugarcoating your opinion, Sister." Morgan glared over at her. "Your reminiscences are not helping my cause."

"Enough!" Angus seated himself at the table. "Let us eat now and then turn our thoughts to courting. I'm blessed near starved, Iona. You know I'm always a more romantic man on a full belly."

"Argh!" Morgan whirled and strode out of the house, back to his lonely manor.

****

"Captain Reynolds, sir?"

The voice came out of the shadows beside his back door.

"Who goes there?" Fresh from defensive behavior in battle, he swung toward its direction, ready to defend himself.

"It's only me, Charlie Ellis, him what keeps yer horses, sir." The lad stepped into view. "I'd like a word with ye, if I may. It's concernin' yer missus."

"Oh, aye? And what could you possibly have to tell me that I do not already know?" His tone reflected annoyance.

"Well, sir, I've perceived...that's a word she taught me...that things aren't exactly as they should be between ye since yer return. I've seen lights in two bedrooms at night when I'm feedin' the horses and, pardon me for sayin' so, sir, but that don't appear right for a couple that's been parted nigh on two years."

"I'm not going to stand here and listen to some urchin's evaluation of my marriage!" He made a move to pass the boy, but Charlie hesitatingly reached and caught him by the arm.

"Again, beggin' yer pardon, sir, but I will have me say. I owe it to Teacher. She's a fine lady, and I'll stand up fer her even if ye choose to knock me on my backside fer doing so...Captain, sir."

"Very well." Impressed and amused by the lad's courage, Morgan relented. "Go ahead. Have your say."

"Well, Captain, sir, I know Teacher has been mighty lonely without you. And no matter what some waggin' village tongues once said about her and that Thatcher fella, I know she was always true to ye. The two of ye belong together, and all it will take...in my opinion...is a bit of wooing."

"Oh, and I suppose you're an expert in that area?" Morgan was all out amused now, leaning against the door jamb to listen.

"Well, no, not exactly, sir, but I do know Teacher is real fond of music. Maybe if ye could sing to her. Ye don't play an instrument by chance, do you?"

"Is that your best suggestion? That I serenade her? Lad, I was expecting better. However..." He dug in his vest pocket and took out a pair of coins. "I believe you offered your best idea, and for that and your good intentions you deserve more than to be knocked on your backside."

He opened the door to his house and was about to step inside when Charlie called out, "Thank ye, sir. But please give my idea a try. What have ye got to lose?"

Then he ran away into the darkness, the coins clutched in his hand.

****

Emma was in her room later that evening when Angus knocked lightly on her door.

"Ye have a gentleman caller, lass." He grinned when she opened it. "He's in the parlor with Iona, all dressed up and proper as can be."

"A gentleman caller?" Emma frowned. "Whoever...?"

"Never mind speculating, lassie. Just come along."

"A moment." She started to turn away toward

her mirror. She'd let her hair down and she hastily began to pin it up.

"Nay, nay, lass. You look pretty as a picture just as you are." He took her arm and guided her toward the stairs.

As Emma entered the parlor, her hand flew her to lips. Standing by the spinet in the flickering candlelight stood Captain Morgan Reynolds, so handsomely arrayed in white shirt and cravat, black frock coat, deep purple satin vest, fitted ebony breeches, and shining boots that he took her breath away.

As Angus guided her into a chair by the fire, Iona, seated at the instrument, put her hands to the keys. A moment later the captain absolutely amazed her by beginning to sing in the most wonderful tenor voice she'd ever heard.

"Flow gently, sweet Afton,

Among thy green braes,

Flow gently, I'll sing thee

A song in thy praise.

My Emma's asleep

By thy murmuring stream,

Flow gently, sweet Afton

Disturb not her dreams."

The words of Robert Burns' love song rang warm and true. Her hand went to her breast and her eyes misted. The song had found Emma's heart.

When it ended, Emma, gazing into the depths of Captain Morgan Reynolds' blue eyes, barely noticed. She wasn't aware of Iona's quiet exit from the room, nor did she see Angus lead his wife gently upstairs.

"Emma." The word was a soft exhale as he came to her, took her hand, turned it palm up, and pressed his lips to it.

The gesture sent a wild gush of sensation coursing through her body. Her breath caught in her throat as an erotic shock wave consumed her.

"Morgan," she breathed as she touched his hair above his temple. "Oh, Morgan, I do love you so."

"Are ye sure, lass?" The Scottish sibilance that broke through when he became emotional flowed like a mountain stream. "Are ye really sure? Ye see, I don't think I can bear to be disappointed again."

"Aye, my fine Highlander, I'm sure."

He drew her up with him to stand before him. "We can go for a wee walk in the moonlight, if you've a mind," he said shyly. "Iona has informed me it is the proper courting thing to do."

"That would be lovely, Captain." She smiled up at him as he took her into his arms. "But don't expect to slide so easily into my bed. It'll take at least another week or two of courting before I'm prepared to allow that to happen."

"Ah, ye wee teasing lassie!" He caught her to him and kissed her until her head swam and her body swirled away into the wild sensuous vortex of his love. "Ye wonderful, wonderful lass! Ye'll make a respectable man out of this Caledonian pirate yet."

"Not too respectable, I hope," she looked up at him coyly through thick lashes. "I rather enjoy a swashbuckling pirate...from time to time."

She grew serious. "But, Morgan, what about the necklace? Its presence in this house still makes me a thief of great magnitude."

"And the fact troubles you greatly, does it not, my fine wee lass?"

"Yes."

"Then we shall shortly set the matter to rights. We'll pay a visit to the French Ambassador in Boston and return it, minus a single, well-spent ruby, to the people of France. Would that satisfy your craving to become an honest woman once again?"

"Yes, oh, yes, it would, Morgan! Thank you so much. Now our children can have a mother they can be proud of!"

"Children. Aye, yes, our children." He looked down at her, his gaze becoming gentle with caring. "What a lovely ring those words have, Mrs. Reynolds. Let us hope the reality will not be too long in the making."

He gathered her into his arms and she knew she would forever belong with her Caledonian privateer.

A word about the author...

The award-winning author of twenty published books, Gail MacMillan is a graduate of Queen's University. Two of her non-fiction books, *Biography of a Beagle* and *Ceilidh's Quest*, have garnered Maxwell Medals. Her short stories and articles have appeared in magazines in Canada, the USA, and Europe. She lives in New Brunswick, Canada with her husband and three dogs.

You can visit Gail at her website:
www.gailmacmillan.com

Thank you for purchasing
this Wild Rose Press publication.
For other wonderful stories of romance,
please visit our on-line bookstore at
www.thewildrosepress.com

For questions or more information,
contact us at
info@thewildrosepress.com

The Wild Rose Press
www.TheWildRosePress.com

To visit with authors of The Wild Rose Press
join our yahoo loop at
http://groups.yahoo.com/group/thewildrosepress/